BITCH SLAP

NOVELS BY MICHAEL CRAFT

Rehearsing

The Mark Manning Series

Flight Dreams
Eye Contact
Body Language
Name Games
Boy Toy
Hot Spot
Bitch Slap

The Claire Gray Series

Desert Autumn
Desert Winter
Desert Spring

Stage Play

Photo Flash

www.michaelcraft.com

BITCH SLAP

Michael Craft

ST. MARTIN'S MINOTAUR
NEW YORK

www.minotaurbooks.com

Library of Congress Cataloging-in-Publication Data

Craft, Michael, 1950–
    Bitch slap / Michael Craft—1st St. Martin's Minotaur ed.
        p. cm.—(The Mark Manning series)
    ISBN 0-312-30530-3
    EAN 978-0312-30530-7
    1. Manning, Mark (Fictitious character)—Fiction. 2. Consolidation and merger of corporations—Fiction. 3. Family-owned business enterprises—Fiction. 4. Newspaper publishing—Fiction. 5. Wisconsin—Fiction. 6. Gay men—Fiction. I. Title.

PS3553.R215B57 2004
813'.54—dc22
                                                                    2004049424

First Edition: August 2004

10 9 8 7 6 5 4 3 2 1

Mon onzième roman,
comme tous les autres,
est encore pour Léon.

Author's Note

Readers accustomed to mysteries written to a certain structural formula may feel they have a loose footing in *Bitch Slap*, as its overall plot arc takes some unexpected and significant turns. My intent has been not to ignore well-known traditions, but rather to broaden the genre in a way that may allow a richer, less predictable story.

Many thanks are due, too many to mention, but I would be remiss in not acknowledging James Dahlman, Michael Neu, and Leon Pascucci for their generous assistance with various plot details. As always, I am indebted to my agent, Mitchell Waters, who has placed ten of my eleven novels, and my editor, Keith Kahla, who has shepherded seven of those to print at St. Martin's Press. Most important, I send heartfelt thanks to you, my readers. Not only have you ensured that the Mark Manning series stands as one of the stalwarts of its genre, but you have truly nourished me with your kind words and sustained enthusiasm.

Finally, my apologies to advocates of the various Eastern studies and disciplines that collectively take a bit of unwarranted ribbing in this story. *Namaste.*

Contents

PART ONE

Vertical Integration

DONE DEAL

Friendly merger of two local firms signals start of new business era

by CHARLES OAKLAND
Staff Reporter, Dumont Daily Register

OCT. 20, DUMONT, WI—Citing the need to trim production costs through the vertical integration of resources and management skills, Dumont County's two largest corporations have entered an agreement to combine forces in "a friendly merger of equals," according to a joint statement issued by both CEOs.

Quatro Press, founded nearly 50 years ago by Dumont's Quatrain family, has grown to become one of the Midwest's largest printing plants, with contracts including several national news magazines. Ashton Mills, the regional paper mill founded by the family of the late Betty Gifford Ashton, has recently built new headquarters in Dumont.

The joint statement notes, "Both companies will benefit greatly from the integration of printing facilities and paper supply. The realities of global commerce in a new millennium demand aggressive strategic planning. The merger is a perfect fit that will reap substantial rewards for Quatro, Ashton, their stockholders, the community, and the environment."

The merged companies, to be known as Ashton/Quatro Corporation, will be managed independently. Ashton shareholders will acquire majority stake of the new stock.

Pending the blessing of Tyler Pennell, an independent accountant and auditor who is performing due diligence on behalf of both companies, a ceremonial signing will be held this Thursday. The two signatories are Gillian Reece, chairman and CEO of Ashton Mills, and Perry Schield, her counterpart at Quatro Press.

Preliminary agreements have already been signed, and according to the joint statement, the deal can now be cancelled only by agreement of both parties. ❏

Chapter One

Our dinner guest dabbed her lips with a white linen napkin. "Christ, Mark, don't be such a tight-ass."

My eyes bugged as I struggled to swallow.

Neil, sitting next to me, came to my defense. With a smile in his voice, he told our guest, "That's not quite fair, Gillian. Mark has always been detail-conscious. That's how he earned his reputation as a great reporter."

"I wasn't talking about his newspaper career. I was talking about all this hokum with due diligence. The merger contracts have already been fine-tooth-combed to death by every hack lawyer in the state. We need to *move*."

"Soon enough," I assured her. "Three days from now, everything's official. Meanwhile, some last-minute preening of the contracts and scrutiny of the books won't hurt anyone; it's for the good of both companies."

She studied me for a moment with a crooked grin. "Your friends wouldn't tell you this, Mark, but word on the street is, you're a prissy snob."

"But, Gillian," I countered with a wink, "you *are* a friend."

She flashed me a stiff smile. "You better believe it."

Neil wrapped an arm around my shoulder. "Well, he may be a prissy snob, but he's *my* prissy snob—and I wouldn't have it any other way. I'm happy to share hearth and home with this man."

Hearth and home. The niceties of domestic life had never been a high priority to me, not back in the days when I had struggled—successfully—to establish my career as one of Chicago's top investigative reporters. My priorities shifted radically, though, when at last I found love in my life. To my considerable dismay, the object of both my affection and my passion turned out to be another man, an architect. Now, some six years after we first met, Neil and I had already seen our way through a number of life-altering transitions.

The first great upheaval had taken place nearly four years earlier, when my professional wanderlust had convinced me to trade my role as a big-city reporter for that of a small-town newspaper publisher in central Wisconsin. Neil eventually made the move with me, relocating his practice and settling with me in the wonderful Prairie-style house that had been built a half century earlier by my uncle Edwin Quatrain, founder of Quatro Press. Until recently, Quatro had held honors as Dumont's largest industry.

So hearth and home—specifically the grand old Quatrain home on Dumont's Prairie Street—had come to represent for me the comfort and stability of middle age. Smugly, I had begun to muse that there was little left for me to prove in life. On that cool October evening, I was content with my career and secure in my attachment to Neil. Which is to say, I was blissfully unprepared for the events that were about to unfold, events that would threaten everything I had accomplished, everything I now took for granted.

"Mark," said Gillian, dabbing her lips again, "I had no idea your talents veered toward the culinary. My compliments." She lifted her glass and sampled a hefty mouthful of plum red Bordeaux, then swallowed the wine with a moan of approval.

"Thank you," I told her, "but the credit goes to Neil. He's the whiz in the kitchen; I just grill the meat."

"He's being too modest," said Neil. "Mark is a dandy chef."

"Sous chef," I corrected.

Neil laughed. "It's a collaborative effort. With Barb gone, we both pitch in."

Gillian's eyes widened with horror. "You've lost your help?"

I explained, "We needed Barb when Thad was here, but now that he's at school, we can manage on our own."

Another daunting turn in the life shared by Neil and me—and perhaps the most significant—was the unexpected role of parenthood that had been thrust upon us. Shortly after moving to Dumont, we had "inherited" a son, my gawky teenage nephew (technically a second cousin), Thad Quatrain. We had made a home for him during his latter years of high school and watched him blossom into a sensitive and intelligent young man. When it came time for Thad to leave for college, just over a year ago, Neil and I realized that a void in our lives was looming. We were back where we had started, "alone together." Thad was now some two thousand miles away, in California, beginning his sophomore year of theatrical study with the legendary director Claire Gray.

(I should mention that while I had become steward of the Quatrains' ancestral home and guardian of Quatrain progeny, I myself am not a Quatrain; my mother was. The man she married was Mark Manning, and they gave me the same name. We did not share the same middle name, however, so I was spared the tag *junior.*)

Neil continued, "So we lost our housekeeper to the world of music. Barb went east last January to study clarinet at the Peabody."

Gillian sniffed. "They can be *such* ingrates. Domestic help is *not* what it used to be . . ." As she yammered on about the sorry state of the world, I studied the woman who sat across from me in our dining room.

In her early fifties, Gillian Reece was just hitting stride at the peak of her career. A skilled business manager with a peerless head for numbers, she had served as chief financial officer at Ashton Mills a year earlier, when Betty Gifford Ashton, our town's benevolent matriarch, had died. In the reshuffling of the corporate hierarchy that followed Betty's sudden passing, Gillian surfaced as the best person for the job of ushering the venerable old company into the challenging business climate of a new century, one that had seemingly rewritten all the rules.

Sitting on the boards of both Quatro and Ashton, I had come to know Gillian well and to respect her shrewd business sense. No doubt about it, she was tough as nails. Less charitably, others described her as a ball-buster.

"It wasn't like that at all," Neil was telling her, reaching to refill her wineglass. "Barb is a truly gifted musician, and we think she has a shot at establishing an orchestral career. She went with our blessing."

Through a smirk, Gillian noted, "You're entirely too lenient and forgiving."

I asked her, "Did you ever meet Barb? I think you'd have liked her. She was not 'just a housekeeper'—she had several business degrees, and she'd worked in the thick of it as a Wall Street money manager. But she eventually burned out. Must've been the tech wreck."

Gillian shrugged. "Survival of the fittest." Primping her steely gray hair, she made the message clear enough: she was the ultimate survivor, and she had little use for those who didn't measure up. Stabbing a piece of tenderloin with her fork, she dragged it through a bloody pool of juice on the plate, lifted it to her mouth, and swallowed—without chewing. Watching the lump slide down her throat, I thought of a giant boa constrictor swallowing a hapless Pygmy whole.

The image of Gillian as a man-eater was, of course, exaggerated as well as unfair. While she was hardly the model of traditional feminine charms, she was intelligent, articulate, and driven. The future of Ashton Mills, I was confident, had never been entrusted to anyone more dedicated or ambitious. On balance, I felt great respect for Gillian as a business associate. If I couldn't quite think of her as a chum, so what?

Ironically, Neil did indeed have chummy feelings for Gillian. And she reciprocated with an affection that conveyed not only friendship but, occasionally, warmth.

"I nearly forgot," she told him, setting down her fork. "The window treatments—has an installation date been set?"

Neil nodded, swallowing a sip of water. "All set. Todd Draper is coming up from Chicago tomorrow night; installation begins Wednesday."

forded a communion wafer. He held the steamy pulp in his mouth for a long moment, chewing it to nothing before swallowing.

He was an odd one, Esmond, and an even odder match for Gillian. He was as meek, ethereal, and taciturn as she was brazen, worldly, and outspoken. He looked a few years younger than she, perhaps in his late forties. While they both dressed with affluence and a measure of style—he in a natty sport coat, she in a silk suit—they shared no physical resemblance, even after twenty-some years of marriage. She exuded a hard-edged vigor and a breezy, if icy, manner. He, on the other hand, was too willowy (he needed meat). Mentally, he seemed adrift on some transcendental plane. I knew from Neil's involvement in planning their new home that they had never had children.

If it's true that opposites attract, there must have been some explosive chemistry between them. Except, you'd never know it—Esmond barely acknowledged Gillian's existence, while Gillian's few references to her husband were tinged with an indifference that verged on contempt.

Nudging the empty bowl a half inch away from him, Esmond repeated, "Sublime."

"Thank you, Esmond," said Neil. "Would you care for more?"

He shook his head, flustered, as if further indulgence was unthinkable.

Gillian set down her fork with a clack, asking, "Is there more meat, Mark?"

"Plenty." I rose, taking her plate. "Neil, more for you?"

"Uh, sure. I'll give you a hand." He rose as well, excusing himself from our guests as we left for the kitchen.

When the swinging door had closed behind us, I blurted, "*Sublime?*"

With feigned umbrage, Neil asked, "You have quibbles with my ratatouille?"

"None." Laughing softly, I wrapped him in my arms. "It's perfect. You're perfect."

"God," he said, nuzzling close, talking into my ear, "the things we do for business . . ."

I shrugged. "The Reeces may not be the most scintillating company,

She groused, "I'm not sure I trust that guy. He—"

"He's the best in the business," Neil told her. "For a project of this scope, I wouldn't *consider* using anyone else. We're lucky he signed on to the project."

The project under discussion was Gillian's new home. She and her husband had lived until recently out in some tiny burg near the mills.

One of her first executive decisions as Ashton's new chairman and CEO had been to begin construction of a lavish corporate headquarters in Dumont proper, the better to align the company for its intended merger with Quatro Press. The reputation of Neil's architectural practice had grown to the point where he was the clear choice for the design contract. (If it would have helped for me to do some string pulling, I'd have readily pulled them, but to Neil's credit, such machinations were unnecessary; his talents alone were sufficient to snare the job.)

So impressed was Gillian by Neil's design for the Ashton Mills offices, she offered him an additional contract for her new home—a whopper of a house that was going up on the edge of town. She knew what she wanted, and she wanted it fast. With her authorization of unlimited overtime, construction had proceeded at breakneck speed. Now, less than a year after Gillian's initial meeting with Neil, the project was nearly complete, in the hands of various decorating crews.

Gillian's husband, Esmond Reece, had had little-to-no input on the house project, having learned to stay in the background. That night at dinner, he was seated at the table with us, next to Gillian and across from Neil, but he had said not a single word since being served. Unlike the rest of us, he was a vegetarian, a bothersome quirk that Neil had accommodated by preparing a hearty ratatouille. For Gillian, Neil, ar me, the delicious concoction provided a tangy accompaniment to t crusty, buttery beef. For Esmond, it sufficed as his main course, ser in a big bowl like a vegetable stew.

At a lull in the conversation, he looked up from the bowl and a spoke. "Sublime," he told Neil. With a smile, he spooned a rem chunk of tomato, lifted it to his nose, and inhaled the pungent before placing it on his tongue with the sort of reverence typi but it does feel good to entertain now and then. With Thad gone, it seems we never have a real sit-down meal anymore—not in the dining room." We usually ate in the big, friendly kitchen or at a restaurant downtown on First Avenue.

Neil groaned. "I didn't realize we'd gotten that desperate. We need some new friends, Mark." He was kidding; we had friends. We simply lacked amiable dinner companions that evening.

"What's with Esmond?" I wondered.

"You'll get used to him. He's into Eastern studies."

"Oh." I had no idea what Neil was talking about, but his explanation seemed as plausible as any for the man's quirky behavior. What's more, I didn't really care. Though Gillian and Esmond were far from my notion of a fun couple, an evening at home with Neil was reward enough. With each passing year, I had come to realize that, ultimately, it was only he who mattered.

Our "marriage" had matured nicely, I thought, and I was proud that we had learned to age gracefully together—no pining over lost youth. When Neil had first entered my life, I was at the brink of forty, with all of its predictable and attendant insecurities. Now forty-five, with another birthday fast approaching, I was beginning to contemplate the next round number, but these thoughts had no sting. I was ready.

As for Neil, he was eight years younger than I. When we met, the gap had seemed considerable, but now, this gap had narrowed. At thirty-seven, he was beginning to contemplate forty, and I never missed an opportunity to let him know how the added years made him all the more attractive. The man I called "kiddo" was now showing a bit of gray, which gave his sandy brown hair a golden cast. Though it may sound trite, he wasn't getting older; he was getting better.

On his last birthday, Neil decided he was due for a midlife lark, so he had one of his ears pierced—nothing outrageous, a single stud. I offered to buy him a diamond, but he hesitated, saying it might appear too dressy or flamboyant or affected. (God forbid!) Besides, he said, he wanted something more distinctive. So we went to a jeweler, and he chose an amethyst. The spot of purple fire has sparkled from his lobe ever since. He never removes it, and we have both ceased to notice it—except in bed, in the semidarkness, where its steadfast glint spices our nights with an unexpected and erotic dash of derring-do.

"Our guests are waiting," he reminded me, stepping out of our embrace.

"And the lady has a taste for more blood." I removed the remains of our tenderloin from the warming oven and sliced a few thick pink slabs, arranging them on a platter.

Neil skimmed some fat from the juices in the pan, then poured the meaty broth into a gravy boat. "If she tears through this, we've got hot dogs in the fridge."

"She could have them for dessert."

"But I slaved all afternoon on that pumpkin thing."

"All the more for Esmond and us—it looks fabulous." It did. Neil had fussed.

Swooping back into the dining room with our bounty, we found our guests engaged in conversation. There was nothing remarkable about their words or their tone, but I found it strange that this was the first direct exchange I'd witnessed between them since their arrival that evening.

Esmond was asking, "And the studio will be ready next week?"

His wife leaned back in her chair. "It should be—assuming everything stays on schedule."

"That's a safe assumption," said Neil, setting down the gravy boat. He took the platter from me and served Gillian a fresh slice of beef. "I've never seen a construction project run like clockwork before, but this one has."

Through twisted lips, Gillian reminded us, "I run a tight ship."

"So I've seen." I winked at her, sitting.

Neil sat as well, covering a laugh with a cough.

Esmond said, "I'm eager to get into the studio." His flat, lifeless tone conveyed no eagerness at all. He was too calm, too serene, as if in a trance. In my mind's eye, he slumped forward, landing his face in the empty bowl of ratatouille.

Blinking away this image, I asked, "Studio? You're an artist, Esmond?"

"My yoga studio," he explained.

"Ah."

Gillian spoke from the side of her mouth, as if confiding to me. "Esmond has been working with swami for ages. Any year now, he may achieve inner peace."

Esmond bristled, but with great self-control. The squint of his eyes sufficed as an outburst of emotion, well masked. "Really, Gillian," he said. "I wish you would not refer to Tamra as 'swami.' It's condescending and disrespectful."

His wife arched her brows innocently. "Why, I always thought 'swami' was a term of *great* respect."

"It is—when it's spoken from the heart."

"Sorry, Esmond. I've never been very adept at matters of the heart." Her tone was more cynical than contrite.

Steering the conversation to safer ground, I told her, "Your new house is the talk of the town, Gillian. I hope you'll allow the *Register* to run a story on it. Our features editor, Glee Savage, is dying to have a look inside. In fact, so am I."

"Well"—she waffled—"I suppose I owe you that much, Mark. Your support of the merger, on both Ashton's and Quatro's boards, has smoothed the way with a lot of wary stockholders."

"The merger seems right for both companies. I've been happy to support it."

"You're welcome to bring over your editor whenever you like."

Neil volunteered, "I'd be happy to show everyone around tomorrow."

"Perfect," said Gillian. Turning to me, she added, "That was a fine story in this morning's paper, by the way."

"On behalf of the paper, thank you." I hesitated. "But in truth, it was little more than a rehash of the press release."

"Nonsense." She flicked a hand, pausing between bites of beef. "It was well written, concise, and told with a real sensitivity to the issues."

"Yeah." Neil nodded. "I was pleased to read that the merging boards expressed their concern for the community and the environment."

"Oh, please." Gillian's lips sputtered with wry amusement. "Let's just say we had the PR department working overtime. I hope it wasn't *too* transparent."

Diplomatically, I told Neil, "I'm sure Gillian is just being glib."

"I'm sure," she echoed. Then she asked me, "Who wrote the story? I didn't recognize the byline—Charles something?"

"Charles Oakland."

"That's it. Obviously one of your more seasoned writers."

Neil burst into laughter.

Both Gillian and Esmond gave a startled blink, confused by Neil's reaction.

He explained to them, "Charles Oakland is Mark's pen name at the paper. *He* wrote that story."

Gillian looked befuddled. "Oh?"

I recounted, "When I took over the *Dumont Daily Register* four years ago, my role changed from reporter to publisher. But writing's in my blood, and occasionally I still like to report stories that interest me. Our readers have come to know my name in conjunction with the paper's editorials—which are opinion, not fact—so I felt I needed a different persona when reporting. Thus was born Charles Oakland. By now, it's pretty much an open secret who he really is."

"Thanks for clueing me." Underlying Gillian's good-natured tone was an implied reprimand for having kept her in the dark till then.

Neil swirled some wine remaining in his glass. "The story mentioned an accountant who needs to give the deal a final blessing. What's that all about?"

"That's a pain in the ass," Gillian said sweetly, through a false smile.

"That's the due diligence," I explained to Neil. "It's pretty routine. When companies merge, 'due diligence' is performed to verify that everyone's accounting is on the up and up. By entering into a friendly merger, Quatro and Ashton are, in effect, buying each other, so the two boards agreed upon the services of a single auditor. Tyler Pennell comes highly recommended."

Gillian sniffed. "He's a rube. He's from Green Bay." She paused before adding, "But I suppose he's harmless."

"Doug recommended him." I was referring to Douglas Pierce, our local sheriff and a close friend. "Tyler is actually a forensic accountant, a specialist in uncovering accounting irregularities relevant to solving crimes. He worked with Doug on a case a few months ago, and Doug was impressed. That's good enough for me."

Neil chortled. "I had no idea that accounting could be so cloak-and-dagger."

"Where large sums of money are involved, there's always room for mischief."

Gillian raised her glass. "I'll drink to that."

And she drained the last of the wine.

Chapter Two

Purple fire.

The sensual images that tickled my sleeping mind that night centered on the purple fire radiating from the amethyst stud that Neil wore. In reality, he lay next to me in our bed upstairs on Prairie Street. In my dream, however, we were running in a park near the house, a craggy green glen of rocks and pines that had been sculpted by a glacier in some frosty eon of the unknowable past.

Side by side, we trot along a path that circles through the park's flat valley floor. The sun hangs low in the evening sky, casting pointed blue shadows from ancient spruces that spring from the ravines surrounding us. The speck of stone pinned to Neil's ear captures the glint of waning daylight, transforms the gentle golden rays to fiercest purple, and wraps us in an aura of pure energy. Our steps are effortless, our breathing easy, as we bound along the familiar course in perfect harmony, our feet barely kissing the ground, crunching the gravel.

Neil wears skimpy, silvery nylon shorts, a pair of well-worn leather running shoes, and no shirt as he pulls ahead of me a pace or two. My running gear is similar, though I generally prefer cotton shorts—these are an old, old favorite, faded yellow, now soft as flannel. Although our workout requires no exertion, we do sweat, and I watch the beads of moisture trickle down Neil's back, collecting beneath the waistband of his shorts. A gray V spreads down the silver nylon, clinging to the crack between his swaying buttocks.

The sight before me is more than sufficient to bring a tingle of arousal to my groin. Although this would logically seem to impede my running, the effect is quite the opposite in dreamland, where I feel propelled and weightless, as if ready to take flight.

Similar dreams have visited me before, most notably six years ago, in the months leading up to my first coupling with Neil. Those dreams of flight, I now understood, signaled repressed longings and my need to escape, to take flight from turbulent inner issues I was unable to face by day. Now, with those issues long resolved and their attendant gremlins consigned to history, the ethereal ramblings of my nights took on an altogether different tone, one of carefree abandon.

What better way to slough off the minor tribulations of waking life than to indulge in such steamy, mindless recreation with Neil? Though aware that he is not physically present in my dream, I sense that he is with me, virtually if not literally. Is he sharing the same dream?

Zipping along behind him, enjoying the sight of him, I chide myself for pondering such inscrutable nonsense—shared dreams, virtual presence, indeed. My mind doesn't work that way, I remind myself; I have little use for such loosey-goosey notions. Perhaps I've been influenced by our dinner conversation regarding Eastern studies, yoga studios, and swami. Did I overindulge in Neil's pumpkin thing? Were these thoughts the result of errant digestive gases?

Stop it. These nasty ideas are counterproductive. The scenario playing out in my dozing mind was meant to be enjoyed. I've taken this excursion with Neil often enough to know where it's leading, to understand that its climax will be a scorcher. So I silence my inner monologue, conquer my thinking brain, and allow myself to drift witlessly into the scripted events that continue to unravel before me in the park.

Rounding a curve in the path, Neil looks over his shoulder at me; the amethyst in his ear is momentarily blinding. He asks, "Had enough?"

"I could use a breather." Though my words sound winded, I am not.

Slowing to a trot, Neil breaks from the gravel path and begins crossing the turf toward a fanciful pavilion that fronts a small lake, a mirror-placid pond. A duck obligingly completes the scene, waddling out of the water to rest on a tiny island just big enough to support a single willow, its slender leaves already brushed yellow by the October nights.

Following Neil's lead, I join him crossing the grass. As our pace slows to a walk, I pull up beside him and drape an arm over his shoulders. I mention, "Beautiful day."

With a sidelong glance, he asks, "Small talk? The weather?"

"Okay, *you're* beautiful. Better?"

"Considerably."

An embankment leads up to a porch that stretches the length of the pavilion. Neil and I trudge up to the porch, where a few park benches are positioned to look out over the pond toward the steep wooded hills. We often rest here, enjoying the scenery, deciding whether our return home will be at a walk or a run.

I approach the middle bench, which has the best view, symmetrically framed by the gingerbread and gewgaws that decorate a colonnade supporting the roof. I deliberately sit at the bench's middle, not only to take full advantage of the view, but to force Neil to sit near my side. It's a familiar routine, a well-rehearsed enactment of innocent flirtation.

As always, Neil slides onto the bench next to me, barely touching. We lean back, relax, and sigh in appreciation of the sylvan slopes beyond. One of us casually shifts his weight, and our calves brush. We've shared far greater intimacies more often than I can count, but this moment of first contact never fails to thrill me, as if an electric spark has arced across the microdistance separating the hair follicles on our legs. Neil nudges his ankle next to mine; our leather shoes squeak as they meet. Then I slide closer to him on the bench, nestling my cotton shorts against his nylon-clad thigh.

It never occurs to us that this public park is not ours alone. With no hesitation—let alone shame—we turn to each other and indulge in a long, openmouthed kiss, the sort of kiss that affirms we can never get enough of each other, the sort of kiss that mimics hunger sated by gluttony. Invariably, my hands find their way to Neil's shorts, and I knead the warm bulge trapped by the silver nylon.

Neil's lips part from mine so he can laugh. "Hold on," he says, catching his breath, "I'd better take care of something," meaning, he needs to pee.

With a be-my-guest gesture, I excuse him. He rises, adjusting the lump in his shorts, then walks the length of the porch, his treaded soles making gummy noises on the bright green enamel. At the end of the porch, he descends a short flight of stairs and disappears around the side of the building.

Stretching my arms along the back of the bench, I splay my legs and enjoy the evening breeze wafting over my body. Out on the little island, the duck appears from under the willow's wispy branches, moves to the shore, and decides to take a swim. I watch for long moments as he circles the island with a lazy lack of purpose, then drifts out of view.

Two hands cover my eyes from behind. "Penny for your thoughts."

I hadn't even noticed Neil's return. "Why, I was thinking of you, of course."

"I didn't realize the thought of me was so relaxing."

"Sometimes. Not always."

"I think you need some excitement. Some stimulation. Close your eyes." His hands slide away from my face.

Is this dreamy, or what? With eyes closed, I hear him move to the front of the bench; then I feel him crouch between my legs.

Both hands grab the waistband of my shorts. "Up," he commands.

I lift my butt an inch or two off the bench as he yanks the shorts past my hips. Instantly, my penis bobs to life in the open air. He moves out of the way for a moment, working the shorts down to my shoes and, finally, free. Resuming his position between my legs, he hunkers before me, resting both elbows on my knees.

I have not yet opened my eyes, the better to fantasize his movements and anticipate his intentions. While I cannot predict his exact ministrations, the object of his attention requires no speculation, and moments later, I feel his warm hand take hold of me. Stiffening to the verge of exquisite pain, I gasp.

"Sorry, didn't mean to hurt you."

With eyes still closed, I assure him, "Didn't hurt a bit."

Then his lips surround me, gobbling the whole length. His probing fingers tickle and toy. As my hips begin to rock gently, I realize from his garbled moans that he's enjoying this workout as much as I am.

With my head lolling back, my eyelids part, and I see the rows of precise, white slats that form the porch's ceiling. He continues to gurgle and slurp, and my rapture intensifies as I draw my chin to my chest, looking down at him; he bobs with abandon, loving his task. Lifting my hands from the back of the bench, I run my fingers through his sandy hair. At my touch, he swallows deeper still.

I wonder, Where's he putting it? Recalling some lame joke about a hollow leg, I begin to laugh, but the noise spilling out of me sounds deep and jerky, like spasmodic suffocation. I'm getting plenty of air, but I do feel light-headed, as if the air lacks oxygen. The sensation isn't frightening; in fact, it's a rush. My hands grope his head all the tighter, feeling the clumps of his now damp hair, the sides of his face, his ears.

Just as the euphoric haze is beginning to block my senses, I hear a familiar sound—the gummy squeak of Neil's shoes drawing near from the side of the porch.

Huh? Fingering the ears of the man who kneels before me, I realize that neither lobe is sporting a stud, amethyst or otherwise. Turning my head toward the approaching footsteps, I confirm that Neil is indeed there, not here, and although I feel suddenly guilty—caught in the act—I also feel perversely clever, as if to say, Hey, Neil, look what I found!

I assume that Neil will feel affronted by his discovery of me with whomever, but my momentary fear is quickly quelled by the look on his face. Far from appearing shocked or angry, Neil absorbs the scene before him with a catlike grin. He pauses just long enough to peel off his shorts, then steps behind the guy who has not yet looked up. Neil slides his penis, which is now plenty hard, into the other guy's mop of hair, enjoying the silky feel and rhythmic motion.

Watching this hot scene unfold before me, I am not only titillated—and how—but intrigued. Neil and the unknown visitor look very much alike, at least as far as I can tell. I have not seen the other guy's face, but he has Neil's build, and they share the same sandy hair.

Here's where it gets *really* good:

Now that Neil is as aroused as he can get (at least without risking an aneurism), he steps up onto the bench, straddling my hips with his running shoes. The shoes themselves have always been a mild, harmless fetish of mine, so they're the icing on this torrid cake. He crouches slightly, lowering his groin till it's level with my face. Like a Pavlovian pup, I get busy.

It doesn't take long. Working in unison, like some well-oiled machine, we three are pumping and groaning. Neil's shoes are squeaking on the slick bench as he shifts his weight from side to side, as if marching further down my throat. Then he catches his breath, freezes for a moment, and with a heaving shout, delivers his orgasm. It races down me, through me, and finding the logical outlet, pulses into the guy on the floor, whose explosion is best described as spontaneous combustion—replete with pyrotechnics, angelic fanfares, a spray of confetti, and one last blinding flash of purple fire.

And then, of course, I wake up.

Not generally one to look a gift horse in the mouth, I could not help wondering what, if anything, my dream had "meant." Though it was fun, to say the least, it was also troubling.

The idea of adding a third sex partner to my relationship with Neil, even if only in the slippery context of slumber, was a tempting prospect that I had previously weighed and dismissed. I'm not sure why the notion of a ménage tugged at my libido from time to time—perhaps it was because Neil had been my first same-sex partner and I had never played the field, while he, in his younger years, had. Did I feel cheated of the experimentation that more curious and less inhibited men took for granted in exploring their emerging sexuality?

I had never broached this topic with Neil forthright. There was no need to ask him about it because he was so convincingly content with me and me alone. Though I felt immeasurable gratitude for his love and commitment—and reciprocated with the same—there was still that nagging wonder. What would it be like? Would he freak if I suggested it? If he were open to the idea, would I later regret it?

The safer course, I knew, was to let well enough alone. Thankful for what I already had, I had come to understand that it would be foolish to threaten my happiness, our happiness, with vague longings for quick, intrusive thrills.

I pondered these matters with some gravity when I awoke that Tuesday morning, Neil still asleep at my side. Similar thoughts traced through my head an hour later as we sat in the kitchen with our friend Doug Pierce, enjoying a breakfast routine that was repeated almost daily. By the time we had parted company, each of us starting our separate days—Doug driving downtown to the sheriff's department, Neil to his architectural office, and I to the newsroom of the *Dumont Daily Register*—by then, thoughts of erotic adventure were the furthest thing from my mind. I had a newspaper to put out, another in the endless march of daily deadlines.

Parking in my reserved spot just behind the building on First Avenue, Dumont's main drag, I barely paused to appreciate the fine October morning with is pristine, azure sky before entering the street-level lobby, waving to Connie, our receptionist, and bounding up the single flight of stairs to the newsroom.

It was here that I always felt most in my element. While the gathering and reporting of news is, by its nature, an excursion into the unknown, the process of journalism had become predictable and second nature to me. Its protocols, ethics, and deadlines had come to represent a sturdy, understood framework not only for publishing, but for life itself. No wonder I always felt so much "at home" upon entering the *Register*'s offices. It wasn't just that I liked my work. I owned the place.

"Morning, Mark," "Hey, boss," "Great tie, Mr. Manning," called various staffers as I zigzagged my way through the maze of desks and moved toward the far side of the room, where editorial offices are separated from the hubbub by a glass wall. Beyond the glass, in the anteroom of my own office, I noticed two men, their backs to me, sitting at the low, round conference table with my managing editor, Lucille Haring—there was no mistaking her bright crop of red hair. Not recalling that a meeting had been scheduled so early, I wondered what was up and quickened my pace.

"Mark! Can I trouble you for a minute?"

Turning, I immediately broke into a smile. "No trouble at all, Glee." Our features editor, Glee Savage, stepped smartly down the aisle in my direction. In her midfifties, she was one of our most senior staffers, having started at the *Register* straight out of college, working for the paper's founding publisher, Barret Logan. Back then, she'd worked on the "women's page," covering weddings and club meetings; now she edited our daily *Trends* section, writing many of the page-one features herself.

She had dedicated her entire career to promoting Dumont's finer, gentler side, and if our little town could be said to have a fashion maven, it was surely Glee. She played the role to the hilt, always dressing to the nines, preferring to risk too much color rather than too little. This morning she wore a neatly tailored suit of nubby silk, ruddy ocher, almost orange. Accenting her autumnal ensemble was a ruffled blouse of shocking yellow. Not a tall woman, she nonetheless strutted with authority atop sensible heels of oxblood calfskin. Incongruously, she carried in one arm a large copper saucepan. Always chipper, always sincere, she was the personification of "perky."

"I hate to nab you first thing," she said, touching my arm with the fingers of her free hand, "but I'm *dying* to know—were you able to set up an interview at the Reece house?" She arched her brows and flashed me an expectant grin, stretching her glossy red lips.

"At your service." I doffed an imaginary hat. "Dinner was rather dull, but yes, I did get Gillian Reece to consent to the feature. We're expected this afternoon."

"We? Keeping tabs on me, boss?"

I laughed. "Never. But I've been itching to see the place myself, and Neil offered to give us both the grand tour. We're expected at one. Care to join Neil and me for lunch before we head over there?"

"Gosh, I'd love to, but I have an eleven-thirty appointment that'll probably run late. Why don't I just meet you at the house?"

"Fine by me. Do you know where it is?"

Glee rolled her eyes. "The whole *town* knows where it is."

"Just look for our car. If we're not there yet, wait, and we'll introduce you to Gillian."

"Perfect. I'm eager to meet her. Thanks, Mark." And she hustled off toward the photo studio, ready to style a recipe picture for the food page.

Lucille Haring had spotted me through the glass wall, and when I stepped toward my office door, she stood, saying, "Gentlemen, here's Mark." Lucy wore a drab olive-colored pantsuit that day, her typical work uniform. Thirty-something, Lucy had joined the *Register*'s staff shortly after I'd bought the paper. Though she had now worked side by side with Glee Savage for four years, none of the older woman's fashion sense had rubbed off on my mannish second-in-command.

As I stepped into the room, the others stood and turned. The two men who had been waiting for me were Perry Schield, chief executive officer of Quatro Press, and Tyler Pennell, the accountant from Green Bay who was performing due diligence in preparation for the merger with Ashton Mills. "Gentlemen," I said, shaking hands with both of them, "what an unexpected pleasure."

"Mark," Perry acknowledged me, returning my handshake and bobbing his head of thinning, silvered hair.

"Morning, Mr. Manning," said Tyler, pumping my hand in an earnest, down-to-business manner. A generation younger than Perry, not yet thirty, Tyler might have passed as the older man's son.

They were cut from the same cloth—literally, wearing dark blue wool business suits that appeared identical, except that Tyler's jacket had an extra button, four instead of three, and Perry wore a starched linen handkerchief in his breast pocket. Tyler was a nice-looking man, in a conservative sort of way. Perry, at sixty-two, looked more distinguished than attractive; a note of fatigue in his bearing hinted that he had passed his prime.

"Mark," said Lucy, motioning that our guests should resume their seats at the table, "Mr. Pennell has raised some concerns with Mr. Schield, and I thought you'd want to talk to them." The tone of her voice, coupled with her uncharacteristically formal use of *mister,* signaled a matter of some importance. Was something wrong?

"Thanks, Lucy," I said through a leery squint as she stepped out of the room. Sitting, joining the two men at the low table, I asked, "What can I do for you?" With an air of nonchalance, I crossed my legs, instinctively trying to lighten the heavy tone I sensed in the room. But I suddenly felt out of place—in my own office, no less—because my casual posture and khaki suit were in such sharp contrast to the staid manner and appearance of my visitors.

"Actually, Mark," said Perry, clearing his throat, "I'm not sure there's anything you *can* do for us—not yet. We just wanted to make you aware of a discussion we've been having. We wanted to alert you to a, well . . . a development."

Tyler raised a few fingers. "I'm not sure *development* is exactly the right word. Let's just call it a 'concern'—a preliminary concern."

I uncrossed my legs and sat upright. "You've certainly piqued my interest."

Perry cleared his throat again, preparing to speak—an annoying habit that had come to nettle me during board meetings at Quatro, which typically lasted three hours. As the company's CEO, he had lots to say at those meetings, punctuated with nonstop hacking. "I'm not sure where to begin," he said, looking agitated.

I suggested, "Perhaps Tyler should explain."

Perry nodded, unfurling the handkerchief from his pocket and covering his mouth for a deep, phlegmy cough.

Tyler said, "This concerns the due diligence for the merger, Mr. Manning."

"You're welcome to call me Mark."

"Thank you, sir."

I cringed. His deferential politeness made me uncomfortably aware of my age. Though my years were midway between his and Perry's, I was sure that in Tyler's eyes, I was already in the same creaky boat.

He continued, "I'm not certain what to make of this—it may be nothing—but I've discovered some accounting blips while examining the books at Ashton Mills."

"Blips?" I asked.

"Inconsistencies. Nothing major, nothing alarming, but nonetheless unexpected. Something doesn't quite add up. It's probably a matter of simple human error, but I'm surprised that it would find its way into Ashton's final, year-end report."

"Yes, that is surprising." I drummed my fingers on the arm of the chair, recalling, "Ashton Mills routinely subjects its accounting to an independent, external audit—precisely to eliminate the possibility of 'human error.'"

"Mark," said Perry, leaning into the conversation again, "if this isn't a red flag, I don't know what is."

"It bears looking into," I agreed.

"Looking into?" Perry's milky eyes widened. "If you ask me, this could be the tip of the iceberg, and we should be extremely wary of the rush to merge."

"Now, hold on," I said, raising both hands in a calming gesture. "This merger hasn't been rushed in the least; it's been in the works for nearly a year. Don't forget, both companies—both boards—have shown great enthusiasm for the merger, which is based on sound business reasons." I rattled off the points that had been covered in the press release.

But I neglected to mention that one of the most appealing aspects of the joint venture was related to Quatro's executive suite. By combining forces with Ashton and sharing management resources, Quatro would be inheriting the dynamic Gillian Reece, who seemed far better equipped than Perry Schield to face the daunting business challenges that lay ahead. I wasn't sure whether Perry himself realized that the merger had been compelled by his own lackluster leadership. Either way, he would soon retire, walking away wealthy.

I turned to the accountant. "Tyler? What's your honest assessment—do these findings amount to a deal-breaker?"

"Gosh, no. At least not yet. I need to do more digging. Most important, I have questions about Ashton's accounting practices, and I need to get answers. Fast."

Perry coughed. "I'm thick with their CFO—met him at the club, and we've played a few rounds of golf together. Maybe I could help set up a meeting."

"Forget the financial guy," I said, trying not to sound too dismissive. "Tyler, I think you should go straight to the top. Time is running short, and there's a lot at stake. Gillian rose through the ranks as a crack accountant, so I'm sure she knows Ashton's books inside and out. If you've discovered inconsistencies, she'll want to be the first to know the details."

Tyler hesitated. "I'm not so sure, Mark. I've always found her to be somewhat, well . . . frosty."

"That may be true"—I couldn't help chuckling—"but she's first and foremost a businessperson. If you have questions, she'll have the answers. There's surely a logical explanation."

Tyler heaved a sigh, then tossed his hands. "All right. I'll try to set something up."

"I'll be seeing her this afternoon. Want me to broach this for you?"

Tyler's features brightened some. "Yes, actually."

Perry cleared his throat. "Careful, Tyler. She's a handful."

"Yes, sir. I've noticed."

Chapter Three

Tuesday had all the makings of a slow news day. It had peaked early, with the worrisome concerns expressed during Perry Schield and Tyler Pennell's visit, but otherwise, I found little else to occupy my time or my mind as the hours slid noonward. Even the morning mail proved humdrum. After one too many strolls through the newsroom, having exhausted all reasonable options for chitchat, I could tell that the staff was beginning to feel pestered, wondering why I wasn't huddled in an important meeting somewhere.

So shortly after eleven, I decided to get some fresh air. I would walk the few blocks to Neil's office, drop in unexpectedly, and pester *him* till it was time for us to move onward to lunch.

Stepping to the desk in my inner office, I donned my jacket and checked my pockets for wallet, keys, pen, and notepad—an old habit, as an experienced reporter had no way of telling when a story might break. I also made sure that a pair of reading glasses was tucked in my breast pocket—a newer habit, one I had resisted, necessitated by the first ravages of middle age. And finally, I plucked a phone from its charger on the desk and slipped it into a side pocket of my coat—a brand-new habit that still made me uncomfortable.

I hate cell phones. Once the cutting-edge technology of heart surgeons and others who might legitimately be interrupted at dinner on a matter of life or death, these intrusive gadgets have become so ubiquitous that most adolescents now carry them—and use them—to the constant annoyance of society at large. I had once thought that the mark of true success was to be *disconnected*. I reasoned that if I was important enough, and if someone needed to reach me, that was his problem, not mine. Now, apparently, I needed to keep myself at the disposal of anyone with the whim to dial my number.

It was Lucy who finally convinced me that my reticence to carry a phone was stodgy and contrarian. Journalism, she lectured, was an increasingly electronic medium; lost minutes could mean missed deadlines. She needed me, the *Register* needed me, twenty-four-seven. So a week ago, against my better instincts, I told her to get me a phone—with the strict caveat that only she would know the number, a condition to which she readily agreed. (Naturally, I shared the number with Neil, but only after securing his promise never to use it.)

As of that Tuesday morning, the gizmo had never once rung. On the one hand, I found its silence a matter of great relief; my fears had been unfounded. On the other hand, I had begun to suspect that the phone simply didn't work, so out of sheer curiosity, before leaving my office, I flipped it open and decided to check the local weather number. It was then that I discovered that the timing of two recent incursions into my life had proved ironically propitious—in my pocket I had glasses at the ready, which I needed in order to read the damn buttons on the phone.

Learning that the afternoon would remain cool but sunny, I decided there was no need for the trench coat I kept at the office, so I pocketed the phone, pocketed the glasses, and headed out, crossing the newsroom, descending the stairs, waving to Connie, and emerging through the glass doors onto the street.

First Avenue was quiet; sleepy little Dumont's noon "rush" was some forty minutes off. There was a snap to my step as I ambled along the sidewalk, peering into shop windows as if they might contain something new. At the corner, I waited for the light to turn, even though there wasn't a moving car in sight. Then, crossing the street, I began to whistle some unnameable tune. Feeling suddenly foolish, I laughed at myself, enjoying the bright fall day. As I headed toward Neil's office, my pace quickened in anticipation of seeing him.

And the phone began to warble.

Good Lord, I thought, had some catastrophe befallen the world? Was Lucy running wild through the newsroom, shrieking to stop the presses, trying desperately to reach me?

I turned on my heel to head back to the paper, then realized the phone was still ringing and decided I'd better answer it. Stepping beneath the awning of a dark corner tavern, I extracted the phone from my pocket, flipped it open, and fumbled with the buttons. Squinting, I couldn't quite read them, but the green one seemed a reasonable choice, so I punched it. Lifting the phone to my face, I asked uncertainly, "Yes?"

"Uh . . . Mark?"

"Yes, Lucy."

"*Lucy?* It's Roxanne. What's wrong, Mark? You sound weird."

Sounding more perturbed than weird, I asked bluntly, "How on earth did you get this number?"

"I called you at the paper, and the receptionist said you'd stepped out. So she suggested I try your new cell phone. Welcome to the twenty-first century, Mark."

I muttered, "More like, welcome to hell . . ."

"Awww. Rough day, sweetcakes?"

Allowing a laugh, I conceded, "Not really. It's been a slow day."

"Then I'm not interrupting. Got a minute?"

"Sure, Rox. For you, anytime." If we were going to talk awhile, I didn't care to loiter in the tavern's shadow, so I crossed First Avenue toward a little park, a patch of green that marked the center of town. A rusty cannon roosted on a chunk of granite with a plaque displaying rows of names etched in bronze. A green-enameled park bench, not unlike the one where I had perched in my dream earlier that morning, sat nearby, affording a partial view of the street, truncated by the cannon's snout. I settled on the bench, alone in this bellicose Eden.

". . . ever since the election," Roxanne was saying.

She was referring to the election of the previous fall, in which her husband, Carl Creighton, had lost his bid to become lieutenant governor of Illinois. They had since resumed their careers as high-powered attorneys in Chicago.

"How's Carl taking it?" I asked.

"The loss? He's fine. You know Carl—unflappable as they come. Besides, it wasn't political ambition that motivated him to run. It was his sense of pubic duty. A lot of people thought he was right for the job."

I hesitated. "And you?"

"What about me?" As she said the words, I visualized her smirk. "Did I think Carl was right for the job? Of course I—"

"I meant, how have you been handling the disappointment of last November?"

"Christ, Mark, that was a year ago. I'm a big girl—and a city girl. Springfield just isn't 'my kind of town.'" She added, "Chicago is."

Roxanne and I were old friends; in fact, she had introduced me to Neil. She and I spoke often, but the opportunity had never seemed right for a heart-to-heart regarding the impact of the lost election on her emotions. I'd been reluctant to ask about it because I'd assumed I wouldn't get a straight answer.

I reminded her, "You were getting into it, the whirl of the campaign. Don't try to pretend you didn't find a certain allure in the prospect of becoming the lieutenant governor's wife."

"Why do you think I *married* him?" she quipped.

Given the timing of their marriage mere weeks before the election, anyone who didn't know her as well as I did might have judged her decision to wed, after several years of foot-dragging, as patently opportunistic. "Nonsense," I told her. "You love Carl for all the right reasons. Rox, you've got a *life* now."

"I'd be insulted if you weren't so insightful. It's true—he fills a void." Her tone was so blasé, anyone eavesdropping would have thought that Carl merely amused her, or gave a good back rub, or helped with a few household chores. But I knew their love to be deep and genuine. Though Roxanne still clung to her veneer of wisecracking ennui, she was, inside, a changed woman. And the changes, I happily observed, were all for the better.

With quiet sincerity, I told her, "We miss you up here."

"I miss you guys, too. Sorry the visits have tapered off."

"Nothing planned? The guest room's always ready for you."

"No, 'fraid not. As you've already noted, I've got a life now."

I laughed. "And Chicago offers a few more social diversions than Dumont. You don't need to drive four hours to find fun with friends."

"To each his own. Dumont seems to work for you."

"We weren't talking about me."

"I certainly didn't intend to talk about *me*. I called *you*, remember?"

"Okay, Roxanne"—I crossed my legs, lounging lazily on the bench—"what can I do for you?"

"Well," she waffled, groping for a topic to justify her call, "I was wondering how the plans for the big merger are proceeding. Everything on track?"

"Hope so. Tyler Pennell says he came across some wrinkle in the Ashton Mills books, but it's probably nothing. When it comes to the numbers, that company is no slouch."

"So I've seen." Roxanne had been involved in some early discussions that were held when both companies were sniffing each other like nosy, horny dogs. It was largely on the basis of her blessing that I had subsequently championed the merger to both boards.

"I suggested that Tyler should voice his concerns directly to Gillian Reece."

"Miss Congeniality?" asked Roxanne through a low chortle.

"She's an accounting whiz as well as a first-class administrator." While singing these praises to Roxanne, I noticed, out on First Avenue, Gillian's husband, Esmond Reece, parking at the curb. He got out of his car, locked it, and strode away with purpose, heading up the sidewalk in the same direction I had been walking when my phone had rung. I told Roxanne, "If Tyler has questions, I'm sure Gillian has answers."

"I'm sure." Roxanne was a true master at infusing agreement with cynicism.

"Don't be so hard on her. I thought you admired strong women."

"Oh, I *admire* her," Roxanne told me. "I just don't much *like* her."

Fair enough, I thought.

"By the way, how goes construction of the mansion? Have they installed milady's drawbridge yet? Have they filled the moat?"

"Neil is hard at work wrapping up the project. I think they're basically down to decorating. I get the grand tour this afternoon."

"Don't make me jealous, Mark. I'm apt to slash my wrists."

"Well, I *have* been eager to see the place. Neil's proud of it."

"Of course he is." No cynicism colored these words. Roxanne loved Neil as much as I did (but that's another story). "Gillian is lucky to have someone of Neil's talents available right there in Dumont."

"Neil is lucky to have such an extravagant client—nothing but the best. They're bringing up some hotshot curtain guy from Chicago."

"Todd Draper?"

"You've heard of him?"

"And *you* call yourself a journalist. Where have you been, Mark, under a rock?"

"Well, I . . . uh . . ."

Roxanne laughed with delight. "Just kidding, precious. I wouldn't have known Todd Draper from Adam, but Neil used him for the rebuild of our condo." After Carl had lost the election, he and Roxanne decided to nurse the wound of defeat by splurging on a complete redo of their high-rise apartment in Chicago, gutting it to the girders. They turned to Neil for the overall design, and he, in turn, chose the various decorating contractors.

"Hngh," I said, impressed, "it sounds as if this Draper guy really *is* good."

"Not only that . . ." Roxanne paused enticingly before telling me, "Todd Draper is quite the dish."

"Really?"

"Mm-hmm," she purred.

"He's driving up tonight—staying at our place."

"My, my, my. Isn't *that* a promising setup? Now, you must promise me, Mark—no sneaking into his room tomorrow to roll in his dirty sheets. Don't embarrass yourself."

"My *God*, you have a lurid mind."

"Don't I, though?"

Chapter Four

Curious thoughts about Todd Draper wafted through my mind as I crossed First Avenue and resumed my walk to Neil's office. Roxanne's phone call had lent an unexpected note of cheery expectation to a day that had seemed, only minutes earlier, too predictable. We had a guest arriving, one whom Roxanne had described as a "dish." Her taste in men was discerning—and uncannily similar to my own—so I couldn't help toying with mental images of the guy who would later land on our doorstep. Also, I wondered, why hadn't Neil mentioned that the impending inconvenience of having a houseguest would be outweighed by the visual stimulation he would provide?

These minor mysteries vanished as Neil's storefront office came into view with its discreet, tasteful sign near the door reading NEIL M. WAITE, AIA. His was a one-man operation, supplemented at times by interns from a local college. These quarters, along with my office at the *Register* and our house on Prairie Street, represented our shared life, our home. The simple act of turning the knob on his door conveyed a message of security and stability, and I chided myself for having found a disagreeable monotony in that morning's unremarkable routine.

Walking inside, I expected to find Neil busy in the rear area of his office, which was devoted to the design and engineering aspects of his trade, replete with a full array of computers and plotters, as well as the traditional drafting table and tools he still preferred to use for residential work. Instead, Neil was seated at a desk near the front of the room, which also contained a conference table for clients. Sitting at the table, talking to Neil as I entered, was Esmond Reece.

Looking every inch the successful small-town architect, Neil wore a crisp, plaid dress shirt with knit necktie and tan corduroys. He broke into a smile as he looked up from his work at a typewriter—a sleek, gray, vintage IBM Selectric from the 1960s. Though his office was thoroughly computerized, he disliked the look of mailing labels on his correspondence, which he deemed tacky, so he used the Selectric solely for addressing envelopes. Its carbon-film ribbon and "porcupine" type ball produced clean, perfect text. That's one of the qualities I love most about Neil—the man has standards, and he sticks to them.

"This is a pleasant surprise," he said, checking his watch. "You're early."

"Better early than late." Closing the door behind me, I moved to the desk and leaned to give Neil a hug.

Esmond stood. "Good morning, Mark. Nice to see you. Thanks again for dinner at your home last night. It was wonderful." Though his words were congenial, they lacked life, as if recited by a golem. Reinforcing this eerie image, he wore an odd sort of suit of stretchy charcoal fabric. Styled without traditional tailoring, it seemed to cling to, rather than hang from, his body. The jacket was buttoned to the neck, showing no shirt. It looked like a uniform for clones in some menacing futuristic thriller.

I stepped to the table and shook his hand. "The evening with you and Gillian was our pleasure. You're always welcome." I sat at the table.

Esmond remained standing, telling Neil, "If this is a bad time, I could—"

"Not at all." Neil fed a large envelope into the carriage of the typewriter. "I'm glad you dropped by. It's important to air your concerns." He typed a few short lines; the machine's metal ball raced along with a muffled rattle.

Esmond sat again, looking perplexed. "I don't want to appear to be going behind anyone's back—certainly not Gillian's—but I don't know where else to turn." He slumped.

The momentary silence was broken by the sound of another envelope grinding through the typewriter carriage. "Uh," I asked anyone, "what's going on?"

Neil answered while typing. "Esmond is worried about some of the cost overruns on the house."

"Ahh." But I was confused. Turning to Esmond, I said, "Pardon a rather personal question, but isn't Gillian paying for the house?"

"Of course. She pays for everything."

"It's her project," noted Neil, pulling the last envelope out of the typewriter and jogging a stack of them on the desk.

Esmond said, "I wasn't talking about just the house. I mean, Gillian pays for *everything,* all the time."

"I see," said Neil, getting up from the desk. He moved to the conference table and joined us, sitting next to me, facing Esmond. "I wasn't aware of your financial arrangements."

I wanted to ask Esmond, Don't you work? What *do* you do? Has Gillian always "kept" you?

This last unspoken query was a long shot. Though Esmond seemed likable enough, a gentle soul, he didn't strike me as an enticing candidate as a boy toy, even in younger years.

Sensing the questions hanging in the air, Esmond said, "I need to share with you some of my background with Gillian. I assume she's left you in the dark."

I explained, "I've known Gillian only in the context of Ashton Mills; we've interacted only at the professional level. She hasn't spoken of her home life, and I've never pried."

"On the other hand," Neil told Esmond, "working on the design of your new house with Gillian, I've had *many* discussions regarding your home life. I don't mean to sound presumptuous, but I get the impression your relationship is somewhat, well . . . 'distanced' or mature."

"You're not being at all presumptuous," said Esmond. "It should be evident to anyone that Gillian and I are hardly lovey-dovey. Those days are long past. When I offered to enlighten you, I was referring to our financial situation, not our romantic status."

"Oh." Neil seemed as unprepared for this discussion as I was.

Sensing we were about to hear words of considerable interest, I reflexively removed the notepad and pen from my inside jacket pocket and set them on the table. As soon as I'd done it, though, I realized that my journalistic instincts were not appropriate to the situation. Lamely, I explained, "Too much stuff in my pockets . . ." And I added my cell phone to the small pile on the table.

Watching me, Esmond said, "Actually, Mark, that's how it all started."

Was he speaking in riddles? If he meant to confuse me, he'd succeeded. Feeling doltish, I asked, "That's how what started?"

"Cellular phones." Then he paused. "I'm sorry. I should back up. You must think I'm addled. Gillian does."

"I highly doubt that," Neil offered.

"Then you really *haven't* covered much ground with her. But trust me, Neil, she has no more understanding of the real me than I have of her."

I reminded him, "You said you'd back up. What are you trying to tell us, Esmond?" I was itching to unscrew the cap of my pet fountain pen, but withstood the temptation.

"This goes back to the days when we first met, more than twenty years ago. We were both living in Milwaukee. Gillian was getting a leg up, so to speak, in the corporate world as head accountant at some widget factory—they made switches for dashboards, which may sound mundane, but it was highly profitable. She would later be promoted to CFO there, then move on to Ashton Mills.

"But I'm getting ahead of myself. Back in her accounting days, she had recently divorced her first husband and sometimes dropped in for a drink after work at this trendy downtown bar—well, trendy by Milwaukee standards. That's where we met. I worked at a research company in a nearby building, and I had just finished a major project. The more we got acquainted—"

"Excuse me, Esmond." I could no longer resist. Uncapping my Montblanc, I flipped open the pad and scratched a few notes. "What sort of research project?"

"I'm an electrical engineer. At least back then I was." Had he told me he was a beekeeper, I'd have been no less surprised. There was simply no reading this man. He continued, "I was involved in developing some key circuitry for an emerging technology that was still in the theoretical stage—still on the drawing board, as it were. My team was getting nowhere, and I thought I had a better idea, so I broke off on my own, renting space and equipment in the research facility. Soon after that, I came up with one of the original circuits that allowed cellular phones to talk to each other."

Neil and I stole a mutual, bug-eyed glance. Was this guy on the level?

"Needless to say, down in Chicago, Motorola was *very* interested in my circuit design. They had big plans for this technology."

"Yeah," I said with a soft laugh and supreme understatement, "the idea sort of took off, didn't it?"

"So, over a drink with Gillian one night, I explained all this, and her ears really pricked up."

"I'll bet they did," Neil said under his breath.

"Gillian offered to negotiate the patent deal for me, and since I had no head for business, I readily accepted her offer. When the dust settled, well, let's just say I never needed to work another day of my life. Gillian and I were jubilant, and at the time, the next logical step seemed to be marriage—a 'partnership of skills,' she called it."

"In other words," I noted, "a merger."

"Yup. And part of the deal—her suggestion—was that she should look after our finances. Having no interest in money management, I saw it as a blessing that my new partner had such a keen head for it, so I turned over the purse strings."

Through a quizzical squint, I asked, "You agreed to this in a practical sense? Or in a legal sense?"

"*Very* legal," he assured me. "Gillian had everything drawn up, signed, and sealed. Ever since, she has invested my nest egg for us and paid me a salary from the dividends."

"Salary?" asked Neil. "Sounds more like an allowance."

With a resigned laugh, Esmond conceded, "I suppose it is. But don't get me wrong—I'm more than comfortable." With no hint of boasting, he added, "It's a very large nest egg." Reaching over the table, he patted my phone.

Scratching behind an ear, I turned to Neil. "Then why the sudden concern about cost overruns?"

"Just what I was wondering." Neil turned to Esmond. "What am I missing here? *You're* set for life, and Gillian has the most lucrative job in Dumont County. Any number of times, I've tried to rein in the construction budget on the house, but her stock response has always been 'Money is no object; timeliness is.'"

Esmond tossed his hands. "I've heard her use those very words. And yet, this very morning, she told me that, because of the cost overruns on the house, she had to reconsider her promised funding of a nonprofit venture that's important to me."

I turned a page of my notepad. "May I ask the nature of that venture?"

"Certainly. You'll recall that last night's dinner conversation touched on my yoga instructor."

I nodded. "Gillian referred to her as 'swami.'"

Neil flashed me a disapproving look.

"Ughh"—Esmond shuddered—"Gillian thinks she's being glib or clever, but anyone with the least sensitivity can tell she's merely displaying her own ignorance. Tamra Thaine is a woman of deep insights and great learning. As her student, I might address her as 'yogi,' but for Gillian to offhandedly refer to her as 'swami' is the height of arrogance and disregard. Belittling ancient teachings with a lack of interest and understanding, Gillian ridicules only herself."

I could hardly disagree with him. At last showing some spunk, he had voiced his position with force and eloquence. And there was no denying that Gillian had a smug, disagreeable edge—was she afflicted with an underlying, lifelong bitchiness, or was she simply indulging in a bout of CEO syndrome?

To be honest, when Gillian had made the "swami" crack, my first inclination had been to laugh. I have never placed much stock in beliefs that have no apparent basis in reality—most notably, religion and other forms of superstition—and owing to my lack of familiarity with yoga, I didn't know what to make of it. Was it truly a discipline rooted in centuries of study, with demonstrable results, or was it mindless nonsense, right up there with voodoo and faith healing? Not knowing the answer, I decided to err on the side of open-mindedness.

So I told Esmond, "Gillian can be a bit much at times, but after spending so many years with her, you've surely come to an accommodation, weighing the bad against the good."

Speaking softly, but looking me straight in the eye, he said, "Over the years, Mark, I've come to the conclusion that there's very little in her that *is* good."

I was tempted to defend Gillian, citing her quick mind, her organizational skills, her head for numbers, but I knew that these attributes would mean nothing to a man whose marriage had withered and whose love had died.

Neil got us back on track. "Esmond, you were starting to explain how the expense of the new house is threatening an important non-profit venture."

"Yes, Neil." Esmond sat back in his chair. As he did so, the high-collared jacket tightened around his neck. He stretched his bony chin for a moment, then continued, "A year ago, when Gillian decided to move the corporate headquarters of Ashton Mills to Dumont, we took a hard look at how the move would affect our lives. We then lived in Harper, a little outpost of a town near the mills. Gillian never liked Harper, and she was eager to move to Dumont. I, on the other hand, had always appreciated the quiet life in Harper, where I first met Tamra, beginning my journey to inner awareness."

"In other words," I attempted to move his story along, "you didn't want to make the move with Gillian."

"Right. And to tell the truth, I saw this as an opportunity to split amicably; we could each follow our separate lives and pursue our own goals. But she wouldn't hear of it, claiming we needed to keep up appearances for the sake of business." Esmond laughed, noting, "It was the first time in many years that she had expressed any need for me whatever, and even though this claimed need was decidedly passive and backhanded, it somehow lent a sense of renewed purpose to our marriage. When she asked what it would take to convince me to move to Dumont, I had a ready answer—Tamra Thaine."

This was starting to sound a tad kinky. Through an uncertain smile, Neil asked, "What about Tamra?"

Sensing our thoughts, Esmond shook his head gently. "Nothing like that. You see, back in Harper, I had come to know Tamra through my private lessons, but she wanted to expand her business and teach classes, so Gillian and I provided the seed money for her to open a small yoga studio in an old storefront. It was nothing lavish, but it served Tamra's purpose well, and she established a modest practice. Tamra's knowledge of Eastern studies goes far beyond yoga, however, and she had been toying with the idea of expanding her class offerings, not in hopes of additional income—Tamra's material needs are slight—but as a service to the community, which could benefit from her wisdom. Trouble is, such an undertaking would require two things that were unavailable to her in Harper: larger facilities, and a larger population base to draw students from.

"I wanted to help Tamra in this venture, so Gillian and I struck a deal. I would move to Dumont with her and maintain the facade of a stable marriage; in return, our new home here would include a private yoga studio, and more important, Gillian would personally set up an endowment allowing Tamra to establish an institute of Eastern and Hindu studies. The property has already been purchased, and conversion of the facilities has begun."

"Here in Dumont?" I asked, looking up from the notes I was taking. In our gossipy little town, this was news—and I'd heard nothing of it.

"It's just outside of town, off the highway that extends from First Avenue. The property was originally a farm; then it was used as some sort of school a few years back. But the school has since shut down, and we were able to pick it up cheap."

I recognized exactly which property he was describing, and I cringed at the memory of my encounters with its previous owner. Flipping to a fresh page of my pad, I said, "Maybe I'll drive out there this afternoon and take a look. This might make a good story."

"I'm certain Tamra would be grateful for any publicity—not for herself, of course, but for the institute. It's quite a challenge, getting everything up and running. The community deserves to know about it."

Neil noted, "Gillian has never mentioned this to me. Funny."

"I'm not surprised," said Esmond. "She's never had her heart in the project. Her support of it is merely meant to humor me. It's not philanthropy; it's a bribe. But now that I've lived up to *my* end of the bargain by moving here lock, stock, and barrel, she plans to renege on her promised funding—specifically citing the cost overruns of the house."

Neil got up, moved to the desk, and pulled a thick manila folder from one of the file drawers. Opening the folder and spreading a few ledger sheets on the desk, he told Esmond, "As of today, everything's still on budget. To my thinking, all the overtime has been outrageously expensive, but Gillian insisted on completing the project quickly, so the extra costs were planned into the budget. You can relax, Esmond—there haven't been any cost overruns."

Esmond stood, looking perplexed. His clingy clone-suit remained bunched around his shoulders and his lap for a few moments, looking anything but fashionable, before falling into place. "Then why," he asked, "would Gillian say just the opposite?"

Neil said, "She was probably having a bad day."

I offered, "Or maybe she was bluffing, just trying to razz you."

Esmond allowed, "She's good at *that*."

Standing, I stepped next to him and patted his back. "Let her calm down. She has a lot on her mind with the merger, but after Thursday, with the agreements signed and the deal done, I bet she'll have everything back in perspective. She can be a difficult person, I know, but Gillian has always struck me as a woman of her word. If she promised to fund the institute, that's that."

"I hope you're right, Mark."

Neil said, "Of course he's right. Would you care to join us for lunch, Esmond?"

"Thank you, that's kind of you, but no. I have an appointment and should run along." He stepped toward the door, turning back to tell us, "I appreciate the time you've given me—and the encouraging words." With a thin smile, he added, "Things are looking up, I guess."

Neil returned the smile. "It's all a matter of perspective. Think positive."

Esmond raised a finger, telling us, "Harmonic convergence." And with a nod of resolve, he left.

Watching him walk past the front window, returning to his car, I asked Neil, "Harmonic convergence?"

"Beats me."

"Esmond and Tamra—do you think there's more to their relationship than yoga?"

Neil repeated, "Beats me."

Chapter Five

Our lunch conversation at First Avenue Grill was dominated by speculation regarding the relationship between Esmond Reece and his yoga instructor, Tamra Thaine. We now knew that Esmond was trapped in a loveless marriage, and his devotion to Tamra was more than evident, so it was not unreasonable to suspect that they might be romantically involved. On the other hand, neither Neil nor I had met Tamra, so we had no means of gauging whether the doting was mutual. What's more, Gillian Reece struck neither of us as the sort who would be willing to look the other way if she thought her husband was involved with another woman. Having observed Gillian and Esmond at dinner the previous evening, I had concluded that their relationship was strained, but I had seen no evidence of the open war-fare that would doubtless be triggered by infidelity.

Leaving the Grill, driving Neil to the Reece house, where we would meet Glee Savage for our one o'clock tour, I thought aloud, "This Eastern stuff—I admit I'm largely ignorant of it, but I get the impression that its practitioners embrace a fairly high standard of morals."

Neil whirled a hand. "The transcendental thing."

"Yeah. So it just doesn't follow that Esmond and his yogi would be horsing around. I mean, it's all about discipline, right? Not sex."

With a low chortle, Neil said, "What about the *Kama Sutra?*"

My eyes moved from the road ahead to glance at Neil. "I forgot about that." My mind was suddenly swimming with images of bizarre yoga contortions that had taken on a mystical, sexual, serpentine twist. Blinking these visions away, I attempted to concentrate on my driving.

Reaching the outskirts of town, we came upon the newer, wooded neighborhood of large houses that had sprung up during the boom period of the late nineties. Doctors, lawyers, and a handful of industry executives had opted to abandon some of Dumont's stately older homes in favor of starting from scratch, building family-size castles in a mishmash of styles that ranged from fake Tudor to plastic Tuscan.

With the general downturn in the economy, however, development of these sprawling homesites had ceased—save one, that of Gillian and Esmond Reece. Gillian not only bucked the trend by deciding to build when others had been stymied by the wait-and-see malaise; she also redefined the trend by raising the bar and setting new spare-nothing standards that would not be challenged anytime soon. Fortunately, in spite of her questionable motivation and unschooled tastes, she'd had the sense and foresight to hire a good architect.

Neil's astonishing Reece residence came into full view as I followed a curve in the road that led to the development's highest knoll. There, perched atop a hillock, was an artful creation of stone, glass, and timber that both blended with and commanded its surrounding vista. I had seen the drawings, of course, and I had visited the site during earlier phases of construction, but now it looked finished, and more important, the house looked as if it had always been there.

"It takes my breath away," I told Neil, braking the car in the middle of the street, gawking through the windshield.

"Thanks, Mark," said Neil, patting my knee. Humbly, he admitted, "I'm pleased with it."

I laughed. "I *hope* so. It's truly a masterpiece—your *latest* masterpiece. Kiddo, you just keep topping yourself."

"Trouble is"—he frowned—"this one's gonna be a tough act to follow. Clients like Gillian don't come along every day."

"Is that a blessing or a curse?"

Thinking over my question, he answered, "The jury's still out on that."

Along the curb in front of the house and lining the long driveway from the street to the garage, trucks and cars were parked at rakish angles by a crew of workers involved in the rush to complete their various construction and decorating jobs. I recognized Gillian's blood-red Bentley—everyone in Dumont knew the car, which was not only conspicuous in our small town, but possibly the only one of its kind in the state. The other vehicles were unknown to me, so I reasoned that Glee Savage had not yet arrived—her prim little hatchback in shocking fuchsia would be hard to miss.

I was still driving the big black Bavarian V-8 I had brought from Chicago. Cruising past the Bentley to park at the end of the block, I was grateful that my car no longer branded me as the rich, gay out-of-towner. Neil and I had comfortably blended into the existing fabric of the town. It was now the Reeces who would take some getting used to.

Just as I turned the key to cut the engine, I noticed the dashboard clock flash one o'clock, and glancing in the mirror, I saw Glee's distinctive hatchback sputtering up the road from behind. "That Glee," I told Neil, "she's always on the dot." We got out of the car and waited on the sidewalk as Glee parked.

She opened the driver's door, acknowledging us with a wave and a yoo-hoo as she leaned to pull her purse from the backseat. She kept it back there because it would not have fit in front. One of Glee's signature fashion statements was the collection of large, flat purses she had amassed over the years. They resembled carpetbag portfolios, easily two feet square, adorned in a variety of colors and patterns that allowed her to coordinate with any ensemble plucked at whim from her closet. Today's specimen sported ferocious black-and-orange tiger stripes, picking up the autumnal hues of the outfit I'd seen earlier in the office.

"Wow!" said Neil. "That's showin'em, Glee."

"Awww, you're such a honey." With her heels pecking the new sidewalk, she rushed to give Neil a hug. They always greeted each other with a transparent affection that seemed to stem from their shared interest in style and design—something of a rarity in Dumont. Anyone watching them embrace on the street that afternoon would recognize that it was fondness, not passion, that underlay their warm greeting. Though Glee was not quite old enough to be mistaken for Neil's mother, she might have passed as a spunky aunt. She told him, "I can't *wait* to see what you've done here."

"Your waiting's over. Come on inside, and let's find Gillian." As Neil led us to the house, Glee fished in her purse for a pen and steno pad.

Approaching the front door, Neil paused to describe his inspiration for the overall design. "My clients wanted a big, comfortable house, and they also wanted to make a 'statement.' The danger, of course, would be in allowing the house to become a mere status symbol; if its main purpose is to reflect the wealth of its owners, it's a trophy, not a home. So I wanted to avoid all the typical visual clues of affluence or opulence—an overscale facade, the indiscriminate use of luxury materials, and most important, succumbing to trendy, thematic design styles that are deemed 'the latest.'"

Glee nodded. "Today's hot trend is tomorrow's white elephant."

"Exactly. And a house is meant to be around for many years—it's meant to be *lived* in as well as looked at. So I steered clear of any recognizable trend or theme." With a sweeping gesture, he told us, "You'd be hard-pressed to give a one-word description of the style of this house."

I had not previously heard Neil articulate the philosophy of his design process, but now I understood how unerringly he had achieved his goal. The building that loomed before me was neither "modern" nor "country," and it was a far cry from "Victorian" or "Mediterranean." But it worked. Everything seemed to fit, nothing was superfluous, and the entire structure was in harmony with its setting.

"Your choice of materials," Glee gushed, "is stunning."

"The stone was quarried in the northern part of the state, and the timbers, though not local, are a reflection of the wooded landscape."

I suggested, "They also tie in with Gillian's involvement with the paper industry—trees."

Neil smiled. "Hadn't thought of that."

Glee was earnestly taking notes, recording Neil's words verbatim. She told him, "What impresses me most, though, is your use of glass. The stone and timbers, in the hands of a less skilled designer, might come across as 'rustic,' but not here. The glass seems to lighten the whole structure and offers just the right counterpoint of sophistication."

With a grin, Neil suggested, "Feel free to quote yourself."

"I just may do that." She underlined something on her pad.

"When we get inside," continued Neil, "you'll see how important the glass is to the overall concept of the living space. The trick was to give the fenestration a look of exterior order and discipline while not allowing the scale and placement of windows to seem 'forced' from the interior. Window treatments will be crucial—did I mention that Todd Draper is doing them?"

"From Chicago? Lord, Neil, there's none better."

"Whether Gillian appreciates it or not, she's getting curtains with a pedigree. Ready to have a look inside?"

By then, Glee and I were more than ready. We eagerly followed Neil as he opened the door and led us into the foyer.

The entrance hall was of grand scale, but its pleasing proportions did not convey the impersonal, commercial feeling of a hotel lobby. Rather, the room seemed warmly welcoming, signaling that we had just entered someone's home. The soft palette and comfortable furnishings contributed to an easy sense of tranquility, though this effect was limited today by the presence of decorating crews who trudged in and out with their wares, calling questions and barking instructions to each other. Conspicuously, the rows of windows had not yet been touched, awaiting Todd Draper's reputed magic, so the acoustics of the room were still harsh and echoing. A rug stood rolled in a corner, not yet covering the rough-hewn floor, probably limestone, which also contributed to the noisiness.

Neil stood with Glee at the center of this activity, answering her queries about square footage, lighting systems, and the decorating subcontractors. While they spoke, I did some snooping on my own, nosing down the halls that led from the foyer—I saw the dining room, a wood-paneled den, and a small sitting room that looked more like a parlor than a full-blown living room. Wondering about the where-abouts of the main room, I returned to the foyer and noticed a tall set of closed double doors directly opposite the front door. Yes, I recalled from Neil's drawings, the living room lay beyond those doors.

Stepping toward the doors, I heard Neil tell Glee, "But I'm proudest of the living room. I've always liked the traditional American concept of the living room, as opposed to newer, less formal incarnations of the space as a 'great room' that opens to the kitchen and family room. To my way of thinking, there's nothing wrong with the old idea that the living room is a special place, filled with the best of everything, off-limits to messy children. And that's what I've created for the Reeces. I'm glad the doors happened to be closed; you can experience the full effect, the 'ah' factor, upon entering."

"Needless to say," said Glee, "I'm itching to see it." She licked her shiny red lips in anticipation.

There was a momentary lull in the noise from workers in the hall, and standing near the crack between the living-room doors, I heard voices within, raised in a discussion that did not sound friendly. One voice was a woman's—Gillian's—and the other was that of a man who also sounded familiar.

I moved to Neil and Glee at the center of the foyer, telling them, "Perhaps we shouldn't go inside right now. Gillian's in there, and she seems to be having a disagreement with someone."

"Par for the course," said Neil, unconcerned. "It'll blow over. So let me take a minute to describe the room for you." Glee turned to a fresh page of her steno pad as Neil explained, "It's not only a living room, but a library. We took the two-story elliptical space at the center of the house and created an island of hushed formality. Surrounding the main furniture grouping, you'll see floor-to-ceiling bookcases, the full two stories high. A balcony rings the room at the second-floor level, accessible from a winding stairway and from several ladders that roll on a track. Tall, narrow windows are interspersed with the bookcases, sur-rounding the room with light. These windows cry for dramatic treat-ment, so I'm especially eager to see Todd Draper's finishing touches."

"Has he shown you drawings?" asked Glee.

"Sure," said Neil. And he continued to discuss various decorating issues with Glee, passing several minutes in the foyer.

Finally, Neil turned to me, asking, "Have things calmed down in there yet?"

Stepping to the double doors, I intended to lean close and assess the situation, when we all heard Gillian shout, "When hell freezes over!"

The man inside retorted loudly, "Does that mean 'no,' or did you have something more subtle in mind?" Now I recognized the voice—it was Tyler Pennell, who had apparently taken my advice to go directly to Gillian with his concerns regarding due diligence for the merger. It was equally apparent that he had been fully justified in his reluctance to deal with the woman.

"Uh . . . ," I told Neil, "I think I know what this is about. Maybe you should show Glee the rest of the house; I'll see if I can't play peacemaker."

Glee's reporter instincts were suddenly on high alert. "What's up, boss?"

"It's just business," I replied vaguely. "Everyone involved with the merger seems to be getting stressed over the details."

"Oh." Glee lost interest the moment I mentioned the merger. She told Neil, "Sure, show me the house, and we'll save the best for last."

Neil gave me a wink. "Thanks, Mark. See if you can't pave the way for us in there." And he escorted Glee down the hallway toward the dining room.

When they were out of earshot, I turned to the double doors and gave them an officious rap, but the voices within didn't miss a beat. In fact, the verbal assault between Gillian and Tyler seemed to be building, not slackening, so I decided I would simply have to abandon my manners, take action, and interrupt them. Giving a sharp knock of warning, I then fumbled with the doorknobs. Being unfamiliar with their mechanism, I inadvertently released both doors at once, swinging them wide open as I swooped in from the hall. It was a classic, campy Loretta Young entrance, which I would have found funny were it not for the serious circumstances.

Both Gillian and Tyler seemed more startled than annoyed by the interruption, turning to look at me with bug-eyed curiosity. Composing herself, Gillian asked archly, "Yes? May I help you?"

"Sorry," I said, "the doors sort of got away from me. I don't mean to intrude, but the conversation seemed to be getting awfully heated in here; we could hear you from the hall. Besides, Gillian"—I tapped my watch—"you have a one o'clock appointment with Glee Savage."

"Who?" she asked, as if I were speaking nonsense syllables.

"The *Register*'s features editor. She's here for the background interview on the new house."

"Oh, that." Gillian flicked her wrist. "That'll have to wait. Something has come up. Your meddlesome 'forensic accountant' has supposedly unearthed a few deadly inconsistencies in the books at Ashton Mills. I don't know whether to be insulted—or amused. Why, the accusation is downright laughable." Proving her assertion, she gave a loud, false laugh, then told me, "I suggest your accountant learn to check his math. Perhaps he should stop counting on his fingers."

Steely-faced, Tyler said, "See, Mark? I told you there was no reasoning with this woman. It's her way or the highway."

"Damn straight, junior." She flashed him a look that could crack granite.

"Let me remind you, Mrs. Reece, the merger with Quatro Press is contingent upon *my* approval of the numbers. You may not like me, but your goals would be better served by a measure of attitude adjustment."

She looked him squarely in the eye, then asked him sweetly, "Attitude adjustment? Why, Mr. Pennell, I do believe you can kiss my ass."

Tyler was momentarily stunned by her pronouncement; so was I. He sputtered, "You're . . . you're even *worse* than they say. You're impossible. And if you're incapable of conducting business in a businesslike manner, then you'd better understand that business will be conducted *without* you." He crossed the room and picked up his briefcase from a side table near the doors. "Perry Schield will be highly interested in learning what transpired here this afternoon. He's getting cold feet, Mrs. Reece, and frankly, I don't blame him." With that, Tyler turned on his heel, huffed out of the room, crossed the foyer, and walked through the front door, slamming it shut behind him.

Gillian instantly wound herself into a rant, pacing the living room's stone floor, flailing her arms, sputtering profanities about "that rube from Green Bay." Workers peered in from the hall, so I moved to the double doors and gently closed them. Crossing my arms, I watched with strained patience as Gillian vented her rage. There was no point in trying to counter her irrational outburst; the best way to quiet her down was to let her wear herself out.

This was a side of Gillian Reece that I had heard rumors about but had never witnessed. While her behavior was appalling, it was also perversely entertaining, so I watched with a measure of satisfaction, feeling smugly superior, like an adult confronted by a child's tantrum. Should I declare a time-out and haul her off to the car?

While musing over the possibilities (e.g., spanking Gillian Reece), my attention shifted from the woman to her living room. Ignoring her hysterics, I took in the magnificent space Neil had created for her—the sumptuous but refined seating area, the massive fireplace, and of course the surrounding bookcases, with their balcony, ladders, and long, elegant windows. Shafts of afternoon daylight angled in from the openings and sliced across the floor.

". . . so he simply has to go, Mark. He *must*."

"Hmm?" I glanced from the balcony to the fireplace, where Gillian stood, reasonably composed, addressing me from the far side of the room. I asked, "Who has to go?"

"Tyler Pennell." She flipped her hands. "Who else?"

Stepping toward her, I said calmly, "You know as well as I do that that's impossible. Both companies have contractually agreed to abide by Tyler's assessment. There's no pulling out now, especially on the whim of one party."

"Whim? Is that what you call this?"

"Gillian, I don't want to get into this with you. The specific issues are beyond my grasp, and I need to back out of the debate. This is between you and Perry Schield. I hope the merger is still on track—I've always supported it—but the whole question is out of my hands now. The contractual mechanisms are in place, and that's that."

"Ugh." She slumped onto the arm of an overstuffed armchair. "I wish I could be so philosophical and practical. How do you do it, Mark?"

"Maybe it's a guy thing." I smiled.

She smirked. "You're calling me feminine?" Her tone implied revulsion.

I could think of no safe answer to her query, so I tapped my watch again. "Your interview?"

"Oh, *that.*" She slumped. "Can't we cancel—or at least postpone it?"

"No, Gillian, we can't." I enjoyed bossing her, and for reasons I couldn't fathom, she seemed to defer to me as an authority figure.

She whined, "But I'm just not in the mood . . ."

"Look, Gillian. You agreed to the interview. I've assigned staff to it, and we've reserved space for it. Besides, a nice feature on the house could be helpful to Neil's career." This last point was a stretch. Neil's practice was sufficiently well established that a feature in a small-town daily was unlikely to bring droves of new clients to his door, but I reasoned that Gillian might find my pitch persuasive because she seemed genuinely fond of Neil. And I was right.

"Well," she conceded, "I suppose I do owe Neil the recognition. He's given me so much"—she gestured at her surroundings—"I can't begrudge him a little well-deserved publicity."

"He'll appreciate it. And so do I." I offered a smile.

A tentative knock drew our glances to the closed doors.

I told Gillian, "That's probably Neil now."

"Waiting in the wings, no doubt." She breathed a little sigh of resignation, stood, and positioned herself at the fireplace like royalty at a throne.

I crossed to the opposite side of the room and cracked the doors open.

Neil peeked in. Under his breath, he asked, "Still on the warpath?"

"No, no"—I chuckled, opening the door wide—"everything's fine."

Neil turned to Glee, who was standing behind him. "They're ready for us. Come on in. I want you to see this."

"Oh, *Neil,*" she said, following him into the room, "it's everything you promised—and more!"

Moving toward the center of the room, Neil acknowledged, "It did turn out beautifully. I'm pleased."

"*Pleased?*" asked Glee, turning to take in the whole space, gazing at the library balcony. "It's first-rate, simply stunning. I can't *wait* to get a photographer in here. Mark, it's page-one material, Sunday's *Trends* section."

"Great idea, Glee. It's quite a house. And now, perhaps you'd like to meet the proud owner." I escorted her across the room, around Neil, toward the fireplace, where Gillian still stood, erect and queenly.

"With pleasure," Glee assured me.

"Gillian," I said, "I'd like you to meet the *Register*'s features editor, Glee Savage. And, Glee, this is Gillian Reece of Ashton Mills."

The two women each took a step toward the other, pausing some six feet apart.

"Glee?" said Gillian, stepping closer. "Glee Buttles?"

Glee closed the distance between them, then froze. "*Gill?*" she asked. "Gill *Dermody?*" Without hesitation, she lifted her right hand. I presumed she was offering a handshake, but I was dead wrong. No, Glee raised her hand higher, stretching her arm behind her for a moment, then hauled off and smacked Gillian in the face with a fierce, stinging bitch slap.

Gillian, Neil, and I watched in slack-jawed silence as Glee turned and marched out of the room, continuing through the foyer.

Her heels snapped at the stone floor.

I swear I saw sparks.

Chapter Six

Neil and I struggled for words as Gillian Reece watched Glee Savage's steamy exit. "I can't begin to apologize . . . ," said one of us. "I can't imagine what got into her . . . ," said the other.

"Well," said Gillian, lifting her fingers to the hot, red welt on her cheek, "at least the interview was mercifully brief."

Her calm reaction to Glee's assault struck me as entirely out of character. I would not have been surprised had she torn after Glee, tackled her in front of the house, and thrown her to the ground, rolling toward the street in a maelstrom of thrashing limbs and torn hair. Instead, her stolid attitude suggested she had found Glee's outburst unremarkable.

I asked her, "What was *that* all about?"

"Who knows?" Gillian shrugged. "No telling with that woman."

With a note of understatement, Neil said, "I gather you two have met before."

"We knew each other in college." She paused before adding a self-evident afterthought. "We didn't get along."

Gillian made it clear she had nothing more to say, so Neil and I extended our apologies, then left.

Returning to my car, we speculated as to the root of the enmity we had witnessed, but we could come up with nothing that would motivate the attack, especially from Glee, whose behavior had been consistently ladylike and cheery during the entire four years I had worked with her. I told Neil, "Gillian doesn't seem willing to enlighten us, but I bet Glee will."

"Is she in trouble?" asked Neil. "I mean, at the office?"

Good question. "I want to hear what she has to say first."

I didn't think it would be productive to confront Glee with my questions right away—better to let her calm down. So I drove Neil downtown, dropped him at his office, and decided to explore the lead Esmond Reece had given me regarding Tamra Thaine's makeover of a compound that lay just beyond the city line.

Heading west on First Avenue (the Reece house was on the other end of town), I followed the main street as it narrowed, then curved, becoming a county highway. A few frosty nights had left their mark on the rural landscape, turning fields golden and treetops crimson. A blue, cool sky arched overhead with such pristine clarity, it was easy to imagine Dumont as the center of a benevolent universe.

But something was brewing, at least in the cosmic sense, and I wasn't sure what. My quiet, routine day had now been marred by several sour notes—all of them tracing back to Gillian Reece. Was I at last getting a peek at the real woman? Had my unflinching support of the merger with Quatro Press been premature?

These thoughts were nipped as a sign came into view on the left side of the road. The rustic placard of weathered, silvery barn boards announced with letters fashioned from twisted twigs, DUMONT INSTITUTE OF EASTERN STUDIES. I couldn't help musing that the name produced an unfortunate acronym.

Still, it was infinitely more welcoming, at least to my eye, than the sign that had previously hung there, heralding A CHILD'S GARDEN, an unassuming name for a crackpot New Age day school. Shortly after my move to Dumont, I'd had some vicious run-ins with the school's founder, a lesbian feminist named Miriam Westerman. Though I harbor no ill will for either lesbians or feminists, this gal had taken both concepts over the top and had attempted, through legal channels, to steal my nephew Thad from his home with Neil and me.

She had failed in that endeavor, and eventually her school had failed as well. Last I heard, she had moved to Washington state, which seems to hold some odd allure for her Wiccan ilk.

Today, turning into the driveway that led from the road, I felt a twinge of anxiety well up from these sore memories, but my overwhelming emotion was the sheer relief of knowing that Miriam had left town. As the trees lining the drive parted and I pulled into the gravel-paved clearing that served as a parking lot, I saw at a glance that things had indeed changed.

Everything was now white. The house, the barn, and the old outbuildings that still dotted the original farm property, as well as several newer buildings of spare, utilitarian design, had formerly been painted by Miriam and her cohorts a horrific shade of screaming green, the color of the eco-movement. Now the only green to be seen was that of the surrounding pines. All the buildings—in fact, anything manmade—was purest white (suggestive, I presumed, of inner peace). The paint job was fresh, barely dry, and I wondered wryly how pure it would look after the stormy rigors of a Wisconsin winter.

Clearly, the institute was not yet up and running, as there were only two vehicles other than mine in the clearing—Esmond's car, which was white, and an SUV, also white, doubtless Tamra's. Both were parked near the entrance of the main building. Cutting the engine and leaving my car, I crossed the clearing, checking my pockets for pen and notebook. My shoes ground the dusty gravel as I approached the building; then my footfalls fell silent as I stepped up to the concrete stoop and opened the front door.

Pausing inside a small vestibule, I first noticed the smell of paint— it *was* fresh—then noticed quiet music drifting through the main hall. Vaguely Eastern, the droning, minimalist melody created a woozy mood reminiscent of the psychedelic days of my college years, like something I'd heard beyond distant, closed doors of anonymous dorm rooms. All that was missing was the smell of pot.

Following the music in search of its source, I walked the hall softly and turned down an adjoining corridor, feeling decidedly stealthy. But I wasn't trying to sneak up on anyone; rather, the aura of the setting, reinforced by the music, seemed to demand a respectful silence, as in a church. It would have been unthinkably boorish to call out, Anybody home?

Passing several rooms, I looked inside and saw that each was still in disarray, with books, supplies, and whatnot heaped in corrugated boxes. Shabby furnishings shoved against the walls suggested a library in one room, an office in another, a classroom in a third. Other rooms, however, were clean, stark, and bare of furnishings, with no apparent purpose.

It was such a room wherein the music played. Stopping in the hall outside the open doorway, I was tempted to rap on the jamb or clear my throat to discreetly announce my presence. Glancing inside, however, I abandoned this notion as too intrusive.

The music was playing from a boom box in the corner of the room. In the middle of the bare floor, Esmond lay on a small rubber mat, faceup, with his left knee contorted to touch the floor on his right side. He wore stretchy gray pajamas similar to the suit he had worn that morning in Neil's office; the workout togs were only slightly less flattering than the suit. Next to him crouched a woman in white leotards. With her back to me, she reached to help Esmond stretch his limbs into various positions, all of which looked plenty painful, but Esmond looked downright serene. What was next, I wondered, a bed of nails?

No, next Esmond rolled away from me, facedown, and pointed his butt upward until he had formed a perfect inverted V, with hands and feet flat on the floor. When Esmond froze in this position, the woman moved out of her crouch and stood on her hands, pulling her legs and torso into a ball that seemed to float above her elbows. It was all quite impressive, in a perverse sort of way, and I wondered how long they could hold these bizarre positions. Aware that yoga poses generally have poetic, descriptive names, I wondered what inventive monikers applied to these particular contortions. Squatting dog? Bloated crane?

And my cell phone went off.

The woman crumpled to her knees and Esmond collapsed onto his mat as I fumbled to retrieve the phone from my pocket, mortified. "A thousand apologies," I sputtered, sounding farcically Mesopotamian. As they helped each other up, I hissed into the phone, "Yes?"

"Hey, Mark, is that you?"

"Neil?" Imagining some dire emergency, I turned into the hall, asking, "What's wrong?"

"Nothing." He laughed. "What's that freaky music?"

"I'll explain to you later; I'm in the middle of something. Why did you call?"

"To ask about dinner. Todd Draper phoned. He can't get away till after five, so he'll be arriving late tonight. Said he'd eat along the way somewhere, so we're on our own. I can cook, if you want."

"Sure, Neil, that's fine. Whatever you like, okay?"

Sheepishly, he noted, "I'm interrupting, huh?"

I allowed a quiet laugh. "You are, in fact. Sorry to be short with you, but I can't talk."

"Understood. Later, Mark."

"Bye, kiddo." I slipped the phone into my pocket and turned back to the room, where the woman had just turned off the boom box. Esmond was walking toward me with a big smile, hand extended in welcome. "Esmond," I said, "I feel like a fool. I came looking for you, but didn't want to intrude on your session—then the damn phone rang."

"Nonsense. No intrusion whatever. We were just finishing." He pumped my hand. "Glad you came, Mark. Let me introduce you to Tamra." His manner was far more vivacious that I'd seen before, leading me to conclude that he was happier in Tamra's presence than in Gillian's—a safe bet (though I did not know Tamra, I was beginning to know Gillian only too well).

"Mr. Manning," said Tamra, padding across the bare room toward me, "welcome to my ashram." She extended her hand.

Esmond clued me, "An ashram is a place of spiritual retreat."

"Ah." I shook the woman's hand lightly, finding that her grip was stronger than mine. "Thank you, is it 'Miss Thaine'?" I didn't know if she preferred some Hindu form of address.

She smiled. "Everyone calls me Tamra." She wore no makeup; a few soft lines creased her face around the eyes and mouth. Her light brown hair, showing some gray streaks, was pulled back in a loose knot. She had an ageless quality about her—the word *inscrutable* sprang to mind.

I honestly couldn't guess whether she was thirty or sixty. Though there was nothing Eastern about her name, her clothing, or her physical features, she seemed blissfully serene and "in the zone." Had she achieved inner peace? Or was she on drugs?

I told her, "And everyone calls me Mark. I hope you will, too."

With the slightest bow of her head, a mere nod, she said, "Thank you, I shall." But I found it odd that she did not repeat my name.

Esmond said to me, "I've already told Tamra that you might want to print something about the institute in the *Register*."

"That would be wonderful," she said with enthusiasm so mild, it could have passed for sarcasm.

"It's definitely news," I told them, "and I think a good share of our readers might find it of interest. Eastern studies are relatively unknown here, but that's the purpose of the press—to inform and educate. I'm ashamed to admit my own ignorance, but I'm always curious."

Tamra said, "I'm pleased to know you have a hungry mind. May we show you around?"

"I was hoping you would, yes."

Esmond took over, saying, "This way, Mark." And he led me back along the corridor I'd already walked. Tamra followed as Esmond explained, "The offices and classrooms, sorry to say, are still a mess, but our energies have been focused on the grounds and the buildings—first things first. We've managed to clear out the studios for the private lessons." He paused at the front door, where he and Tamra stepped into their sandals, then led us outside.

"What sort of lessons, specifically?" I asked, pulling out my notebook and uncapping my pen.

Standing in the slanting afternoon sunlight, Tamra answered, "Hatha yoga has been the mainstay of my practice and will, at least at first, be the primary discipline taught at the institute. It is a system of physical exercises for the control and perfection of the body—based on asanas, or postures—but yoga is only one of the four chief Hindu disciplines. I also have a keen interest in ayurveda, sometimes called the sister science of yoga, which seeks to inform wellness decisions based on both diet and exercise. Lately, I have been studying reiki, a healing discipline based on touch, deriving not from India but from the Far East. My journey has barely begun, but these are all worthy disciplines, and I hope to share my knowledge of them with the people of Dumont."

Making note of these terms, I said, "Yes, there's definitely a story here." My tone may have sounded ambiguous because my open-mindedness was still struggling to overcome my skepticism.

"Come this way," Tamra again addressed me without saying my name.

Esmond and I followed as she led us from the parking area to a narrow path that skirted one of the buildings, then disappeared into the trees. The gravel underfoot gave way to matted pine needles as we ducked beneath branches and were seemingly swallowed by the deep, cool shade. The legs of Tamra's tight white leotards scissored ahead of me as she moved swiftly through the trees, then stopped. Turning back to us, she asked with a stilted inflection, "Is this not sublime?"

Catching up with her, I saw that we had arrived in a small clearing, perfectly circular, with the ashy remnants of a campfire at its center. The tall, slender trees surrounded us like a wall leading upward to a pinched circle of sky, giving me the uneasy feeling that we were standing inside a chimney. I asked, "Sublime?"

"I discovered this space after we acquired the property. It's perfect—utterly perfect—for drumming."

"Drumming?"

Esmond amplified, "Drumming in the woods."

Scratching a few notes, I told both of them, "I'm sorry, but I must be dense. I have no idea what you're talking about."

Esmond and Tamra exchanged a crooked smile. Their meaning was not difficult to decode—they agreed that I was, in fact, dense, and they felt not derision but pity for this woeful shortcoming.

Tamra took a deep breath, held it for a long moment, then raised her arms to the circle of sky and exhaled noisily. If this demonstration was meant to evidence a healthy body and spirit, it was unconvincing. The rattle of her lungs suggested she indulged in chain-smoking, though this seemed unlikely.

Thus purified (or whatever she had done), she turned to me and explained, "Drumming in the woods is an ancient practice, rediscovered in our own age, stemming from both Native American and holistic traditions. In the quest for harmonic convergence, drumming can be usefully combined with pranayama, or regulated breathing. The breath, we know, is a manifestation of the life force."

I wasn't sure what to make of this. It sounded thoroughly loony, but I thought I should take notes. "Could you define harmonic convergence?"

"According to Quetzalcoatl, it's the fulfillment of the prophecy of thirteen heavens and nine hells, when humanity will experience an unprecedented new age of peace. The convergence began in 1987 and will end in 2012, with the culmination of the cycle of evolution."

"Really?"

"So they say. In the yogic tradition, harmonic convergence relates more to chakras, which are energy points in the body corresponding to glands and emotions. Yogic practices, combined with drumming and pranayama, can help to balance the energy of the chakras."

I surmised, "The goal being . . . what, inner peace?"

"Something like that, yes."

Esmond added, "So naturally, Tamra intends to include drumming groups among the classes offered here at the institute."

"Naturally," I agreed, putting a period on my notes and closing my pad. "It seems we've barely scratched the surface of all this, so I'd like to assign this story to one of my writers, who can take the time to sort it out and do it justice."

"Mark"—Esmond beamed—"that would be wonderful. As you know, Gillian has threatened to withhold her promised funding of Tamra's important endeavors here. I still don't know if Gillian was just blowing smoke, but either way, the publicity will help. By raising the community's awareness of the institute, we can attract not only students, but other funding sources."

Leaving the drumming circle, we retraced our steps through the woods and emerged into the full daylight of the parking court. As Esmond and Tamra were walking me to my car, he asked, "Can we expect to hear from your reporter, or is there someone we should call?"

"I'll talk to our features editor about it. She'll either take the story herself or assign it to someone else. In any event, she'll phone you to set up an interview. What number should she call?"

I opened my pad again to take down the number Esmond gave me. Then he asked, "May I borrow your pen, Mark? I'd like to make note of your editor's name."

"Sure." I turned my pad to a new page and passed it to him with my pen. "Her name is Glee Savage."

He nodded, writing the name; I noticed that he was left-handed. When he finished, he tore the page from the notebook, which he returned to me with my pen.

Replacing everything in my pockets, I extended my hand, thanking Esmond for the tour. Then I turned to Tamra, thanked her as well, and waited to see if she would offer her hand.

Instead, she brought her hands together in the Hindu gesture of prayer, lowered her head, and said to me, *"Namaste."*

Esmond translated, "'I bow to the divine in you.'"

A charming sentiment, I thought, but why hadn't Tamra spoken my name?

"Likewise," I told her with a nod.

Chapter Seven

Lucille Haring's jaw dropped as she listened, sitting across from me at my desk. "You mean, Glee actually *hit* her?"

"Smack in the face. It was her palm, not her fist, but still . . ."

Lucy scratched her stubbly copper-colored hair with the eraser of her pencil. "I can't believe it. It's so *unlike* her. Do you want me to have a talk with her?" As managing editor, Lucy outranked Glee, but Glee was older, with a far longer history at the paper. Lucy also understood that I preferred a management style based on trust and delegation, not hierarchy, so the issue of reprimanding Glee was touchy.

I told Lucy, "I'd like to hear what Glee has to say for herself. Her behavior was a poor reflection on the paper, certainly; much to my surprise, Gillian was more indifferent than indignant. She said that she and Glee knew each other in college and didn't get along. I have no idea what's at the bottom of this, but I didn't get the feeling Gillian would call the cops or start suing anyone."

"Thank God." Lucy crossed the legs of her olive-drab pantsuit and wrote a note to herself on the yellow legal pad that rested on her knee.

I recalled a detail that I'd found curious. "When Gillian recognized Glee today, she referred to her as Glee Buttles. I've always wondered if Glee Savage was her born name, but I've never asked."

"Me neither. As far as I know, she was never married." Lucy noted this fact with a measure of approval. She herself had never wed, but her reason for remaining single was different from Glee's. Glee was a woman who had devoted her life to her career; Lucy was equally committed, but more to the point, she was a lesbian.

"Where *is* Glee?" I asked. "Have you seen her?" It was nearly three o'clock, and activity in the newsroom beyond the glass wall of my office had begun to pick up as deadlines approached for our morning edition (the *Register*'s only edition). The hard-news pages would not be put to bed till later that evening, but features and advertising were already being locked up.

"Now that you ask, no, I haven't seen Glee. But that's not unusual. She keeps her own schedule—and she's never missed a deadline." Lucy checked her watch. "She's bound to show up soon; she has stories to file."

"And I've got a new story I want her to look into." Opening the reporter's notebook that sat on my desk, I added, "You're not going to believe this."

Lucy eyed me skeptically. "There's more? I thought I'd heard it all. Don't tell me—after Glee bitch-slapped Gillian, she went on a rampage and robbed a bank."

"No, no. Nothing like that—this is a different story entirely. Have you heard anything about the Dumont Institute for Eastern Studies?"

Lucy thought for a moment, shaking her head, then looked up from the notes she was taking and spelled out the acronym. "D-I-E-S? Catchy."

With a laugh, I added, "I presume that was an oversight on their part."

"Whose?"

I filled her in regarding Tamra Thaine's newly established school, Esmond Reece's role in securing funding for it from Gillian, and my visit to the compound only an hour earlier. "I got an earful, and it all sounded like nonsense. But I have no background in these disciplines, so I'm reluctant to judge beliefs that are supposedly based on learning that predates Western culture by thousands of years."

"Or maybe," said Lucy, "it's just nut stuff."

"Maybe. And if so, that's part of the story. We need to go slow with this one and get our facts straight. I'd like Glee to handle it."

"Back up, Mark." Lucy was drawing a grid on her notes, a technique I'd often seen her use when trying to establish the facts of an emerging story. "What's the connection between Tamra and Esmond?"

"She's been his private yoga instructor for several years now. She moved here from Harper, Wisconsin, as did the Reeces."

Lucy's pencil tapped a square on her grid. "Obvious question: Are Tamra and Esmond 'involved'?"

"Just what I've been wondering. On the surface, I've seen nothing to suggest that they're romantically linked, but they do seem to have a 'spiritual kinship,' which may—or may not—draw the line at sex. What bearing does any of this have on the story? I'm not sure."

Lucy's pencil moved to another square on the grid. "Esmond and Gillian—how's their marriage?"

"Not good." I recounted the background Esmond had shared with me in Neil's office, and I described my observations of Gillian in action, concluding, "She's one tough cookie, and frankly, if I were Esmond, I'd find Tamra a tempting alternative."

"This is starting to sound like a soap opera, complete with catfights and—"

"Ah!" I interrupted. "Here comes Glee."

Lucy turned to watch Glee make her way from the stairs through the newsroom. She apparently knew we needed to talk, as she was beelining toward my office. I stood, leading Lucy away from my desk to the conference area of my outer office. Glee rushed through the door; her big, floppy tiger-striped purse trailed her like a kite on a short string.

"*Mark*," she blurted, "I hope you can forgive my unprofessional behavior today. I don't know what got in to me. I'm truly sorry." Her head bowed; her shoulders slumped; her purse dropped to the floor.

"Glee," I said gently, approaching her, "of course I forgive you. In the years I've known you, I've never seen you make such a gaff—and I presume it won't happen again. The bigger question is: Will Gillian forgive you?"

Glee's head bobbed up again. She answered offhandedly, "Oh, I doubt it."

Stepping into our conversation, Lucy asked, "What's this all about, Glee?"

I noted, "Gillian said you didn't get along in college."

Glee folded her hands, explaining calmly, "That's the gist of it, yes. The details aren't important, not after so many years. When I said that Gillian won't forgive me, I was referring to our general ill will, which goes back more than thirty years. As for my slapping her this afternoon, she knows as well as I do that I owed her one. I understand she's become a whiz in the business world with finances and accounting; if so, she wouldn't lose track of a thing like that."

"A thing like what?" I persisted.

"Mark, it's personal. Today I evened the score a bit." Pausing in thought, she then stressed, "A *bit*." Her red lips pinched at some memory.

"Still," I said, "I think you owe the woman an apology for the incident, if not out of your own sense of courtesy, then at least for the good name of the *Register*."

"I agree," said Glee without hesitation, blinking away her vexing thoughts of the past. "I'll phone her this afternoon, then visit her at the house tomorrow so I can apologize in person. Besides"—she grinned—"I don't want to jeopardize the story on the house. It'll be a great feature, and Neil deserves the recognition."

"Can't argue with that." I breathed a quiet laugh.

"So here's my plan: I'll play kissy-face with Gillian in order to get her back in our good graces. And I'll file a teaser column this afternoon for tomorrow morning's paper, extolling the Reeces' new home and whetting readers' appetites for a full-blown photo feature on Sunday."

Lucy said, "Sounds good to me, but you'll need to write something fast. I'll tell the desk to save you some space. How much do you need?"

Glee paused to calculate. "No more than twelve inches of text. You can cut it if you need to."

Lucy nodded. "Done." And she took her leave, disappearing into the maze of desks in the newsroom.

Glee stooped to pick her purse off the floor, telling me, "I'd better make tracks. Can't stop the presses."

Wryly, I reminded her, "I can. Sit down a moment, Glee."

"Uh-oh." She eyed me askance. "It seems I'm in for a lecture."

"No, nothing like that. I want to discuss a new assignment with you." My words were true enough, but I was also determined to get the dirt about Glee and Gillian. Motioning toward the low, round table, I asked, "Shall we?"

"You're the boss." Her tone carried a hint of skepticism. Choosing the chair nearest the door, she opened her purse on her lap and pulled out a pen and notebook. Under her breath, she told me, "After what happened this afternoon, I'm surprised you'd trust me with anything more meaty than 'Dog Bites Man.'"

"Oh, it's meaty," I assured her, sitting in the adjacent chair. "In fact, it's related to the Reeces."

She squinted. "Is this a feature—or an exposé?"

"Possibly both. Ever heard of the Dumont Institute for Eastern Studies?"

She wrote the name on her pad, then grimaced.

I nodded. "I know. Someone wasn't thinking. I'm not sure how we'll make repeated references to it in print—but now, that's *your* problem."

"Hey, Mark, back up. Let's not sweat the stylistic details, not yet. To answer your original question, no, I've never heard of this joint. What's the story?"

I gave her the same background I had just given Lucy, concluding, "So the institute is very much tied to the Reeces. Not only is Esmond Reece in thick with Tamra Thaine, but Gillian has threatened to withhold her promised funding of the project, claiming to be cash-strapped by cost overruns on the new house—which Neil says is bunk."

Glee rolled her eyes. "Consider the source."

"But the bigger story, at least from the perspective of our local readers, is twofold. First, the founding of the institute is news in itself, and the various disciplines taught there are largely unknown in Dumont, requiring incisive explanation. Second, and more tantalizing, is the question of whether the whole operation is on the level. So it's not your typical features story, Glee." I paused, adding, "Of course, you can assign it to someone else if you like."

She smirked. "Are you kidding? I smell a story." She had used the same expression years earlier, on a cold winter morning when we had first met, describing a hunch she couldn't shake regarding a sordid detail of my family's past. To my dismay, her hunch later proved to be accurate. I soon learned that when Glee's reporting of fashion and food occasionally strayed into the realm of hard news, our readers always benefited from superior journalism. Looking up from her notes, she now asked, "Have a contact for me?"

Rising, I stepped into my inner office for a moment, grabbing the notebook from my desk. "Right here," I said, returning to sit at the table with her. "Tamra is the person to interview first." I gave Glee the number that Esmond had given me.

She copied the number, then slipped her pen and notebook into her purse and snapped it shut. Chipper as ever, she rose and moved to the door, telling me, "I've got my work cut out for me."

Broaching my intended topic, I said, "I'm sure you can handle it, Miss Buttles."

She froze in the doorway, then stepped back into my office. "Oh." She sat again, facing me. "You, uh, . . . you caught that, huh?"

Airily, I wondered aloud, "Who would name a child Glee Savage? It seems so contradictory. It seems like a name that someone might have made up."

She crossed her legs and leaned forward on her knees, countering, "Who would name a child Glee *Buttles?* I'll tell you who—Mr. and Mrs. Russel Buttles. God, isn't it *awful?*"

I thought it judicious not to answer.

She saved me the trouble. "As a little girl, I couldn't *stand* that name. You can well imagine the jokes. At least, growing up in the fifties, I had the comfort of knowing that a Prince Charming would one day rescue me with some other name. Smith, Jones, Johnson—it didn't matter which prince, so long as he wasn't Prince Buttles." She sighed. There was humor in her voice, but it had a bittersweet overtone as she continued, "Things didn't go quite as planned. Coming of age in the sixties and graduating from college in the early seventies, I was still Miss Buttles, or Ms. Buttles, which was none better. So when I got my first job out of school, right here at the *Register,* the paper's founder, Barret Logan, asked me, 'And what byline will you be using?' His tone implied that it was not only permissible to change my name, but desirable. Well, that was all the prodding I needed. And to this day, I have happily been known as Glee Savage."

"You tiger, you." I growled.

"That played into it, I admit. Back then, reporting was *still* dominated by men, so I felt it would be to my advantage to juice up my byline. And you know what, Mark? This is odd, but I think I actually became more aggressive, as if I were living up to the name."

I paused before noting, "You were decidedly aggressive this afternoon."

"Who, *me?* That wasn't Glee Savage; that was Miss Buttles."

"I see. And you didn't slap Gillian Reece; that was Gill Dermody whose face got in the way of your hand."

"Very good, Mark. You catch on fast." She reached to pat my fingers. "No wonder everyone thinks you're so clever—not that I ever disputed the point."

"I'm clever enough to understand that your breezy manner is more than idle pleasantry; it's an evasive maneuver." I looked her in the eye. "Right?"

She fidgeted with the lip of her purse. "Evasiveness is a subtle skill I fear I've always lacked. I tend to be direct."

"An admirable quality in any writer."

"Thank you."

I smiled. "Then 'fess up, Glee. What's this tumultuous background between you and Gillian?" I wasn't being nosy. As an investigative reporter, I was trained to dig instinctively, so I could justify my prying on professional grounds.

With a sigh of defeat, she said, "I suppose I'll *never* file that story if I don't clear this up with you, so I might as well get it over with. Would you prefer the short version or the whole grisly story?"

"Why, Glee, you already know—any story worth telling is just long enough."

"True. And the most difficult sentence is always the first."

With a pensive nod, I suggested, "Perhaps I could give you some help with the opening line. At the risk of being presumptuous, I have an inkling this relates to the elusive Prince Charming."

Her eyes bugged. "You *knew*. You already knew."

"Nope. But hey, you just made reference to the dashing hero who would rescue you from your maiden name; then you said, 'Things didn't go quite as planned.' I already knew that you and Gillian had known each other in college and didn't get along. Considering the raw emotions that were bared this afternoon, I doubt if the run-in was precipitated by two sorority sisters tussling over a tennis bracelet. So I put two and two together and sniffed man trouble." Glibly, I concluded, "Elementary."

"Cripes," she said under her breath, "you *are* clever."

I grinned. Though I appeared to be gloating, my true intention was to put her at ease with a difficult topic. And it worked.

"It was all so long ago," she said, shaking her head softly, "it hardly seems worth the fuss, not now. But back then, I could've killed that woman. We weren't sorority sisters, Mark—you got that detail wrong—but we lived in the same dorm. I was a senior at Madison, and Gill was a freshman, so we knew each other for only a year. But wow, that was more than enough."

Since I still had my notebook in hand, I was tempted to jot a few details while Glee spoke, but I resisted.

She continued, "Yes, all the trouble goes back to a man—well, a grown kid, really, at that age. We'd been seeing each other for two years, and he was a year younger than I was, so when I reached my senior year, we had to face the question of my graduation—what then? I decided to stay on for a year of grad school, basically to put me 'on hold' while Hugh finished his degree. That was his name—Hugh Ryburn. We weren't exactly engaged, but we knew we had a future together.

"Then along came a spider, and her name was Gill Dermody. She was a business major, not very common for a woman back then, so even as a freshman, she stood out. She happened to be in the floor lounge one evening when Hugh and I were watching TV, and . . . well, you can figure out the rest. She flat-out stole him. Worse yet, she made no secret of her intention to do it, and after she'd done it, she missed no opportunity to crow about it. She even resorted to trickery—the oldest trick in the book—claiming to be pregnant by Hugh that spring.

"He was torn, but wanted to do the 'honorable' thing. When I graduated, I forgot about grad school and left Madison. Shortly after, Gill discovered she'd had a 'false alarm' (surprise, surprise), but since I was out of the picture, Hugh married her anyway. A few years later, I heard that Gill had chewed him up and spit him out. He'd meant everything to me, but to Gill, he was merely a conquest.

"Meanwhile, I got on with my career here and found it more rewarding, or at least more predictable, than romance. I tried to forget about Gill Dermody—the conniving Mrs. Hugh Ryburn—and I never knew that she'd become the Gillian Reece who was setting up shop here in Dumont. She, of course, had never even heard of Glee Savage, so our meeting this afternoon came as a shock to both of us.

"Maybe I should be grateful to her. If she'd never come along, I might have become Glee Ryburn, but I probably wouldn't have landed in Dumont, and there would never have been a Glee Savage."

Setting down my notebook, I stood, offering open arms. "I'm more than happy with the Glee we've got."

She rose, readily accepting my hug. "Thanks, Mark," she said with a sniff. Then she stiffened. "It's just the *way* that damned woman went about it."

"I agree. It was unconscionable."

Glee patted my chest. "I haven't spoken of this in years."

"So you decided to unload yourself to a reporter?"

She backed up a step, crossing her arms. "You *forced* it out of me."

"Coaxed, certainly. Cajoled, maybe. But forced? Never."

"You're splitting hairs, mister." She grinned, picking up her purse. "And *I* still have a story to write."

I tapped my watch. "Then get cracking."

She blew me a little kiss, a sincere gesture conveying true fondness, then left my office and headed to her desk.

Retrieving my notebook from the table, I carried it back to my inner office and set it open on my desk. The blank pages conveyed none of the soul-baring I'd just heard, but one of Glee's statements still rang in my ears.

"Back then," Glee had said, beginning her story, "I could have killed that woman."

No doubt about it—my view of Gillian Reece was growing darker by the minute.

Chapter Eight

That evening, Neil cooked dinner for the two of us at home. I helped with the preparations, but basically kept out of the way, contributing with the lion's share of the cleanup afterward. We found this arrangement mutually agreeable, and the routine was a comfortable reminder of the simple joys of being home alone together. With Thad away at school pursuing a degree in theater and our housekeeper following her own quest to establish a career in music, Neil and I had feared that the occasional open evening with nothing booked— not even a dinner reservation downtown at First Avenue Grill—might leave us feeling adrift and abandoned. We were pleasantly surprised, though, to discover that the return to our original state, "just us," was neither depressing nor boring. On the contrary, we had rediscovered those very aspects of each other that had attracted us in the first place. Our "empty nest" now felt more like a "love nest" than it had for several years.

Though we had dined alone tonight, the intimacy of our evening would not last. Our houseguest, Todd Draper, was due to arrive later, driving from Chicago. He had phoned along the way, reporting his progress, and we estimated his arrival at nine-thirty. While Neil gabbed with him on the phone, confirming directions for the remainder of the trip, I recalled my conversation that morning with Roxanne, who had caught my attention with her description of Todd as a "dish."

Waiting for the hour when he would land on our doorstep, I tried not to dwell on imagining what he would look like. I also tried to avoid wondering how I would react to having him bedded in the guest room, just down the hall from Neil and me, upstairs on Prairie Street. Instead, I built a fire.

"It's not *that* cold," said Neil, entering the den from the front hall, carrying a tray of liqueur bottles. He set the tray on a coffee table in front of the fireplace, where I hunkered at the hearth, fussing with kindling and matches.

I turned from my task to tell him, "It's mid-October already, and we haven't had a fire yet. Today was getting nippy. Anyway, it's all about atmosphere."

"Ahhh, atmosphere," he acknowledged, grinning as he poured a finger or two of cognac for each of us. Then he frowned and sniffed. "Try opening the flue—or you'll get way more atmosphere than you bargained for."

"Good idea." It was our first fire of the season, so my technique was rusty. So was the flue, which creaked like a crypt as I screwed it open.

While I finished with the fire, Neil settled on the studded-leather love seat that anchored a cozy group of furniture at that end of the room. Cracking open a book, he slipped off his shoes and pulled up his feet, curling into the corner of the sofa like a cat.

Flicking some grime from my fingers, I asked, "Do you mind if I do a bit of desk work?"

"Hm?" He looked up from his reading, already engrossed. "Oh, sure, Mark. No problem." And his nose was again buried in the book. The glow of the fire turned his mop of hair impossibly golden.

Taking both snifters from the tray, I handed one to Neil and skoaled him gently as if bidding adieu. It was a sketchy farewell, as I wasn't going far. Sipping from the glass, I stepped to the opposite side of the room, which was dominated by the enormous partners desk that had belonged to my uncle Edwin—and hadn't been moved since.

When Edwin Quatrain had built this house some fifty years earlier, employing the talents of a Taliesin architect from Spring Green, he reserved a special space for himself on the first floor, just off the front door. His den was a masculine but artful lair that occupied a prime corner of the house, with windows facing both the street and an expansive side yard. The desk, as well as the mantel and indeed all of the home's ornamental detailing, had been designed by Wright's protégé in the hallmark Prairie style that melded Art Nouveau, mission, modernist, and Oriental influences.

Other rooms Neil had taken a free hand in decorating, but Uncle Edwin's den, now my own home office, didn't offer much leeway. The fireplace, bookcases, paneling, doorway surrounds, and massive desk were all fixed architectural statements—and charming ones at that. Neil simply added the grouping of leather furniture, in a traditional chesterfield style, creating a conversation area near the fire. He also hung the tall windows with white, sheer end panels, claiming the room needed softening, but grumbling that they weren't quite right. And that was that. Other than the modern telephone and sleek new computer, the room must have looked much the same when Uncle Edwin had first settled into it.

Placing my snifter on the leather blotter, I sat in my clubby desk chair, also leather, and opened a file of papers I had brought home from the office. Checking my watch—it was eight-thirty—I noted that I could get in an hour's work before our guest's expected arrival. I took a sip of cognac, holding the liquor in my mouth for a long moment as it assaulted my tongue before sliding down my throat. Neil, I noticed, had set his glass on the coffee table without drinking from it. Lifting the top batch of papers from my folder, I saw that it was the draft of a series of local election profiles being readied by the *Register* staff, so I removed the paper clip, sorted through the profiles, and began to read.

Not until I heard the squeak of brakes, the purr of an engine, did I look up.

"He's here," said Neil, setting down his glass, which was now empty. Tossing his book on the sofa, he got up, stepped into his shoes, went out to the hall, and opened the front door.

I quickly jogged my pile of papers together and closed the folder as if hiding a mess—company was coming. Rising from the desk, I crossed to the coffee table and set both of our glasses on the tray. The fire was low, but still glowing, so I added another log or two to the embers.

"Hey, Todd!" I heard Neil call from the porch. His feet squeaked the few stairs leading down to the sidewalk. "Sure, that's fine, just leave it in the driveway." A car door slammed. The trunk popped open.

Crossing to the front windows behind my desk, I tucked aside the sheers and peeked into the darkness, feeling ridiculous, like some withered busybody crone. Neil stood at the rear of the car, helping our visitor unload things from the trunk, which was lit. I could clearly see their hands moving, but I couldn't get a look at our guest's face, hidden by the raised deck. The car was a full-size Mercedes, I noted—apparently this guy *was* good.

When the trunk closed with a thud, I stepped aside, fearful of being caught peeping. Standing at my desk, I tidied a few pencils and pens that stood in a cup, then untangled a knot in the phone cord.

"Traffic bad?" asked Neil, leading our visitor up the front stairs.

"Nah. Once I got past Milwaukee, it was open road."

They paced across the porch. Stepping through the doorway and into the front hall, Neil said, "Whew! You don't exactly travel light, do you?" The metal feet of several heavy bags clacked as they hit the floor.

"Sorry. Must be my Boy Scout training. 'Be prepared.' "

"Right!" They both laughed.

Emerging from the den and joining them in the front hall, I asked Neil brightly, "Who's your friend?" I already knew, of course, but since Neil was so adept at social niceties, I preferred to let him handle the introductions.

He dispatched these duties with ease: "Mark, this is Todd Draper, *the* best curtain designer in the business. Todd, this is Mark Manning, my better half."

"Well," I hedged, reaching to shake Todd's hand, "let's just say I'm Neil's 'other half.' "

Todd laughed again. "It's a pleasure, Mark. I've long wanted to meet you."

"Then tonight's your lucky night, I guess." My lame attempts at humor generally made me squirm, and this hackneyed retort was no exception.

But Todd grinned graciously, telling me, "I guess it *is*." He had shaken my hand with warm enthusiasm, hanging on a moment longer, and only now let go.

"Todd," said Neil, "I assume you need to freshen up. Then we can all sit down and have a drink. Mark lit a fire."

"Sounds perfect. Have any Scotch?"

"Name your brand."

He did. Then Neil walked him down the hall to a bathroom before slipping into the dining room to raid the liquor cabinet.

Watching them move away from me, I noted that both men were about the same height and build. Like Neil, Todd was in good shape, no stranger to the gym. He was probably in his early forties, a few years older than Neil, a few years younger than I. For his drive that cool night, he'd worn a lightweight V-necked sweater, charcoal gray, over a white T-shirt. He also wore a pair of heavy, starched khakis, deeply wrinkled at the knees and the lap from his four hours in the car. I had always taken special pleasure at the sight of a man in khakis, and Todd, I noted, wore them exceptionally well.

Coincidentally, Neil and I were similarly attired that night, having dressed down after returning from our offices.

Returning to the den, I poked the fire, shifted a log, and got the flames going. Then I poured some more cognac for Neil and me. As I set down the bottle, Neil entered from the hall with a bottle of single-malt Scotch and a small ice bucket.

Putting these on the drinks tray, he asked, "Well, what'd you think?"

"Todd? Seems like a nice guy—certainly pleasant enough."

"Not too hard on the eyes, either." Neil twitched his brows.

"No," I agreed vaguely, "I suppose not." Changing the topic, I wondered, "Isn't it a little unusual for Todd to come so far to install a project? Did he drive all the way up here as a favor to you?"

"Not at all. His Chicago workroom produces orders for designers all over the country. Whenever possible, Todd and his own crew take care of the installation, often returning after the first 'fitting'—not unlike tailoring a custom-made suit. He's done work in California."

"There's a crew coming as well?"

"Tomorrow. They'll drive up in a truck, delivering the finished curtains. But Todd wanted to spend the night and get a fresh start in the morning."

Todd breezed in from the hall. "Talking about me?" He flashed a big, perfect smile. I couldn't imagine what he'd done in the bathroom, but he did indeed look refreshed. Was it my imagination, or had his pants lost their wrinkles?

"Yes," Neil told him, "we were talking about you."

"Secrets from your past," I kidded.

"Oh, dear," he said, raising his fingers to his lips. "Nothing *too* tawdry, I hope."

"Just tawdry enough," I told him.

"Ice?" asked Neil.

"Two cubes," Todd answered. "No twist, no water."

Neil poured the Scotch. "You're too easy."

"That's what *you* think." Todd took the glass with a nod of thanks.

Neil and I lifted our snifters from the tray, touched them to Todd's glass, and joined in a toast. "Welcome to Dumont," Neil told him.

"To friendship," I added.

"Why, Mark," Todd said demurely, "I hardly *know* you." He winked.

I laughed as he and Neil took the first sips from their glasses; then I joined them, downing a bracing swig of my brandy.

I was instantly comfortable having Todd in our home, and this feeling had nothing to do with his good looks. (In fact, handsome men sometimes leave me ill at ease, as I'm ready to assume an air of superiority on their part.) No, my comfort with Todd was unrelated to physical attraction. Rather, it stemmed from his affable nature, his quick wit, and, yes, his easy, flirtatious manner, which came across as unremarkable and unthreatening. In short, the man had a certain sophistication about him, a self-confidence he wore well. He struck me as . . . *urban,* a quality rarely encountered here in Dumont. With a measure of surprise, I realized that I now missed people like Todd, who were an everyday aspect of my former life in Chicago. I told him, "Now that you're here, I'm sure friendship will follow."

"It already has," he said over the rim of his glass. Then he swallowed more Scotch.

Neil suggested, "Let's get comfortable."

Todd asked, "Are you trying to get my clothes off—*already?*"

I choked on my drink.

Feigning a stern voice and hard features, Neil answered, "Hardly, Mr. Draper. I was merely inviting you to sit down."

"Too kind of you. I've had my ass strapped to that autobahn cruiser for hours on end, but sure, I'd be happy to set a spell with you boys."

So we settled on the furniture in front of the fireplace. Neil resumed his previous position at one end of the love seat, moving the book he had left there. I waited, allowing our guest to choose the spot he would find most comfortable; he chose to sit next to Neil on the love seat. Two chairs remained, situated on either side of the coffee table, at right angles to the small sofa. I chose the one nearer Todd, as it seemed friendlier for Neil and me to flank our guest than to "gang up" beside him. Easing into the armchair, I cupped the snifter in one palm and blinked at the image of Neil and Todd sitting together. I hadn't previously noted Todd's sandy hair, but it now picked up the fire's glow with the same intensity as did Neil's.

Neil asked him, "So what do you think of sleepy little Dumont?"

"Seems nice enough." Grandly, he expostulated, "It's not *where* one lives, but *how.*" Then he laughed. "No, seriously. You've got a wonderful place here. As for the town, I haven't really seen it yet; I arrived in the dark."

I asked, "Have you seen the Reece house?"

"Just Neil's plans, which look fabulous. I'm eager to see the real thing."

"You won't be disappointed." I shifted my glance to Neil. "Seriously, kiddo, you really outdid yourself this time."

"Shucks," he drawled, "jest doin' m'job."

I told Todd, "The features editor of our paper, Glee Savage, is planning a big photo spread for this Sunday."

Neil elbowed Todd. "So we'd better get those curtains up."

"Yes, massa." Todd squinted. "Glee Savage? What a handle."

I agreed, "It is, isn't it?" I was tempted to explain how the name had come about, but refrained, deciding that Glee's story had not been shared with me so I might lob it about as cocktail chat. Besides, Todd's comment about Glee's name brought something else to mind.

"Todd Draper . . . ," I said. "Speaking of handles, that one's not bad for someone in your line of work."

He nodded wearily. "Everyone asks about the name, but I didn't make it up. I was born Todd Draper."

"Really? I just assumed—since you're in the drapery business—"

"Mark, Mark, Mark," said Neil, shaking his head pitiably, exchanging a sigh with Todd, "one never says 'drapery.'"

Todd explained, "In the trade, anything hanging at a window is 'curtains,' not 'drapes.'"

"Ah." There are areas of knowledge that should be the birthright of all gay men, but I was still learning.

"Ergo, the name Draper is almost *inappropriate* to my work. Even so, it has that heritage—a pedigree, if you will."

My look of blank ignorance prompted Neil to remind me, "Dorothy Draper was one of *the* great interior designers of the last century. I'm sure you've heard of her, Mark."

Actually, I had. Neil often spoke of her as the doyenne of American decorators. With arched brows, I asked Todd, "You're related to Dorothy Draper? I'm impressed."

"Distantly. Well, *supposedly.* My father, who founded Draper Studios in Chicago, always claimed there was common blood, so you'll have to take his word for it, not mine."

"Is your dad still in the business?"

"No, he's long gone. Up until two years ago, Geoff and I ran it, but now that *he's* gone, I run the whole show."

Tentatively, I asked, "Geoff . . . ?" Was he an uncle of Todd's? A brother?

"Mark," said Neil quietly, "Geoff was Todd's lover. He died in an auto accident."

"Oh, gosh," I said, leaning forward to place my palm on Todd's knee, "I'm so sorry."

"Thanks, Mark." He placed his hand over mine. "It was rough—especially the suddenness—but I'm coming out of it. Friends make all the difference." He squeezed my hand, then drained the Scotch in his glass.

A log popped and collapsed in the grate, spraying sparks against the screen.

"More?" I asked.

"Please." He handed me the glass. Without getting up, I poured his refill from the tray on the coffee table.

Neil asked him, "Are you back in the dating game yet?"

Todd grinned. "Oh, not actively, but yeah, I've been looking."

"You won't have a *bit* of trouble," I said offhandedly, then wished I hadn't been so quick with the comment.

Neil seconded, "Trust me—anyone would jump at the chance."

"Thanks," said Todd. Then he added coyly, "Because I'm more than ready."

I handed him his drink.

The three of us gabbed for another half hour or so, covering topics ranging from business to politics. We discovered a few mutual friends from my days in Chicago, and Neil compared notes with Todd on some of their shared clients. Throughout this banter, Todd's manner was uniformly lighthearted, with laughter punctuating his words—until the name of a particular client was mentioned.

"First thing tomorrow," said Neil, "I need to introduce you to Gillian Reece. She—"

"*Ughhh*, what a bitch," Todd interrupted.

"She can be difficult," I allowed.

"I mean, even on the *phone*, you can just tell that this woman is one nasty piece of work. She's pretentious, opinionated, overbearing—and she has *no* taste. Zero. None."

I mentioned, "But she's awfully good with numbers," knowing this would do little to sway Todd's open-and-shut opinion of her.

Neil shrugged. "At least she had sense enough to hire *us*."

Todd put his arm around Neil's shoulder. "She hired *you*, my friend. And *you* had sense enough to hire me. But now that I have a sense of the woman, I can't imagine how you work with her."

"Somehow, we seem to get along. There have been no major battles, and our few minor skirmishes, I've won. Don't worry, Todd. If anything comes up, I'll play referee."

"It *has* come up—and it's bugle fringe. She wants it!"

Neil flumped back in the love seat. "You're kidding."

"Would I make light of something so heinous as bugle fringe?" At last Todd cracked a smile.

"So tell me," said Neil, "as long as we're being brutally honest, what do you think of the sheers in this room?"

Though out of my element, I quipped, "I thought they were curtains."

Todd explained, "Sheers are *always* curtains, Mark, and curtains are *sometimes* sheers, but neither sheers nor curtains are *ever* drapes."

"Ah." Still learning.

Todd turned to Neil. "They're, uh . . . adequate. Perfectly adequate."

"You liar." Neil cuffed Todd's shoulder. "They're god-awful, and you know it."

Todd smirked. "Well, at least I didn't *say* it."

"They're cheesy. And I'm man enough to admit I need help. Think you could draw something up for us?"

"Depends."

"On what?"

"Your *budget*, of course!" Todd yelped a loud laugh.

He and Neil continued in this vein, debating possibilities for redecorating my den. I had sense enough to stay out of it.

Besides, I enjoyed just watching them, sitting there together on the sofa, engaging in their bout of manic creativity. Taking a long look at them, I realized that Roxanne had been right. Todd Draper was indeed "quite the dish."

What's more, he looked a lot like Neil.

More to the point, he reminded me of the third party in my dream that morning.

PART TWO

Joint Venture

THE 'AH' FACTOR

Workers reaching completion on stunning new local residence

by GLEE SAVAGE
Trends Editor, Dumont Daily Register

OCT. 22, DUMONT, WI—A magnificent new home being built on Dumont's east side has been the talk of the town since ground was broken for construction late last year. Decorating crews are now rushing to complete the project, and soon its owners, Mr. and Mrs. Esmond Reece, will move into their lavish new residence.

The *Register* was recently treated to a preview tour, conducted by the architect, Neil Waite of Dumont. "My clients wanted a big, comfortable house," he said, "and they also wanted to make a 'statement.' The danger would be in allowing the house to become a mere status symbol."

Mr. Waite has clearly succeeded in avoiding any such pitfall, producing a home that is both visually arresting and meant to be lived in. What's more, the structure blends seamlessly with its setting. The architect explained, "The stone was quarried in the northern part of the state, and the timbers, though not local, are a reflection of the wooded landscape."

In the hands of a less skilled designer, these materials might have come across as "rustic," but not here. Mr. Waite also included in his materials palette the sensitive use of glass, which lightens the whole structure and offers just the right counterpoint of sophistication.

Remarkably, the inside of the house is even more jaw-dropping than its exterior. Centerpiece of the interior space is a sumptuous two-story elliptical living room that also serves as a functioning library.

Without a doubt, Neil Waite has now established himself as one of the finest residential architects in the Midwest. See for yourself in Sunday's *Trends* section, which will carry a full-color photo feature. ❏

Chapter Nine

Wednesday dawned later than we had intended. Our conversation with Todd Draper the night before had kept us up beyond our normal hours, and I had failed to heed a lesson learned from previous experience—that one brandy before retiring is more than sufficient. So I lingered in the shower that morning while Neil traipsed down to the kitchen, started the coffee, and admitted our friend Doug Pierce, the sheriff, who paid a routine breakfast visit, delivering pastry fetched on the way from his early workout at the gym.

When I arrived downstairs, Doug had just set a copy of the *Register* on the kitchen table, folded open to Glee's column. "Congratulations," he was telling Neil. "That's quite a valentine—and a well-deserved one at that."

Skimming the story, Neil shook his head with a soft laugh. "Glee barely mentions Gillian, referring to her as Mrs. Reece."

Strolling over to the table and into their conversation, I said, "I admire Glee's restraint, considering what she probably *wanted* to call Gillian."

"Trouble?" asked Doug, looking over the rim of his coffee mug. He always dressed in business clothes, rather than a uniform, and that morning he was wearing a jacket I particularly liked on him, a tweedy green blazer.

"Long story," I said, dismissing Doug's question, tired of the topic. At dinner the night before, I had confided to Neil the history of Glee's college romance, wrenched by Gillian.

Doug couldn't stay long, needing to go downtown for an early meeting of the public-safety commission, so we weren't able to introduce him to our houseguest that morning. Todd, exhausted from his long drive on Tuesday evening (and doubtless no less groggy than I from too many nightcaps), slept through breakfast and, when he finally did come downstairs to meet us in the kitchen, asked if he could take some coffee in the car with him.

"Don't you want to try some kringle first?" asked Neil, referring to the large horseshoe-shaped Danish that Doug had brought. "It's a specialty up here."

"Maybe tomorrow, thanks. I need to get over to the Reece house; my crew may already be there. Besides"—he eyed the pastry and patted his stomach—"need to watch my figure."

He looked just fine to me. In fact, fresh from the shower, he looked even better than the night before.

Even though Todd was last to rise that day, he was first out of the house. Leaving through the back door with his go-cup, he gave a cheery wave, telling us, "See you there!"

"Okay, Todd," said Neil, "we won't be long. Sorry—I'd wanted to introduce you to Gillian."

Todd rolled his eyes. "I'm sure I'll find her." And he was gone.

Both Neil and I planned to join him at the Reece house, Neil because he was on the job and needed to oversee the completion of various projects, and I because I was curious. Lying in bed after our long conversation with Todd the previous night, Neil had told me, "Don't spread this around, but the curtains for Gillian's living room *alone* cost nearly fifty thousand dollars." *This* I had to see.

Though we were all headed to the Reeces', each drove his own car, as Todd and Neil had unpredictable schedules, and I didn't plan to stay long, needing to spend the rest of the morning at my office. After sprucing up the kitchen, Neil and I left the house. I followed him to the outskirts of town, to the magnificent new home that had been written up in that morning's paper.

Perhaps because of the publicity, there seemed to be more traffic than usual in the secluded, woodsy neighborhood where the Reeces would soon reign as homeowners nonpareil. As publisher of the local paper, I liked to think that our modest daily journal held that sort of power, though in truth, the extra vehicles might simply have signaled an intensified rush to finish the job.

Neil and I cruised along a line of parked cars and trucks that included Gillian's conspicuous Bentley, Todd's sleek Mercedes, and a large van with Illinois plates. Elegant gold lettering on the side of the truck trumpeted DRAPER STUDIOS. Neil parked in front of the truck, and I pulled in beyond Neil.

Getting out of our cars, we noted that the back doors of the truck were wide open. Inside were several large corrugated cartons, marked REECE. It was apparent from their arrangement that these were merely the last of the boxes; many others had already been unloaded. At the moment, none of the Draper's crew were present at the curb, though we saw two men with a dolly carting a similar corrugated box into the house through the garage.

"Let's find Todd," said Neil, leading me along the sidewalk toward the front door. A landscaping crew was trimming rolls of sod to fit the front lawn like a moist, loamy carpet. Precise rows of boxwood, not present yesterday, now lined both sides of the stone walkway. Workers ducked in and out of the house, some of them pausing to take notes as they gabbed on cell phones.

As we stepped through the front door, Neil encountered several contractors who immediately nabbed him, asking questions while scribbling on clipboards. The foyer rug had been laid, dampening the previous day's din. Painters in white overalls were touching up the room's heavy wooden trim. Cartons from Draper Studios were placed beneath each window; a stack of them stood near the double doors leading to the living room.

Above it all, drifting through the house at random intervals, was the warble and chime of cell phones, sounding like birds in an electronic aviary, one of which kept attempting an anemic rendition of the *William Tell* Overture (specifically, a measure or two of the section cribbed by *The Lone Ranger*). Who, I wondered, could possibly be addled enough to program a phone with such an insipid ring? Had he no sense of dignity, self-respect, or at the very least, shame?

Extricating himself from a knot of workers, Neil crossed the foyer to me and repeated, "Let's find Todd."

I nodded. "I wonder if *he's* found Gillian."

"Has he ever!" said a guy trundling by just then with a Draper's box on a dolly. He broke stride long enough to jerk his head toward the living-room doors, then continued down a hall toward the other end of the house.

Neil and I shared a brief, concerned glance, then stepped together to the double doors. I wasn't about to repeat a performance of yesterday's awkward entrance, so I told Neil, "She's your client." Neil gave me a quizzical look that seemed to ask, So? Then he turned one of the knobs and opened the door.

That's when we plainly heard the yelling.

"I already *told* you," Todd shouted, "beaded fringe is *wrong* for this room."

"And who the hell are *you*," said Gillian, "to tell *me* what's right or wrong for my *own* fucking living room?"

"Unless you plan to use it as a bordello—and for all I know, you may—beads are simply inappropriate. You can't have them." Todd stamped a foot. *"Period."*

By then, Neil and I had rushed into the fray. Todd and Gillian stood near the center of the room, with perhaps a half dozen workmen stationed near various windows. Two extension ladders had been set up on either side of one of the two-story windows, and a single panel of drapery—excuse me, curtains—had just been installed. I wasn't sure what Todd and Gillian were arguing about, and at the moment, I had lost interest, as my attention was instead riveted by the long, sensuous panel of fabric. A workman reached from the library balcony to steam wrinkles from the upper portion of the curtain while straightening its folds. The nozzle in his hand hissed and gurgled.

Reading the look on my face, Neil stepped me aside, saying, "They're incredible, aren't they? *No one* does work like Todd Draper." Gillian was still yapping and yelling in the background.

I told Neil, "I admit it—I don't recall *ever* seeing curtains so drop-dead beautiful. I've never even thought much about curtains, but these—wow."

"They're hand-loomed Italian Scalamandré silk," Neil explained, "and this room took *hundreds* of yards of it, with taffeta lining and *two* interlinings of English bump. The pattern is a subtle tone-on-tone vertical stripe of gray and silver; that's what gives the folds such depth, as well as the overall effect of shimmer. It's perfect for these high, narrow windows, especially in contrast to the dark wood of the surrounding bookcases and balcony."

"There's fringe," I noted, "and it's gorgeous. What's Gillian complaining about?"

"She wanted *bugles*—small, hollow glass rods, strung like beads— but Todd refused, giving her classic bullion fringe—silk threads twisted into cords, with handmade bobble tassels. It's all custom work, a foot deep, top and bottom, perfectly matched to the colors of the fabric and the paint palette of the room. Yes, it's expensive, but for work of this caliber, Todd's prices are not only customary, but reasonable. He's a genius."

"Listen to me, smart-ass," barked Gillian, "I was very specific in telling you how I wanted my drapes made."

Todd countered, "I was equally specific in telling *you* exactly how they *would* be made. The curtains are aesthetically correct as delivered—with bullion fringe."

"Bullshit! You seem to be unfamiliar with the concept, but *this* customer is *always* right."

"Let me remind you, Mrs. Reece, that you are *not* my customer. I was contracted by your architect, who also holds a stake in the finished appearance of this room."

Gillian crossed her arms, fuming. "But *I'm* paying the bills, dammit, and for fifty grand, I expect to get *exactly* what I want."

Todd paused, then stepped to within inches of Gillian, telling her flatly, calmly, "Then I suggest you phone Decorating Den. Not only will they be happy to give you exactly what you want, but they will charge you considerably less. You will *never*, however, know the satisfaction—or the prestige—of living with curtains so artfully fabricated as those from Draper Studios." Harrumph.

Standing ramrod stiff, Gillian took in his words, considered his ultimatum for a moment, and then, without flinching, stepped back for better balance, took aim, and stung him with a flesh-searing bitch slap.

Only a day earlier I'd witnessed the depth of Glee Savage's anger, which had allowed a perky little woman to deliver a surprisingly powerful punch, but now Gillian made Glee look like a welterweight, forcing me to wonder if Todd's jaw was broken. During the seconds of breathless silence that followed, Todd raised his hand, feeling his face. I fully expected him to return Gillian's slap.

Instead, Gillian shrieked at him, "Get *out!*"

With more restraint than I could have mustered, Todd glanced at one of his workers, presumably the installation foreman, signaled a thumbs-down, then walked straight from the living room, through the foyer, and out to the street.

The other workers gathered with the foreman, discussing their next move—should they drop everything and leave, or pack up everything and haul it back to the truck, or simply wait?

Neil, meanwhile, confronted Gillian, telling her point-blank, "I'm ashamed of you. Do you have *any* idea of the reputation of the man you just insulted? Do you have *any* idea how lucky you are that Todd Draper himself consented to take on this job, up here in the middle of nowhere? If you want to play with the big boys, Gillian, you'd better learn to *work* with the big boys. You've told me that your goal is nothing less than to have this house published. Fine. But if that's the case, you're playing by *my* rules. If you think *Architectural Digest* is going to beat a path to your door, you're sadly mistaken, especially after word gets out that you've . . ." And so forth. I'd rarely seen Neil with raised hackles, and I was glad to note how adroitly he handled this more aggressive edge to his personality—he was being forceful with Gillian, but objective.

Adding to the general atmosphere of consternation that filled the room, cell phones kept ringing, including that vapid, tasteless one that was still beeping its nasal rendition of *William Tell*.

"Hi-yo, Silver!" said one of the workmen, passing by me. "I think that's you, buddy."

I may have choked. As if in a state of suspended animation, all activity and noise in the room ceased, save the ringing of the phone in my pocket. As it galloped through another measure of its hackneyed melody, my mind raced through a spectrum of emotions that began with denial and ended with mortification. Had I *myself* caused this, fussing with buttons whose functions were unknown to me? Why in hell hadn't I studied the instruction booklet that Lucy had given me with the phone? (Because it was two hundred pages long, that's why, and why should a phone—a *phone*, for Christ's sake—require instructions in the first place, huh?) Managing to get the damn thing out of my pocket, managing to flip it open and find the green button, I said into it, dry-throated, "Yes?"

"Mark! At last—why haven't you picked up?" It was Lucy.

"Never mind. What do you need?" My wording might have struck Lucy as curt, but it was less testy than a more spontaneous question that leapt to mind, its phrasing inappropriate when addressing a lady (even Lucy).

She said, "I just wanted to let you know that Perry Schield was here this morning, and he's on the warpath."

"Oh . . . cripes. Now what?" The chief executive officer of Quatro Press had always struck me as pleasantly avuncular and disappointingly ineffectual, two qualities that were difficult to associate with a man on the warpath.

"The merger, of course. He's been talking with Tyler Pennell, and . . . well, Perry can tell you himself. That's why I've been trying to reach you. When I told him you were over at the Reece house, he said, 'Great, I can kill two birds with one stone.'"

"What'd he mean by *that?*"

"I presume he meant he could talk to both you and Gillian at the same time. Anyway, he's on his way, and I thought you'd want to know."

"Okay, Lucy, thanks. I'll see you later." I disconnected, then squinted at the tiny buttons, well more than the necessary ten, wondering how to change the damned ringer. Fumbling to get out my reading glasses, I dropped the phone on the limestone floor. Satisfied that the question of the ringer was now moot, I returned both the phone and the glasses to my pockets.

Gillian was saying to Neil, ". . . so I *hope* you'll forgive me. I've been under an enormous amount of stress lately."

"Gillian," said Neil, offering a smile, "of course I forgive you, but will *Todd?* You slapped the man."

Her shoulders slumped as she heaved a weary sigh. "He probably won't even listen to me. Can't you intercede on my behalf?"

"Then you *do* want him back on the job?"

"Well . . . ," she hedged, "I *do* want a shot at the *Digest.*"

Both Neil and I understood that these words were tantamount to contrition, at least when uttered by Gillian. If we expected a more sincere expression of penitence for her behavior, we were unlikely to hear it. So Neil told her, "I'll see what I can do."

"*Thank* you, Neil," she gushed, wrapping him in a mechanical embrace. "The main thing is, we just need to *finish.*"

I couldn't help asking, "What, exactly, is the big rush, Gillian?"

"It's a matter of—" she began, but stopped, as if something else had occurred to her. "Well," she told me, "I understand your paper is planning a photo feature for this Sunday. We wouldn't want to disappoint your readers, would we, Mark?"

"No, Gillian, we certainly wouldn't." But her reasoning struck me as iffy. Though I took justifiable pride in the *Dumont Daily Register,* it was a far cry, in the world of interiors, from *Architectural Digest.* No, the truth behind Gillian's rush was simply that she wanted something, and she wanted it now.

Neil was saying, "First, I have to *find* Todd. I doubt if he tore out of town yet; his things are at our house. Maybe his crew has some idea where he went." So Neil went over to talk to the group of workers, now assembled near the spiral stairway to the library balcony.

Gillian turned to me. "You're so fortunate, Mark, to have a man like that in your life." With a snort, she added, "I'll trade you for Esmond *any* day."

It was an odd sort of compliment, and I wasn't sure how to respond. After a moment of grasping for words, I found that I needn't bother—we were interrupted just then by Perry Schield, who blustered in from the foyer, telling someone, "I'm quite capable of finding them on my own, thank you."

"Oh, Christ," Gillian told me under her breath, "here comes death-warmed-over. Who woke *him* up?"

"Gillian, please—if you're serious about this merger, it's important to recognize Perry as half of the deal. You wrote the press release, remember. It's a 'friendly merger of equals.'"

"I suppose you're right," she said, sounding bored. Obliquely, she added, "At least for a while."

"Mark. Gillian. We need to talk," said Perry, huffing toward us through the living room, the very picture of agitation. I had rarely seen him exhibit much energy, physical or otherwise, so I was surprised to note that Lucy's description had been accurate—Perry was on the warpath. Instead of a tomahawk, however, he wielded his linen handkerchief, hacking into it every few steps.

I asked, "What's wrong, Perry?"

"Yes, Perry," added Gillian, her voice dripping with concern, "whatever is the matter?" I marveled at her ability to switch gears so fast and play nicey-nice.

"Well, I think you already know," said Perry, pausing to clear his throat. "It's Tyler Pennell."

"Ah, yes," said Gillian, nodding. Leaning close, she said in a confidential tone, "Pennell *is* a problem, I agree. It's astute of you to pick up on that, Perry. I meant to have a word with you about him."

Perry trembled where he stood, barely controlling his anger. "Pennell *himself* isn't the problem. It's the reports I've heard from him. First, he claimed to discover some irregularities in the accounting at

Ashton Mills. Second, and worse, when he tried to bring these matters to your attention yesterday afternoon, you invited him to . . . to . . . to *kiss your ass*." Bug-eyed as if choking, Perry dislodged a knot of phlegm from his throat and balled his handkerchief to his mouth to catch it.

Gillian gave him an admonishing grin. "*Really*, now, Perry, I'm sure that's an exaggeration." She laughed airily.

But Perry was not amused. "Tyler Pennell assured me that he was quoting you verbatim."

"Then his memory is as questionable as his accounting skills. Perry, I've said it before—he's a rube, and he has no place on the merger team."

Stepping in, I reminded Gillian, "You, along with the entire Ashton board, agreed to retain Tyler for due diligence."

"We were sold a bill of goods. He's *awful*, Mark."

"His credentials are first-rate, and both boards have agreed to abide by his findings. Ashton/Quatro Corporation won't be created tomorrow without his blessing."

"And he's getting cold feet," Perry piped in.

"Funny," said Gillian, "that's just what he said about you, Perry. *Surely* that's not true. You *know* that AQC is a match made in heaven. And it pains me to mention this, but with retirement looming so near for you . . . well, let's just say that it's very much in *your* best interest to help shepherd this deal to completion." She turned to me with a plastic smile. "Right, Mark?"

Though I did not appreciate her manipulative manner, I could not argue with her premise. I told them both, "I've supported this merger from the start."

"Well, then," said Gillian, flipping her hands, "it seems we're all in agreement. And all of these so-called problems and issues are merely fabrications of a third-rate bookkeeper's overactive imagination. Maybe Pennell feels that he needs to *find something* in order to justify his fee, which I suppose is commendable. The important thing is, after tomorrow, we're rid of him."

Perry had listened quietly, but his stern expression said he hadn't bought much of Gillian's act. He told her, "I wouldn't be so sure about tomorrow. This isn't over till it's over." With a brisk nod, he bade both of us, "Good day." Then he turned and trundled out of the room, his exit prolonged by the wake of coughing and hacking that trailed behind him.

Watching him leave, Neil returned from the curtain crew, telling Gillian and me, "I get the impression Perry Schield is a less-than-happy camper."

"Perry Schield," said Gillian, "is a boob."

"And Tyler Pennell," I recalled, "is a rube."

"That's right"—Gillian nodded emphatically—"boobs and rubes. We're *surrounded* by them. Philistines at every turn."

Wearily, I asked Neil, "What's the consensus on Todd?"

"His crew thinks he just went somewhere to cool off. Maybe he went to have breakfast—or took a drive to the park. I'll start looking." Neil leaned to give me a good-bye peck.

"Gillian!" said a voice from the foyer. "We need to talk." These were the same words that had announced Perry's entrance. Now what?

We turned to see Esmond Reece enter the room with Tamra Thaine at his side. He wore the same ill-fitting gray suit I'd seen him wearing at Neil's office the previous morning; she wore a similar outfit in white. I didn't know if they had a yin-and-yang thing going on, or if the light and dark signified some rank of achievement in their studies, or if they simply preferred dressing in these colors.

Gillian groaned. "*Now*, Esmond? Can't you see I'm busy?"

"It's important," he assured her with no apparent emotion. Then he brightened a smidge, greeting Neil and me, "Hello, gentlemen. So pleasant to see you again."

As Neil had not met Tamra, I introduced them, telling Neil, "I had a chance to visit the Eastern studies institute yesterday. It's quite a project."

"That's why we're here," said Esmond. "The institute—"

"Ughhh!" interrupted Gillian. "'The institute, the institute'—that's all I ever hear!" She clapped her palms over her ears, as if protecting her delicate senses from the assault of a jackhammer. It escaped no one that it was she who was making most of the noise.

"Well," said Esmond, stepping up to her, "I'm afraid there's more to be said on the subject. Tamra and I have been working day in and day out, getting our project off the ground, but our—"

"*Your* project? What the hell about *mine?*" She gestured about the sumptuous, surrounding room, as if it lay in shambles. "Do you think this just *happens?*"

"But our future success at the institute," Esmond persisted, "is contingent upon the funding you've already committed to. If you don't deliver, Gillian, I may be forced to reconsider your stewardship of my assets; I may be forced to reclaim control of my own finances."

With a sharp laugh, his wife asked, "Do you honestly think I was dumb enough to leave you any loopholes?"

"A bargain's a bargain, Gillian, and you've—"

"And I've hit a few snags!" she snarled.

"Cost overruns? Neil tells me everything's on budget."

As Neil was standing right there, Gillian was in no position to contradict him, so she took another tack, skirting the facts and launching a personal attack on her husband and his yogi.

Sneering, she asked, "Just how long do you intend to keep this up, Esmond? These damn 'lessons' have been going on for years now, and what do you have to show for it? Back in Harper, when you first told me you were taking up yoga, I thought, Sure, why not? Maybe some good will come of it. What the hell's to lose? But here we are, and you *still* haven't learned any tricks."

"Tricks?" asked Tamra, the first word she had uttered to Gillian.

"Yeah, *tricks.* You know—like wrapping your ankles around your neck." Gillian turned to Esmond. "I thought you'd have mastered *that* by now."

He asked, "What possible interest do you have in the asanas I've mastered?"

"Their entertainment value, of course."

The rest of us exchanged a bewildered glance.

Gillian explained, "Say, for instance, we're throwing a party. You could provide some entertainment, Esmond, by wrapping your feet behind your head and walking on your hands. Better yet, you could serve cocktails that way, balancing the tray on one hand, hopping on the other. Our guests would get a kick out of it. Hell, I'd get a kick out of it."

"Mrs. Reece," said Tamra, sounding truly appalled as she approached the woman, "yogic practices are not undertaken for the amusement of an audience, but rather for the student's own spiritual and physical well-being."

"And how 'bout the instructor?" asked Gillian. "There's some enrichment there, too, isn't there, swami? And I'm not talking about spiritual enrichment. Catch my drift, swami?"

"Mrs. *Reece*," said Tamra, flushed and shaking, "that's an insufferable insult. I won't take it."

"Oh, really? You won't take it, huh? Then take *this*." And with no further warning or provocation, Gillian bitch-slapped Tamra.

Covering her face with her hands, the yogi slumped to the floor and burst into tears. Neil and I stepped forward and knelt with the woman, trying to comfort her.

But Esmond snapped. Gillian had apparently pushed him beyond the limits of his serenity training. Without hesitation, he stepped in front of Tamra, raised his left hand, and bitch-slapped his wife.

"Why, Esmond," she said, utterly unruffled, "I didn't know you had it in you." Her tone, for once, was anything but snide; she sounded proud of her wimpy husband for standing up to her.

"Yeah, well, it seems there's a *lot* you don't know about me—and never will." He leaned down and helped Tamra to her feet, telling her, "Let's get some air. The stench in here is nauseating."

Tamra stared for a moment at Gillian's face as if looking into a mirror. The stinging welt on Tamra's left cheek matched the one Esmond had planted on Gillian's right. Tamra opened her mouth, intending to speak, but quickly reconsidered. Turning, she steadied herself on Esmond's arm, and he led her from the room.

"Are you all right?" I heard him ask as they reached the foyer.

I didn't hear Tamra's mumbled answer.

"Gillian," said Neil, "I hope we've seen the last of these outbursts. Try that on the wrong person, and you could find yourself behind bars."

She smirked. "I highly doubt that. Besides, it was almost *worth* the payback from Esmond." She rubbed her cheek, wincing. "Now, at least, I know how to get a rise out of him."

Needless to say, I now wished that my curiosity about the curtains had not prompted me to visit the Reece house that morning. I'd seen far more than I'd bargained for, and most disturbing of all was the perverse pleasure Gillian took in being struck by her husband. I now seriously questioned the wisdom of my endorsement of the impending merger. Did I really want to put this woman at the helm of the company my uncle Edwin had founded?

Without elaborating, I told Neil and Gillian, "I need to go."

"Me too," said Neil. "I've got to find Todd before he blows out of town."

With perfunctory good-byes to Gillian, we took our leave and stepped from the living room to the foyer. Opening the front door for Neil, I told him, under my breath, "Let's get the hell out of here before there's any *more* trouble."

"Oops," said Neil, looking down the sidewalk. "Too late, methinks."

And up from the street strutted Glee Savage. Today's ensemble was black and white, stark and tasteful. Her oversize purse sported zebra stripes.

Meeting her halfway along the brick walk, we greeted her with hugs. After a round of hellos, I asked inanely, "What brings you to these parts, Glee?"

"Have you forgotten? I need to talk to Gillian."

"Uh," said Neil, "this morning may not be the best time for that. Gillian seems a tad—shall we say—vexed at the moment."

Glee shrugged. "Then my visit should lighten her emotional load. I'm here only to apologize for yesterday's unfortunate run-in. I feel terrible about it. And I'll be sweet as pie—I want that photo feature for this weekend." She winked.

"Good for you, Glee." I laughed. "Work your magic on her."

And she stepped up to the front door.

As Neil and I walked back to our cars, he shook his head, muttering, "If photos are running this weekend, let's hope they show curtains."

Then we got into our cars and went our separate ways, I to my office at the *Register,* Neil in search of Todd Draper.

Chapter Ten

My morning at the office turned busy, not with breaking news, but with the everyday minutiae of running a business—a meeting with bankers, another with a potential new advertiser we were courting, and a third with representatives of our writers' guild, whose contract was up for renewal. Everything went routinely; in fact, the proceedings were dull. But I was grateful for the distraction, which occupied my mind and prevented my thoughts from lingering on the disturbing confrontations that had jump-started my day with a surge of adrenaline that caffeine couldn't match. My nascent hangover from the previous night's cognac had been nipped in the bud, and I was cruising noonward at warp speed.

Sometime after eleven, when my last meeting ended, I returned to my office to check proofs and read mail at my desk. Adrift in this sea of printed words—an altogether pleasant experience, compatible with my calling in life—I was rattled to the bone when my cocoon of silence was shattered by the twangy strains of the *William Tell* Overture seeping from my trousers.

I instantly stood, as if I'd discovered a venomous reptile in my pocket and needed to be rid of it—fast. I'd forgotten I was even carrying the phone, convinced that I'd broken it, rendering it harmless. But there it was, resurrected, taunting me from the warm, dark depths of my pants. Esmond Reece, I recalled, was partially responsible for this intrusion, having invented some crucial thingamabob that had changed the world. I cursed him as I plucked his demon spawn from my pocket and flung it on the desk.

It continued to chirp, like some large black insect, and I decided the only way to silence it was to answer it. So I lifted the phone gingerly and flipped it open, wondering who was calling. It wasn't Lucy; I could see her through the glass wall of my outer office, leaning over someone's desk in the newsroom. Perhaps it was Neil, reporting on his search for Todd Draper. Curious to hear his update, I punched the green button and answered, "Yes?"

"Good morning, sir. I understand from our database that your investment portfolio—"

I punched the red button.

Then I stepped out to the newsroom. *"Lucy,"* I called across the hubbub. When she looked in my direction, I motioned her inside.

"Yes, Mark?" she said, stepping into my office. "What's up?"

"This *phone,"* I groused, pointing to it on my desk, not wanting to touch it.

She picked it up. "Something wrong with it?"

"It rings *entirely* too often."

She grinned. "Welcome to the twenty-first century."

"That's exactly what Roxanne told me."

"Really?" she squeaked. Lucy was normally on an even keel, nose to the grindstone, but just mention Roxanne, and lesbian Lucy went ditsy. She could barely conceal her infatuation with my Chicago friend, now a married woman. Roxanne, in turn, took this doting as a profound compliment, a response rooted not so much in tolerance as in vanity.

"She sends her best, by the way," I lied.

Lucy beamed. When her feet touched ground again, she asked, "So what's the problem with the phone?"

I sighed. "It's not just that it rings too often; it's *how* it rings. It's doing *William Tell.*"

"Huh?" A computer whiz, a crack researcher, and a true-blue techie, Lucy was left-brain all the way. Artswise, she was clueless.

I sang, "Ta-da-*dump*, ta-da-*dump*, ta-da-*dump-dump-dump* . . ."

"Hi-yo, Silver!"

"Yeah. Can you fix it? *Please?*"

She shook her head out of pity for my helplessness, studied the phone for a moment, then tapped a sequence of buttons so quickly you'd have thought she was dialing her own number. "What would you like? They've got Brahms' lullaby . . ."

"Just make it *ring*," I said wearily, "like a *phone*."

She shrugged—I was hopelessly square. "How's this?" She played a demo.

"Fine, Lucy. Thanks."

Placing the phone in its charger on my desk, she said, "As long as I'm here, I was wondering about our coverage of the merger tomorrow. Can I assume Charles Oakland will attend the ceremonial signing?" She winked, acknowledging the open secret of my pen name.

I laughed. "He'll be there." Then I frowned. "Unless . . ." I strolled to the conference area in my outer office.

Lucy followed me. "Hmm?"

"Those due diligence issues raised by Tyler Pennell—let's just say that Gillian Reece and Perry Schield don't see eye to eye on the best means of addressing them. Truth is, Gillian doesn't want to address them at all."

"The signing is scheduled for tomorrow at noon, so I'm holding most of page one for Friday morning's edition."

"I hate to say it, but I think we should have an alternate layout as backup." Trying to be helpful, I suggested, "Between now and then, *something* will blow up in the Mideast."

Lucy's eyes widened. "The deal's in jeopardy?"

I sat at the round table. "I don't know. I hope not." Reconsidering, I added, "I'm not sure what I hope."

Sitting in the next chair, she asked warily, "Should I be taking notes?"

"No, but let me fill you in." My mounting concerns fell into two categories, so I detailed for Lucy, first, what I knew of the accounting inconsistencies discovered by Tyler Pennell in his perusal of the books at Ashton Mills. Second, and even more disturbing, was the animosity and physical violence that seemed to be spreading from Gillian Reece like a virus. "Until yesterday, I'd only seen bitch slaps on soap operas, but—"

"Since when do you watch soap operas?"

"Well," I admitted, "I used to watch *Dynasty*."

Lucy grinned. "Joan Collins fan?"

"Of course. And, brother, she could really smack 'em. What a hoot. Point is, till yesterday, I'd never witnessed the real thing, and it was anything but funny. I've now seen four of these assaults, all involving Gillian Reece—twice pitching, twice catching."

"Really, Mark, sports metaphors just *aren't* your strong suit. Don't even try." Lucy crossed her trousered legs.

"And oddly"—I paused before I gave words to my thought—"Glee started it."

Through a skeptical laugh, Lucy said, "Glee? You make her sound like a playground bully."

"It's a disturbing image, I know. Glee gave me the whole story—a romantic feud with Gillian during their college days. Though I don't approve of physical aggression, I can understand what motivated her. More to the point, it seems Gillian also understood, as if she knew she had it coming. Unfortunately, it didn't end there. Now it's open season."

"Well, at least Glee's out of the fray. She apologized by phone yesterday, and her piece on the house ran this morning."

I nodded. "Neil and I ran into her as we were leaving the Reeces' today. Glee was heading inside to make amends in person—and to set up a photo shoot for her Sunday feature. I warned her she was walking into a hornets' nest."

"I wonder how Glee made out." Lucy reached for the phone on the conference table. "If we're serious about running a photo feature on Sunday, we need to get hopping." She tapped in Glee's extension, waited a moment, then groaned. "Voice mail. I'll try Connie." So she dialed again, asking the downstairs receptionist, "Is Glee in the building?" She listened, then said, "Thanks, Connie," and hung up.

I asked, "Well?"

Fingers to chin, thinking, Lucy reported, "Glee hasn't been in the office since she left for the Reece house—hours ago."

I instinctively stood. "I'm going over there."

Lucy stood. "I want to go with you."

So I grabbed my keys and my phone, and we left.

Chapter Eleven

Driving Lucy to the edge of town, I wondered aloud, "Wouldn't Glee let us know if something had . . . gone wrong?" My question was prompted not by a premonition of what, precisely, might have gone wrong, but by the series of confrontations I had witnessed that morning. I wasn't sure of the exact definition of "bad karma" (perhaps Tamra Thaine could explain it to me), but I knew it when I saw it, and I had seen it in the Reeces' living room.

"Of course she would," said Lucy, trying to sound convinced. "Besides, you know Glee—she keeps her own schedule. It doesn't mean a thing that we haven't heard from her."

Ironically, Lucy's reassuring words seemed only to heighten our concerns. We rode the rest of the way in silence, our somber mood within the car seeming at odds with the colorful autumn landscape that blurred past the windshield.

As we entered the wooded development, I asked, "Have you seen the house yet?" I inflected the question with a bouncy tone, as if the purpose of our drive had no more urgency than sight-seeing.

Lucy shook her head. "From everything I hear, I'm in for a treat."

"That's putting it mildly." I tried not to sound facetious.

When we turned the last corner and the new house came into view, Lucy gasped. "Wow, I see what you mean." The lilt of her voice con-

veyed not only her enthusiasm for Neil's impressive architecture, but a
sense of relief that our fretting seemed unwarranted. It was apparent at
a glance that Glee was not there; her fuchsia hatchback, conspicuous
anywhere, was nowhere in sight. In fact, the only vehicle parked at the
house was Gillian's hulking Bentley.

"That's odd," I said, pulling to the curb in front of Gillian's car.
"When I was here this morning, there was hardly room to park, with
trucks all over the place." Among those trucks had been the Draper
Studios van, now gone.

Removing her seat belt and opening the door, Lucy suggested,
"Maybe they all went to lunch; it's noon."

With a sidelong glance, I told her, "I didn't know tradesmen 'did'
lunch."

"You snob."

"I *mean*, don't they generally bring something to the job?"

"Beats me. I'm an office gal." This was a first—Lucy referring to herself as anything other than a *woman*.

As we got out of the car, I paused, looking up and down the vacant
stretch of curb. "I'll bet the job is done. Gillian was really cracking the
whip, and she knew about that photo feature. Shall we ask her if
everything is ironed out with Glee?" I gestured toward the brick walk
to the front door.

"Lead on," said Lucy, and I escorted her up the walkway to the styl-
ized but unpretentious portico that framed the home's entrance.

When I had visited twice before, Neil had accompanied me, walking through the front door unannounced. Amid the surrounding activity of landscaping and decorating crews, this seemed appropriate. Now,
however, with the work finished and the lady of the manor home
alone, the construction site had been instantly transformed into a private residence. Standing at the door, I rang the bell.

As we waited, Lucy looked about, taking it all in. "Now I understand what Glee meant in this morning's headline about 'the "ah" factor.' It's breathtaking."

I was delighted that Lucy shared Glee's enthusiasm for Neil's work; I
shared it as well. But at the moment, I was wondering how long it

would take Gillian to answer the door. Had she not heard the bell? Was she soaking in the tub? Or was she simply ignoring us? I pressed the button again.

Lucy said, "I didn't hear chimes. Maybe they're not connected yet. Try the knocker."

Nodding at this reasonable suggestion, I grasped the handsome, massive brass knocker (which Neil had sent to a metal finisher for nickel plating, claiming, "Yellow metal always looks cheap") and gave the door a couple of solid clanks. As I did so, the door opened gently before us; though it had been closed, the lock had not caught. Poking my head inside, I called, "Gillian? It's Mark Manning." Hearing no response, I added, "Anyone home?"

Under her breath, Lucy told me, "Maybe she's on the crapper."

Wincing at the image Lucy had conjured, I told her, "Gillian's not the type."

"What does *that* mean?" asked Lucy through a blurt of laughter.

I wanted to shush her, but I wasn't sure why. For some reason, I felt as if our presence there, with my foot through the door, was stealthy. Sidestepping the issue of Gillian's bodily functions, I wondered, "Where is she?"

Lucy grinned. "Maybe she's out on a lunch break with the paper-hangers."

"No," I said, looking through the doorway, glancing about the foyer, "the walls are finished." Meaningfully, I added, "But the windows are not." I stepped inside.

Lucy followed. "My God," she said, moving to the middle of the foyer, "it's a palace!"

I doubt if Neil would have appreciated the description, as his quest had been to build a home of understated elegance, with the emphasis on *understated*. To Lucy's eyes, however, it was glamour beyond reckoning—and she had seen only the front hall. "Wait till you see the living room," I told her.

She wandered about the foyer, running her hand over the marble top of a sideboard. "Why, we could get a photographer in here yet this afternoon—except for those boxes." She wrinkled her nose at the cartons from Draper Studios that stood unopened beneath each window.

I explained, "I don't know whether Neil caught up with Todd Draper, and if he did, whether Todd agreed to stay on the job. In any event, the curtains aren't hung. The installation was supposed to take several days."

Lucy arched her brows. "Those must be *some* curtains."

"Fifty grand worth—in the living room alone. Care to have a peek?"

"Try and stop me."

"In here," I said, stepping her to the double doors that led from the front hall. "They were just getting started this morning, and that's when all hell broke loose"—in case the lady of the house was nearby, I lowered my voice—"with Gillian."

Lucy bumped up behind me as I stopped at the doors, cracked one of them open, and looked inside. "All clear," I told her, now feeling decidedly stealthy, traipsing through someone else's home. Opening the door wider, I whispered, "Come on. Let's take a quick look."

And in we went.

Leading Lucy through the middle of the long, elliptical room, heading straight to the fireplace on the far wall, I explained, "Neil designed the living room as a functioning library, surrounding the perimeter with two-story bookcases, accessible by rolling ladders and the winding stairway." I pointed while continuing, "Full-length windows circle the room. Todd Draper's crew managed to get one of the curtains up before Gillian threw a fit. *There*—I've never paid much attention to curtains, but are those drop-dead, or what?"

Hearing no gushy reply, I glanced over at Lucy, whose wide eyes were riveted not upon the curtains, but on the floor beneath them. Following her gaze, I caught my breath.

There lay Gillian Reece with her limbs at tortuous angles, unmoving, on the cold expanse of limestone. I wasn't sure if she was dead, but I knew she wasn't napping, not like that, twisted at the torso with her face flat against the floor.

Lucy and I rushed from the fireplace to the body on the floor, then knelt, both to get a closer look at the woman and to show our respect for her presumed condition. Lucy was a seasoned journalist who'd had close encounters with unexplained death; I didn't need to warn her not to touch anything; I didn't need to explain to her that this was not only a front-page story, but a police case.

Had there been any hope of reviving Gillian, we would have attempted CPR. But I found no pulse in her neck, and the purple cast of lividity had already begun to discolor the side of her face against the floor—her right side.

The left side of her face, away from the floor, was gaunt and ashen, except for the cheek, which still seemed rosy, as if burning from the welt of another bitch slap.

Reaching inside my pocket, I found my phone.

Within half an hour, the street outside the Reeces' house was filled again, not with tradesmen's vans, but with an array of police vehicles.

Inside, the focus of activity was on the dead woman who lay on the floor. Towering over her was the shimmering, silken expanse of Todd Draper's magnificent curtains.

Sheriff Pierce, who headed Dumont's combined city and county police force, stood aside with Lucy and me. Pulling a notebook from the inside pocket of his green blazer, he asked, "There was no one else in the house when you arrived?"

"We didn't see anyone," I told him. "We knocked and gave a shout or two, but no one answered. I assume no one else was here, Doug, but it's not as if we checked every room. We came to the living room directly from the foyer."

He squinted. "And, uh, why exactly were you here?"

"As you saw in today's paper, we were planning to run a photo feature on the new house. Lucy and I wanted to confirm the scheduling." I didn't mention that we were concerned about the meeting that morning between Glee Savage and Gillian, nor did I mention their confrontation of the previous day. I did detail how we'd found the door unlocked and how it opened when I knocked. "I wouldn't normally walk into someone's front hall like that, without being let in."

"And what brought you into the living room?"

Sheepishly, Lucy answered, "I wanted to see the curtains."

We all looked at the single panel of silk that hung near the body. I now noticed that the fringe had come loose or been torn from the top edge of the curtain, hanging to the side. Sealed cartons of more curtains were placed about the room, as earlier that morning, except one of the cartons, which had been opened—up on the balcony, nearest the partially finished window. A bundle of silk hung over the edge of the box; another had fallen or been dropped to the floor, near the rolling library ladder that was parked at the end of the balcony, next to the window.

"The guy who's staying at your house," said Doug. "Didn't you tell me he made these curtains?"

"Todd Draper." I nodded. "Well, his workshop in Chicago made the curtains. Todd has a crew to handle the installing, and he's up here to supervise. Since he's worked with Neil on previous jobs, he's staying at our house. The crew must be at a motel."

Huddled around Gillian's body was a police team consisting of medical and evidence technicians, directed by Dr. Vernon Formhals, who served Dumont County as both coroner and medical examiner. As he rose from his task, his knees cracked. Stepping in our direction, he told Doug, "Too early to draw any conclusions, but it looks accidental."

A powerful-looking but mellow-voiced black man, Dr. Formhals had a dignified air about him that always struck me as slightly professorial. He spoke with the trace of a Caribbean patois, an accent so barely perceptible, I'd known him at least a year before noticing it. I asked, "Did she fall?"

Formhals glanced at Doug, unsure if he should discuss such details in front of Lucy and me, the press. But Doug and I were known to be close friends, and in fact, we'd cooperated on several previous cases. He had become my primary news source regarding local stories of suspicious death, and I had lent whatever investigative skills I'd acquired during my reporting days at the *Chicago Journal*. He trusted my professionalism and knew that I would never violate his confidence, in print or otherwise. With a grin, he gave the coroner a go-ahead nod.

Formhals told us, "Yes, I presume she fell, sustaining serious injuries.

With no one else present to help, she died. The victim isn't far from the foot of that ladder, and the contorted position of the body indicates a fall. Had she been standing on the floor and been stricken by some sudden, catastrophic condition—say, a heart attack, stroke, or brain hemorrhage—she'd have collapsed, certainly, but the limbs and torso would not have been so twisted. A complete medical-legal autopsy is called for, and I suspect we'll find internal injuries consistent with those of an uncontrolled fall. Obviously, she wasn't shot, stabbed, or bludgeoned; there was no external bleeding."

By then both Lucy and I had opened our steno pads, joining Doug in taking notes. Lucy asked the coroner, "Then you don't suspect foul play?"

"Not at the moment. If the victim fell from the ladder, it was an accident. If she was pushed, it was murder. My cursory examination, however, reveals no signs of a struggle."

I asked, "Did you notice that . . . that 'blush' on her left cheek?"

Formhals rubbed his chin. "I did. That's somewhat odd, I admit. An intriguing detail."

"What if someone slapped her? Hard."

"That might account for it, yes, but the rosiness could have any number of causes. I'll need some time to determine that."

"Speaking of time," said Doug, "what about time of death?"

"Less than two hours ago, perhaps around eleven. Her body temperature has dropped only two or three degrees, and the livor mortis—the purple cast caused by stagnation of blood in the dependent or downward parts of the body—is still in its early stages, blanching to the touch. No signs of rigor mortis." Summarizing, he repeated, "Less than two hours."

Doug looked over his notes. "I'll need to check with the various contractors who were here this morning—exactly when did they leave, and why?" Turning to Formhals, he asked, "You'll let me know when you have a complete report?"

"Certainly, Douglas." With a bob of his head, the doctor took his leave, returning to the team of techs who still busied themselves around Gillian's body.

"Doug," I said tentatively, "can I talk to you about something?"

Surprised by my tone, he said, "Sure, Mark. What is it?"

I motioned that we should leave the room. Lucy stayed, taking notes as Dr. Formhals spoke with his crew.

Out in the foyer, I asked Doug, "Do you think it's an accident?"

"Vernon does. Till he comes up with something conclusive, I'll have to proceed on that assumption. Why?"

I exhaled noisily. "Let's just say that Gillian Reece was not generally well liked."

Doug studied me for a moment. "I thought you were one of her biggest fans—with the merger and all."

"I was. But a lot of weird stuff has been brewing in the last few days, all of it stemming from Gillian. I was here earlier this morning, Doug, and I'm telling you, it was nonstop confrontations. She actually hauled off and *slapped* a few people. I've seen her on the receiving end, as well."

Doug was taking notes again. "Which explains her pink cheek."

"No, I'm afraid it doesn't. The last person I saw slap her was her husband, Esmond, who's left-handed, so he slapped her right cheek. But the body's pink cheek is on Gillian's *left* side, meaning, if it's a welt from a slap, it came from someone's right hand."

"Which doesn't help us much—the vast majority of the general population is right-handed."

"Exactly. What's more, we don't know if the welt on the body is from a slap, and even if it *is* from a slap, we don't know if it had anything to do with Gillian's presumed fall from the ladder."

With a soft laugh, Doug noted, "Which puts us back at square one."

"I know, sorry. But I thought you should at least be aware of this background."

He put a hand on my shoulder. "Thanks, Mark. I appreciate it. For now, I'm working on the theory that this death was an accident, but just for the record, tell me about the confrontations you saw this morning."

Doug clicked his ballpoint and proceeded to take detailed notes as I described the earlier series of run-ins: Arguing about curtain fringe, Gillian had slapped Todd Draper. Then Gillian had verbally sparred with Perry Schield regarding accountant Tyler Pennell and the merger. Finally, when Esmond Reece and his yogi, Tamra Thaine, arrived and challenged Gillian on money matters, Gillian slapped Tamra; then Esmond slapped Gillian.

"Whew!" said Doug, struggling to write fast enough. "Some morning."

"I admit, it threw me. I thought I had known Gillian Reece. Now that she's gone, I'm not sure *what* to think of her."

"Sorry, can't help you with that." Doug again put a hand on my shoulder. "But, hey. Thanks for the insights." Referring to his notes, he added, "No telling yet, but this could be important."

I was happy to help.

I was also grateful that Doug had specifically asked me to describe the confrontations I had seen "this morning." On a technicality, I felt justified in omitting from my report the incident of the previous afternoon—when Glee Savage had bitch-slapped Gillian.

And where, I still wondered, had Glee been all day?

Chapter Twelve

I lunched alone that day. Lucy needed to run errands before returning to the office, so I dropped her downtown after returning from the Reece house. Neil had told me at breakfast that he needed to drive to Green Bay to meet with a subcontractor on an upcoming project, so I still hadn't heard whether he had caught up with Todd Draper. For all I knew, our houseguest had skipped town.

Sitting alone at "my" table at First Avenue Grill, I ate quietly without noticing my food, still shaken by the grim discovery of Gillian's broken body on the limestone floor of a brand-new home in which she had never slept.

"No, thank you, Berta, nothing else," I told the plump waitress in white when she offered dessert.

Returning to the *Register* and learning that the whereabouts of Glee Savage were still unknown, I went straight to my inner office and closed the door, which was not my habit—staffers noticed, glancing through my glass wall from their desks in the newsroom. I needed to think. More precisely, I needed to talk, and the woman whose counsel I sought was in Chicago.

Hoping I'd catch Roxanne at her desk (it was well past one, nearly two), I sat at my own desk, reached for the phone, and began to dial.

Then I paused. This was to be a free-form conversation—stream of consciousness—the sort of brainstorming that might be enhanced by my ability to pace about, thinking aloud. The springy cord of my desk phone would act as a tether, a needless restriction, so I hung up the receiver and, astonished by my own decision, reached for the cell phone that still nested in my pocket.

Standing, I slipped on my reading glasses, opened the phone, and punched the tiny buttons that led to a direct line at the law firm of Kendall Yoshihara Exner.

"Roxanne Exner," she answered on the second ring.

"Got a minute?" I asked. "It's Mark."

"Well . . . ," she said, taunting, "it's a *horribly* busy afternoon, but for you, babe, anytime. What's up? Wait—don't tell me." With a laugh, she guessed, "Death stalks Dumont."

"Unfortunately," I informed her, "you're right on the money."

"Oh, dear," she said, sobered. But she couldn't resist adding, "That sleepy little cow town of yours must have the highest murder rate in the Midwest."

"Don't jump the gun." I began pacing my office. "It may not be murder, but at this point, it's an unexplained death."

"I hate to sound glib, but—anyone I know?"

With a gulp, I told her, "Gillian Reece."

"Uh-oh." Roxanne hadn't met Gillian, but she was well aware of the woman, having studied an early proposal for the merger, advising me on its feasibility.

"It appears her death was an accident." And I detailed for Roxanne the events of that morning, including the series of confrontations, the coroner's initial findings, and the sheriff's assumption that there had been no foul play. "Except," I continued, "I have a nagging suspicion that there may be more to this, and unfortunately, Glee Savage has a role in it."

"*Glee?*" said Roxanne. "You've *got* to be kidding."

"I only wish." Then I recounted for her the story of the bad blood between my features editor and the paper-mill CEO, their mutual shock upon meeting again yesterday, and finally, the bitch slap. "Most troubling of all, the last person I saw enter the Reece house this morning was Glee, and she hasn't been seen since."

"It sounds as if *lots* of people had a bone to pick with this woman."

"True, but *they* don't work for me." Tired of pacing, I perched on the edge of my desk.

"Hmmm . . . I see your point."

"So if the coroner should conclude that Gillian's death was *not* accidental—"

"Hold on," Roxanne interrupted. "I just thought of something. What effect is Gillian's death likely to have on the impending merger?"

I stood again. "Good God."

"Unless I'm mistaken . . ."

"It's *off*, Roxanne. I just realized—the whole deal is now off. I don't know if you saw the final agreement, but its terms were explicit. Gillian was to sign on behalf of Ashton Mills, Perry Schield on behalf of Quatro Press. Neither one could back out individually, so the deal could go forward without Gillian's signature, but I'm virtually certain that Perry will view her demise as just the out he's been looking for. With neither signature, there's no merger."

"Perry was looking for an out?"

"He was getting cold feet, based on some issues raised by due diligence. He was also getting an unvarnished picture of Gillian's personality, so he couldn't have relished the prospect of working with her. Sure, he was looking for an out."

My inflections must have been transparently upbeat, since Roxanne then noted, "You don't sound too disappointed yourself, Mr. Manning." Though smirks aren't audible, I'd have sworn I heard one.

I admitted, "Though I regret Gillian's untimely passing, yes, I'm relieved the merger won't happen tomorrow. I was beginning to have serious doubts about it."

"Hmmm," said Roxanne, grinding her mental gears (I heard that as well). "If Gillian's death was *not* an accident—"

"And if her death killed the deal," I continued Roxanne's thought, "this opens a variety of possibilities regarding motive."

With a skeptical laugh, she asked, "Are you saying you suspect kindly old Perry Schield of offing the dragon lady?"

"Of course not. We don't even know if Gillian died of foul play. But if she did, these business issues seem to point away from the ancient ill will that stemmed from Gillian's stealing Glee's boyfriend."

"In other words, if there's a killer on the loose in Dumont—*again*— you'd prefer for that person not to be on your payroll."

"Well," I noted, perhaps too pragmatically, "it would be dreadful PR for the paper." Softening this view, I added, "It wouldn't do Glee any good, either."

"Yeah, nothing can spoil your day quicker than a murder rap. It's a real bitch."

"Exactly. Roxanne, it's reassuring to know that, after all these years, you and I are still on the same wavelength."

"We have the same taste in men," she noted. "Speaking of which, how's Neil?"

"He's great. Busy as can be."

Someone rapped on my glass wall. Turning, I saw Glee standing outside my office. She waved.

Roxanne said, "Give him a kiss for me, okay?"

"Sure thing, Rox. Thanks for listening. I need to ring off now."

"*Ciao*, love." And she hung up.

Setting the phone on my desk, I opened the door and stepped to my outer office, where Glee awaited me.

"Hi, boss," she said. "Sorry to interrupt, but when I came in through the lobby, Connie said you'd been looking for me."

"Uh, yes, I was." I tried to sound neither agitated nor accusing as I asked through a smile, "Where have you been, Glee?"

She shrugged. "Appleton."

When she mentioned the town, I recalled her telling me something about it, but the details didn't click.

Reading the confusion in my face, she explained, "I was following up on an earlier story about that big charity do that will benefit several area hospitals. I drove over there today to interview the organizer of the gala, but it was a wild-goose chase—the woman, a Mrs. Dresen, wasn't home. Must've had our wires crossed."

As Glee recounted this, I remembered both the earlier story and Glee's follow-up plans, so the explanation of her absence was perfectly plausible. Getting ahead of myself, however, I was now concerned that if Glee eventually needed an alibi for the time of Gillian's death, she wouldn't have one because Mrs. Dresen hadn't been home. Obliquely, I asked, "Did you speak to anyone else in Appleton?"

"Don't think so. Why?"

"No particular reason. Do you happen to recall when you left Dumont for Appleton?"

"Right after I left the Reeces' house—sometime before ten."

"Good." The coroner had said Gillian died no earlier than eleven.

"Good?" Glee's features wrinkled. "Mark, what are you driving at?"

"Let's sit down, Glee." We stepped to the chairs surrounding the low conference table. Glee took a seat, setting her zebra-print purse on the floor. Sitting next to her, I asked, "How did your meeting go with Gillian?"

"Not well." She expelled a long breath, almost whistling, before she continued, "I'm sure you recall that I arrived at the house just as you were leaving, around nine o'clock. Gillian was in the living room, barking something at a decorating crew; I think they were there to hang curtains. When she saw me, she said, sweet as pie, 'Ah! Glee! Can you wait a moment, please? I have something to attend to.' She then proceeded to lecture *all* of the work crews, who were finishing various tasks. She informed everyone that their work was to be completed within one hour, and she wanted them *out*. The curtain crew left right away, and she badgered the others until they, too, had all gone. She kept me waiting all this time, and she yammered straight through, barely pausing to breathe. It was a nonstop harangue."

"Sounds like fun," I said grimly. "So when the two of you finally talked, you were alone."

"Right. The house was suddenly empty, and to tell the truth, as beautiful as it is, it was also sort of creepy—but that was the company, not the architecture. Gillian listened quietly as I apologized for my behavior yesterday. It was a good grovel, Mark—I took full blame and made no reference to the background issue, Hugh Ryburn. I paused, giving her an opportunity to accept my apology, but she simply nodded, saying, 'You may continue . . . ' It was a challenge to remain civil, but I did. Getting down to business, I told her how much the *Register* was looking forward to running the photo feature on her new home, and I asked when we might send over a photographer."

"What'd she say?"

"Plenty. She informed me brusquely that she was withdrawing her permission for the feature. I assumed she was having second thoughts because of privacy issues, so I tried to assure her that we wouldn't shoot anything she considered off-limits, and I even offered to let her review the photos before we printed them. But she was unconvinced. In fact, she laughed at me, saying that she'd never intended to go through with the feature. The only reason she gave her initial okay was to cause me the professional embarrassment of promising the feature in my column this morning."

"She *told* you that?"

"In so many words, yes. Needless to say, our meeting was over, and the atmosphere was tense."

"You didn't, uh . . . slap her again, did you?" As Glee was right-handed, her parting blow might have accounted for the welt on the left cheek of Gillian's body.

Glee shook her knotted hand. "Believe me, Mark, I was tempted to do more than slap her. But no, I managed to control myself, and I simply left—*without* saying good-bye." Glee gave a sharp nod, as if her parting breach of etiquette was tantamount to fisticuffs.

"I can hardly believe it," I said with a sympathetic shake of my head. "It's unthinkable that Gillian would set you up that way. It's so . . . premeditated and mean." I paused, recalling the many incidents that had reshaped my view of the woman over the last two days. "On second thought, maybe I *can* believe it. I'm sorry, Glee."

"It's not *your* fault, Mark. The story was my idea, and even after I realized who Gillian was, I wanted to proceed with the feature. It was *my* mistake thinking that I could work with the woman, that I could trust her. So I'll just have to eat crow with our readers."

"Actually, Glee, that won't be necessary. We wouldn't run the story anyway, not after what's happened."

"What's . . . happened?" she asked with a quizzical squint.

I reached to the arm of Glee's chair and touched her hand. "Gillian is dead. We found her this afternoon—Lucy and I went over to the house, wondering if you were still there."

Glee's brows arched. "Really?" Her tone carried no shock, no disbelief, but the lilt of pleasant surprise. She asked outright, "Who killed her—do they know yet?"

"Why do you assume she was murdered?"

"Because she looked plenty healthy this morning; she wasn't on her deathbed. Besides, we're talking about *Gillian*. She was a shrew, Mark. What goes around comes around." Glee tossed her hands, pleased as punch.

"In fact," I told her, "the investigation is in its early stages, but Coroner Formhals thinks Gillian died accidentally—a fall from a ladder."

"What a shame." Glee's inflection was so ambiguous, I couldn't tell whether she regretted that Gillian had fallen or she regretted that Gillian hadn't been pushed.

Suspecting the latter, I said, "Forgive me, Glee, but I must say, you don't seem very upset by this news. I can understand that you feel a measure of relief, knowing you can now explain to our readers that the Sunday feature has been cancelled in light of an unexpected turn of events, but—"

"No, Mark"—she wagged a finger—"that's not it at all. It may be coldhearted of me, but I'm not the least upset by your news of Gillian's 'accident' or whatever it was." Glee stood. "Let's not mince words. I'm glad she's dead."

I stood as well, offering a weak smile. "I know you too well, Glee, to think you're coldhearted. I simply hadn't understood the depth of the pain Gillian caused you."

Glee sighed. "I hadn't either, Mark."

We stepped to each other and embraced for a moment. Then Glee picked up her purse from the floor, telling me, "I'd better check with Lucy. We'll need to come up with a new Sunday feature. I have a few 'anytime' stories on file."

I gave her a wink. "I'm sure you do."

Glee returned the wink. "I'll get right on it." She started out the door to the newsroom, then stopped, turning back to me. "I just thought—with Gillian gone, does this foul up the merger? I'm sorry, Mark. I know how hard you've been working on it."

"I appreciate your concern, but I suppose these things happen for a reason. Let's hope it's for the best."

She nodded, thinking a moment before echoing, "Let's hope." And she left.

As I watched her retreat toward the far end of the newsroom, I was mulling something I'd just said. When I'd told Glee that "these things happen for a reason," I was speaking in the broad, metaphysical sense of fate or destiny. But my words also had a literal meaning, suggesting that I already believed there had been a *reason* for Gillian's death, a *motive* that was possibly linked to the merger.

These thoughts were nipped by the ring of my phone—my desk phone, the one with a cord. Moving to my inner office, I lifted the receiver and answered, "Yes, Connie?"

"It's Sheriff Pierce, Mr. Manning." And she connected us.

I said, "Hi, Doug. Any news?"

"No, Mark, nothing on the autopsy, not yet. I was wondering if you know how to reach Esmond Reece. We need to notify him of his wife's death, but don't know where he is. Do you happen to know where he works?"

"He *doesn't* work, doesn't need to."

"Ah, the perks of having a rich wife, I guess."

"Truth is, he made his own fortune quite a while ago. In recent years, he's occupied his time with yoga and other Eastern studies. I'm pretty sure where you can find him." I was about to tell Doug the details, but instead, I offered, "Want me to take you there?"

He laughed; my tagalong ploys had become transparent. "Sure," he said, "if you have time."

"I always have time to help." While my civic-mindedness was doubtless admirable, we both understood that I was angling to be an eyewitness to a developing story.

"Tell you what. I'm in the car right now, so I can swing by and pick you up in about two minutes. Meet me in front of the building?"

"Great. I'll be there. Two minutes." I was about to hang up when I remembered something. "Oh, Doug. By the way. I have a cell phone now."

"I'm stunned. Welcome to the twenty—"

"Yeah, yeah, I know. Do you want the number?"

Chapter Thirteen

About two minutes later, an unmarked tan cruiser rolled to a stop at the curb in front of the *Register* building. Sheriff Douglas Pierce leaned to open the passenger door, and I hopped in. We greeted each other as I secured the seat belt across my chest. Then Doug asked, "Where are we headed?"

"West, just outside of town. Take First Avenue to the highway."

As he roared away, the souped-up cop's engine plastered my back against the seat. Doug, accustomed to his car's ferocious acceleration, didn't notice my blanched knuckles gripping the edge of the armrest. He casually glanced over to ask, "You said something about yoga?"

I nodded. "Back in Harper, Esmond Reece took up yoga with an instructor named Tamra Thaine. When Gillian decided to move the corporate headquarters of Ashton Mills to Dumont, Esmond didn't want to make the move, so they struck a deal. Gillian agreed to endow a nonprofit venture that Tamra wanted to establish here, an institute for Eastern studies."

"You told me earlier that Gillian slapped Tamra at the house this morning."

"Right. Gillian was backing out of her promised funding. Esmond brought Tamra to the house, and together they confronted Gillian, who didn't budge. In fact, she became so verbally abusive, I was tempted to slap her myself." As an afterthought, it seemed prudent to add, "But of course I didn't."

A question pinched Doug's features as he watched the road. "You also told me Esmond had made a fortune and didn't need to work. Why doesn't *he* bankroll the institute? Why go begging to Gillian?"

I explained how Esmond's cell-phone circuit had made him a wealthy man. "But since he had no head for business, he transferred control of his assets to his accounting-savvy wife. It's a bizarre setup, at best."

Doug corrected me, "It *was* a bizarre setup."

As we neared the edge of town, the road curved out to the highway. Doug gripped the wheel, taking the turn without braking. Swaying toward the center of the car, I glimpsed the speedometer. Though the driving conditions were perfect and there wasn't another car in sight, I couldn't resist noting, "You're ten miles over the limit, Sheriff."

He looked at me as if I'd just suggested he should wear high-button shoes. "Yeah? So?" He grinned.

I myself never appreciated backseat drivers, so I understood his reaction. Still, I did feel that he was driving too fast, and since he was sworn to enforce the law, he should be the first to observe it.

"Well," I said, joking, "it's a minor infraction. I'll let you off this time."

He shook his head, laughing. I could almost hear his thoughts: I was hopelessly square.

Sometimes, I realized, my thinking was indeed too rigid and inflexible. During private moments, Neil had occasionally cautioned me against being "priggish." Coming from anyone else, that word would have been insulting, but coming from Neil, it was said, I knew, in the earnest belief that I was sometimes too exacting for my own good.

Though I trusted Neil's judgment, which sprang from love, not from a desire to be critical, I still found it hard to buy into the notion that my life would be in any sense better or more joyful if I were to abandon certain standards of thinking and behavior that had served me so well in the past. My attention to detail, my commitment to play by the rules, my scrupulous nature, had allowed me to excel in school when I was young and, later, to establish a successful career, first as an investigative reporter in Chicago and now as a publisher and businessman in Wisconsin.

I reasoned that if I occasionally erred on the side of fastidiousness—even priggishness—I had done no harm, and in fact, I had demonstrated integrity to my own principles. Was I really to chuck my long-established code of personal ethics just to satisfy those who might feel I could afford to loosen up?

"How far?" asked Doug, bringing me back to the moment.

"Just beyond that next stretch of trees." Offhandedly, I added, "You'll barely recognize the place."

As my meaning sank in, Doug turned to me with a blank expression. "Don't tell me—Miriam Westerman's old property?"

"The same."

"Whatever happened to that nutcase?"

"She joined a new coven in the Pacific Northwest."

"Good riddance." With a chortle, Doug added, "What a loon."

I didn't say anything, but to my way of thinking, the jury was still out on whether the property's old loon had been replaced by a new one.

The twiggy sign came into view: DUMONT INSTITUTE FOR EASTERN STUDIES. I told Doug, "Same driveway, through that first clearing."

He slowed the car and turned onto the gravel drive, following it through the woods to the parking area at the middle of the compound. As during my visit of the previous afternoon, we found only two vehicles parked there—Esmond's car and Tamra's SUV, both white, near the entrance of the main building, also white.

Getting out of Doug's car, we both took care not to slam its doors. We instinctively lowered our voices while walking to the building, as if entering hallowed ground. Not that Doug or I placed much credence in the holism and cosmology that was once preached there—and apparently still would be. Rather, it was precisely because of our skepticism that we felt uncomfortable and out of our element in such surroundings.

As I gently opened the building's front door, music wafted from a distant hall. The twangy, mystical strains of a sitar, punctuated by the beat of a tabla, suggested Tamra was giving Esmond another lesson. I told Doug, barely above a whisper, "They must be in the same studio where I found them yesterday."

"A music studio?"

"No, a yoga studio. The music's for mood, I guess." As I led him through the hallways, I noticed paint cans and tarps along the way; the efforts to spruce up the place had progressed since a day ago. A lingering scent of turpentine hung in the air, blending with the woozy music. The mixture seemed oddly appropriate, as the pungent smell of paint thinner took on the character of incense. "They should be in here," I told Doug, indicating the doorway from which the music flowed.

Quietly, Doug and I approached the door along the adjacent wall; we actually tiptoed, which lent a sinister, though cartoonish, quality to our escapade. Peeping around the jamb, we saw Tamra and Esmond inside, engaged in a lesson, as predicted. It looked for all the world as if she was trying to teach him to wrap his ankles behind his head, following up on Gillian's earlier suggestion, but they were having a rough time of it, as he just wasn't that limber.

My inclination, as on the day before, was to wait quietly until they finished, but Doug felt constrained by no such protocol. Rapping on the doorjamb, he cleared his throat. "Uh, Mr. Reece? Excuse me."

Esmond's legs snapped back to the mat on the floor as Tamra bolted to her feet and crossed the room in a fluster to switch off the boom box. "Ah, Mark!" said Esmond, struggling to stand (his legs were doubtless feeling a tad rubbery). "Welcome back."

Stepping into the studio, I told both him and Tamra, "We're sorry for the intrusion, but I'm afraid this is important. Have you met Sheriff Pierce?" I was sure they hadn't. My mention of the sheriff underscored the gravity of our visit, and accordingly, both Esmond and Tamra moved forward, sober-faced, as I introduced them to Doug.

Tentatively, Tamra began, "I hope there's not a problem with our renovations, Sheriff. We made a point of securing all the permits before beginning our work on the facility. Our first students haven't enrolled yet, but if safety is an issue—"

"Don't worry, Miss Thaine," said Doug. "It's nothing like that. I'm sure everything's in order." He turned to Esmond. "I'm here because of an unfortunate accident that occurred this morning. It's most disturbing."

Esmond's complexion, pale at best, turned whiter. "Good God, Sheriff, what's happened?" He reached for Tamra; she came to his side and grasped his hand.

"You may want to sit down," Doug began, but then realized there was no furniture in the room, so he continued, "or just brace yourself for some very bad news. Mr. Reece, I regret to inform you that your wife, Gillian, died this morning of an apparent accident at your new home. It seems she fell from a ladder. Allow me to offer my sincere condolences."

Esmond and Tamra turned to look at each other, their faces conveying no emotion other than mild surprise, as if Doug had just told them we were in for a hard frost that night. Esmond returned his gaze to Doug. "You're kidding."

"I assure you, Mr. Reece, I wouldn't kid about such a subject."

"It's true," I added. "My editor and I went over to the house around noon, and that's when we found Gillian—on the living-room floor, at the foot of one of the library ladders."

Esmond shook his head, repeating, "You're kidding."

Tamra asked Doug, "Are you sure someone didn't *push* her?" Her tone carried no dismay that Gillian was dead, only incredulity regarding the manner of her death. What's more, Tamra had raised the very question that I myself kept asking.

Doug told her, "At the moment, we have no reason to suspect foul play, but the coroner's findings could change the course of our investigation."

"Coroner?" asked Esmond. "Investigation?" His voice at last conveyed concern.

"A death from any unnatural cause, including accidental causes, will always trigger an investigation."

"Maybe we *should* sit down," said Tamra. "Let's go to my office."

With a wordless nod, Esmond followed her out of the studio and into the hallway, as did Doug and I. Tamra's and Esmond's bare feet gently slapped the vinyl floor as we made our way past the cans of paint and filed into a room near the front door, the same room I remembered as the headmistress's office during the kooky, tyrannical reign of Miriam Westerman. But Miriam was gone, and so were all her trappings.

The room was now white, of course—blindingly so in the afternoon sunlight that slid through the bare windows in broad, hot shafts. Tamra's desk was a simple plank of white laminate suspended over two file cabinets, also white. The only other furniture in the room consisted of several director's chairs, all with slings of natural-colored canvas. One of the chairs was behind the desk; the others were clustered in front of it. "Gentlemen?" said Tamra, suggesting we sit as she seated herself at her desk.

Esmond sat toward the end of the desk, nearest Tamra. Doug and I sat side by side, loosely facing the other two. I instinctively removed my notepad from my jacket pocket and unscrewed the cap of my pen.

Esmond heaved a sigh, as if clearing his thoughts. "Now, then," he said to Doug, "perhaps you could describe what happened. Back in the studio, you took me unawares. I'm afraid nothing registered." He now looked flushed instead of pale; beads of perspiration dotted his forehead. Had the news of his wife's death finally made an impact, I wondered, or was he simply reacting to the heat of the sun-filled room?

"Of course," said Doug. He reviewed the events of that morning—the presumed time of death around eleven, the discovery around noon, and the coroner's initial theory of the fall, which did not imply foul play. Having established this timeline, he then asked Esmond, "You and Miss Thaine were at the house this morning, correct?"

"Yes. It was most distressing. We had words. Gillian was on particularly bad behavior today—on a rampage, one might say. She was horrible; she slapped Tamra. Then I behaved badly; I slapped Gillian."

"What time was that?"

"I'm at a loss to say. It was earlier rather than later."

Tamra said, "It was around nine, Sheriff. A newscast was starting on the car radio when we drove away."

"And where did you go?"

"We drove directly here to the institute."

Esmond added, "We've been here all day, working—painting and such."

I asked, "Has anyone else been here?" My meaning was transparent enough; I was asking if they'd had witnesses who could verify their whereabouts.

Esmond replied, "No, unfortunately, we were alone the whole time—not much of an alibi."

"Who said anything about alibis?" asked Doug. "I'm assuming Gillian's death was accidental."

Tamra folded her hands in front of herself on the desk. "To be perfectly frank," she said, "if Gillian's death was accidental, there was an element of serendipity to it—kismet, if you will." She turned to Esmond, telling him, "I'm sorry. I mean no disrespect for the spirit of one who has passed, one you have loved, but in the case of Gillian, it's difficult to take a charitable view of her 'divine consciousness.' Her meanness of spirit was coupled with a propensity toward physical aggression, a combination altogether at odds with the cosmic energy that creates and maintains the universe."

Esmond nodded forcefully, in full agreement. "Gillian's shakti was way out of whack. Her death has restored a certain harmony to the absolute."

Under my breath, I asked Doug, "Taking notes?"

Struggling to ignore me, he told Esmond, "I'm glad you're taking this so well. I can appreciate that there were problems with your marriage, but still, your wife played a prominent role in the Dumont business community. I'm sure she'll be missed."

I wasn't so sure of that, but I echoed stock sympathies to Esmond, concluding, "It was a privilege to know Gillian. Say what you will about her, but I have never known anyone with a keener mind for numbers and the intricacies of finance."

Esmond listened patiently, bobbing his head in deference to my testimonial, if not quite buying into my flattering assessment of his late wife's skills. Then his eyes bugged open and a smile lit his face. "Hey!" he said with a finger snap. "Speaking of numbers and finances, I just thought of something. With Gillian gone, our previous arrangements are now null and void. Control of my assets reverts to me." With an odd noise, something between a laugh and a growl, he added, "I should never have agreed to her trusteeship in the first place."

Sitting back in her chair, absorbing the implication of Esmond's words, Tamra broke into a smile. "Unless I'm mistaken, there could be far more at stake here than the patent monies you earned twenty-odd years ago. Gillian became a wealthy woman in her own right."

Doug agreed, "Wisconsin probate law is always partial to the surviving spouse."

"Well, then!" Esmond sat up straight, squaring his shoulders. "Tamra, fret not. Your worries are over. *Our* worries are over. I promise here and now"—he raised his right hand—"to fund personally the Dumont Institute for Eastern Studies. And I assure you, this worthy endeavor will be funded *very* generously." With a wink at Doug and me, he added, "I've got witnesses."

Though I felt he was counting unhatched chicks, it did seem a reasonable assumption that, one way or the other, Esmond would profit from his wife's death. As I mulled the implications of this as a possible motive for a possible homicide, Tamra pulled from a file a long handwritten list—presumably the institute's wish list—and began checking off certain items. Esmond scooted his chair to the back of the desk, next to Tamra, and grabbing a pencil, he began working with her, amending the list.

I again noted that Esmond was left-handed.

Tamra was right-handed.

As Doug and I had delivered our "devastating" news, our mission there was complete, so we rose, taking our leave. Engrossed in their planned spending, Esmond and Tamra barely looked up to say good-bye.

But just as I was heading out the door, Esmond called, "Oh, Mark?"

Doug and I stepped back inside the office.

Esmond continued, "Gillian was making an awful fuss about those curtains, but they looked just fine to me. Please extend my compliments and apologies to Neil and the designer."

"I will, thank you."

"And please do tell them to proceed. The entire project is a go."

Tamra's eyes moved from Esmond, returning to the list on her desk. She gave his free hand, his right hand, a fond squeeze.

Chapter Fourteen

I never did hear from Neil regarding the outcome of his search for Todd Draper that morning, so when I returned home from the office sometime after five, I was surprised to find Todd waiting for me, but not Neil.

Entering the kitchen through the back door, I called, "Anybody home?" I knew the answer, as I'd already seen Todd's car parked in front of the house, so the question was simply meant to announce my arrival.

"Hey, Mark!" said Todd, stepping into the kitchen from the dining room with a towel tucked through one of his belt loops. "Neil said he might be late, so I thought I'd get dinner started." Sure enough, grocery bags lined one of the counters, and a heap of fresh produce peeped out from the sink.

"Todd, you're a *guest*," I protested. "You shouldn't bother with that."

"Don't be nuts. I had all day to myself, so I thought I'd make myself useful."

With an uncertain smile, I asked, "What about the Reeces' curtains?"

"Oh, that." He rolled his eyes, stepping to the sink and running some cold water. "Neil caught up with me after Gillian threw me out this morning. He spotted my car at that coffee shop at the edge of town. We talked. He explained that Gillian wanted me back on the job, and he agreed to lay down the law to her—the curtains are to be installed as delivered. After we shoot the photos, she can do whatever she wants, but till then, this project is *ours*. My crew can get a fresh start in the morning."

"So Neil returned to the house?" I slipped off my sport coat and hung it over a chair at the kitchen table.

"I assume so." Todd began breaking up a head of lettuce and rinsing it. "I didn't hear back from him, so everything must be on track. He needed to drive over to Green Bay to meet a cabinetmaker, so he said I should make myself at home if he wasn't back by five." Wiping his hands on the towel, Todd turned from the sink. "Can I get you a drink?"

I laughed. "I should get *you* one. What would you like?"

He thought a moment. "Oh, keep it simple—vodka, rocks."

"My anytime favorite. Have you ever tried it with a twist of orange peel?"

"No, but it sounds . . . interesting."

So while Todd returned his attention to the vegetables in the sink, I moved to the refrigerator, took out an orange, and pulled a frosty bottle of Japanese vodka from the freezer. As I was reaching to get glasses from a nearby cupboard, the back door swung open.

"My," said Neil, entering with a grin, "isn't this a domestic scene?"

"Welcome back, stranger," said Todd.

"Hi there, kiddo." I stepped to the door, wrapped Neil in a loose embrace, and gave him a quick kiss. "What took you so long?"

"Ugh!" He hung his keys on a hook near the door, tossed a few files on the counter, and loosened his tie. "I keep forgetting that Green Bay is a full two-hour drive from here. And there were some problems with the cabinet guy; we needed to work on some changes. And *then*—"

"Never mind. You're back. Ready for a drink?"

"*Please.*" He slipped off his corduroy blazer and hung it on another chair as I set about pouring our drinks.

Todd told Neil, "I've got the salad going, but I wasn't sure about the sauce for the meat."

"No problem. I'll handle it." Neil opened a drawer and pulled out a wire whisk, asking, "Is your crew lined up to give it another try in the morning?"

"All set. And how was your man-to-man with Gillian?"

"It went just fine. In fact, she even agreed to stay clear of the house tomorrow so you can work in peace."

"Sounds perfect."

Clearly, neither Neil nor Todd had yet heard that Gillian was no longer in a position to pester them—or anyone else. I felt compelled to deliver the news quickly, but decided that downer could wait until everyone had a drink in hand.

Moments later, the three of us stood facing each other at the center of the kitchen, glasses raised. "Well," said Neil, "the day got off to a rough start, but this is decidedly better. Cheers, everyone."

"Cheers," echoed Todd. "To friendship."

Wordlessly, I joined them touching glasses. We drank.

"Say, now," said Todd, eyeing me over the rim of his glass, "the orange twist is a wonderful touch. I'll have to remember that."

"We've always liked it," said Neil.

I took another sip—more precisely, a hefty mouthful—and swallowed.

"Cat got your tongue?" asked Neil.

"Uh, no," I said. "Guys? Something happened today, something quite disturbing, and it seems you haven't heard about it."

They glanced at each other with raised brows. Skeptically, Neil asked me, "More disturbing than the flurry of bitch slaps?"

"Much worse, I'm afraid. Gillian Reece will have nothing more to say about the curtains, the fringe, or any other aspect of the new house. She died today. Apparently it was an accident, a fall from a ladder in the living room."

Neil and Todd again glanced at each other, but this time their faces fell.

I added, "The circumstances struck me as suspicious, but Doug and Vernon are working on the assumption there was no foul play."

Neil explained to Todd, "Doug and Vernon are the sheriff and the coroner." Then, as the full impact of my news hit Neil, he gave a pained groan. "I'm . . . I'm stunned. Gosh, poor Gillian. I'm first to admit, the woman had some 'issues,' but who doesn't?"

"I can't believe it either," said Todd, shaking his head. "Lord knows, I didn't much *like* the woman, but hey, I'm used to working with difficult clients."

Thoughtfully, Neil added, "After all's said and done, I actually *did* like Gillian. She was a pistol, but we got along, and no client has ever given me freer rein. We built a great house together."

I wrapped an arm around Neil's shoulders. "I'm sorry, kiddo. I know you liked her. But truth is, I can't think of anyone else who did."

Todd asked, "And that's why you find her death suspicious?"

"Well, sure. She may have fallen from the ladder, but she could also have been pushed. And she didn't fall far—maybe ten or twelve feet. It seems strange that such a short drop would be fatal."

Neil said, "I assume there's an investigation under way."

"Absolutely. Doug's crew was conducting the usual search for physical evidence, and Dr. Formhals is conducting an autopsy. We should know more tomorrow."

"Speaking of tomorrow," said Todd, raising a finger, "I hate to sound too pragmatic, but with Gillian gone, what about the curtains?"

"Yeah," chimed Neil. "What about the whole *house?*"

Setting my drink on the table, I explained, "I happen to know the answer to those questions. Doug and I met with Esmond this afternoon, and he mentioned that I should ask both of you to proceed. He specifically said I should compliment you on the curtains, Todd."

"Oh? Nice of him to think of that when he's faced with such personal tragedy."

I paused before reporting, "He didn't exactly seem grief-stricken. In fact, he said Gillian's death restored harmony to 'the absolute,' or words to that effect."

"Oh, brother," said Neil. "Sounds more like his yoga pal, Tamra."

"She, too, had a few choice cosmological observations."

"Huh?" asked Todd.

As Neil filled him in regarding Esmond's background with Tamra Thaine, the three of us pitched in, preparing our evening meal.

News of Gillian's death effectively squelched the party atmosphere that had filled the kitchen when I was pouring our first round of drinks, and the mood became subdued, if not quite somber, as we fussed with dinner. When three gay men conspire to cook, it's inevitable that a few *bons mots* will be lobbed about, so we weren't above injecting our kitchen duties with a note of levity. Still, we limited our laughter to convivial chuckles, eschewing the shrieks and howls that might otherwise have colored the preparations.

When our meal moved from the kitchen to the dining room, I opened a bottle of wine and Neil lit a pair of candles on the table. In light of that day's events, I couldn't help feeling that the flickering tapers, a festive touch, also projected funereal overtones. Neil and I took our usual chairs, and when Todd sat down, we both realized that he now occupied the spot where Gillian had sat only two nights prior. Strangely, this simple observation seemed to reinforce the reality of Gillian's death, the surety that she would not return, the knowledge that she was no longer of this world.

Our dinner conversation covered our appreciation for Todd's salad and Neil's roast, then moved on to a variety of topics—Neil's meeting with the cabinet guy (too long, but productive); Todd's experience working with our Chicago friend, Roxanne Exner (a perfect client, though Neil had coached her); my day at the *Register* (other than the main event, dull); and Glee's planned photo feature in the Sunday paper (now spiked).

Although we tried not to dwell on Gillian, her unexpected death had an irresistible tug on our conversation, which kept drifting back to her. At one point, Todd put down his fork and knife, heaved a long, breathy sigh, and told us, "I wish I'd kept my anger in better check this morning. My God, now she's dead. I shouldn't have let her rile me so."

"Todd," I reminded him, reaching across the table to pat his hand, "the woman slapped you."

"And then you left," said Neil, taking Todd's other hand. "You acted with great restraint, more than I could have shown."

Anyone walking in just then would think we were having a séance.

"You guys are so supportive," Todd told us, jiggling our hands.

"What are friends for?" said Neil. "Besides, I'm feeling a bit guilty myself. I was awfully hard on Gillian today."

She had it coming, I thought, letting go of Todd's hand, sitting back. I told Neil, "Let's just say you delivered a much-needed dose of tough love."

Neil allowed a soft laugh, sitting back also. "You wordsmith, you." Under his breath, he said to Todd, "Mark's a writer—as if you couldn't tell."

"As if I didn't *know*. Your reputation precedes you, Mark."

Embarrassed by this flattery—from a friend, in my own home—I quickly changed the topic, asking Todd if he'd had any ideas for the curtains in my den.

He replied coyly, "I've been horsing around with some sketches."

"Oh?" asked Neil, on full alert. "Anything you'd care to share?"

"Not just yet."

Neil persisted; Todd stood firm; I laughed at their good-natured banter. We had successfully set aside the grim subject of Gillian's demise.

Engaged in pleasant conversation, we lingered at the table for well over an hour, closer to two, before Neil rose, saying, "I'll go put dessert together."

"Oh, don't fuss," said Todd.

"Trust me, it's no big deal." Neil lifted a few plates from the table.

"I'll take care of cleanup," I told him, grabbing more dishes.

"I'll help. I insist." And Todd joined the effort.

Moving to the kitchen, Todd stood with me at the sink, loading the dishwasher, while Neil concocted his standby, no-fuss dessert—ice cream, berries, and a drizzle of booze.

"That looks terribly elegant," said Todd, looking over his shoulder.

Neil primped. "I'm nothin' if not elegant." He stuck his thumb in a bottle of Cointreau and tipped it, letting the liqueur drip over the berries.

Working in tandem at the sink, Todd and I made quick work of the mess. Taking things from me as I rinsed, he leaned and bent to stow them in the dishwasher, brushing his hip against mine—more than once. It didn't quite feel like a come-on, and I'm not sure how I would have reacted if I'd suspected these little "accidents" were anything other than the happy result of the proximity of friends. Besides, this was all taking place under Neil's nose, and I'd noted the night before, when Todd arrived, that his flirtatious manner seemed no more than an innocent manifestation of his friendly nature. So I made no effort to increase the distance between us at the sink.

Before long, we were back in the dining room with coffee and ice cream. No cognac tonight—the bit of Cointreau would suffice as a bracing, but less lethal, finish. The spirit of camaraderie around the table was deep and genuine. Todd had all the makings of a good friend, and I was grateful that Neil had invited him to stay with us. Already I regretted that Todd's time in Dumont would be so brief.

Perhaps that curtain project in the den would require several return visits . . .

When the ice cream was finished, we continued to sit and talk, nursing our coffee. Todd sat back with a satisfied smile, telling Neil, "What a great meal."

"Thanks," said Neil, "but you helped."

"Yeah, I guess I did. We *all* pitched in. You know, we work well together. I mean, we really sort of click, the three of us. Don't you think?"

Hmmm . . .

"Absolutely." Neil turned to me. "See, Mark, I told you you'd like Todd."

Roxanne had made the same prediction. Mulling this, I said nothing.

With a laugh, Neil prompted, "You do like Todd, don't you, Mark?"

Through a crooked smile, Todd echoed, "Don't you, Mark?"

Something stirred in my pants, and it wasn't my cell phone. What's more, my brain was spinning. "Well, uh, *sure*," I answered clumsily.

"Hey, guys," said Todd, leaning forward, arms on the table, "this is sort of awkward, but we're friends here. There's something I want to ask you about."

"Of course, Todd." Neil mirrored his position, leaning into the table. "What's on your mind?"

I leaned forward as well, closing our circle.

Todd cleared his throat. "Like I said, sort of awkward. This goes back to Geoff, in a way."

"Awww." Neil gave a sympathetic cluck. "All this talk tonight of Gillian and unexpected death, it got you thinking about—"

"No, Neil." Todd wagged a hand. "That's not it at all. I'm talking about something we broached last night. You asked me about getting back in the dating game, and I said that I've been looking. I'm more than ready. So here's the deal:

"I have no idea what sort of ground rules you guys have in your relationship, and the last thing I'd want is to cause trouble, but I figure it can't hurt to ask. I've been coming out of a long dry spell lately, and for all I know, it may be slim pickin's for you guys up here. I mean, Dumont is a charming little town, and you're obviously very comfortable, but sometimes, you may need other gay companionship—or more—and I imagine it's hard to find here."

With an uncertain laugh, he continued, "Well, in case you haven't noticed, *I'm* here. You guys are great together, and I can tell you're happy, but I thought maybe, occasionally, you might enjoy . . . spicing things up. If so—and I can't believe I'm saying this—I would welcome any sort of intimacy that may interest you." He stopped for a moment, looking back and forth to Neil and me. "Oh, God," he groaned, "I can tell from your stunned silence that I've just embarrassed myself."

I struggled to speak, but didn't know what to say. I knew what I *wanted* to say (Let's help Todd out of his dry spell), but I thought I'd better let Neil take the lead.

"Well," he finally said with a warm smile, "I'm a little surprised, but certainly not stunned—and there's no reason at all to feel embarrassed."

"None at all," I seconded.

"But . . . ?" wondered Todd.

"But I think maybe you've misread our friendship."

Drat, I thought. Under the table, I was raring to go.

Neil continued, "Truly, Todd, if Mark and I were looking for someone, we'd jump at the chance to be with you. Right, Mark?"

"Uh, right," I croaked. "Absolutely."

"But we've never experimented with our relationship that way, and

I don't think we've even considered it." Neil looked at me, expecting some backup.

I gave a weak, stupid smile.

"Guys"—Todd stood (looking downright edible, to be perfectly honest)—"say no more. I'm really, *really* sorry. Will you forgive me?"

"Of *course*," I gushed.

"Todd," said Neil, standing, "there's no need to apologize. Your modest proposal—or *im*-modest proposal—is a profound compliment."

"Hmmm," said Todd with a cagey grin, "it sounds like I still have a chance."

Neil returned the grin. "Only time will tell, I guess."

What did he mean by *that*? Was he simply buying time, waiting to discuss this unexpected option with me in private?

"Well, if you change your mind, you know where to find me. It was a rough day—emotionally—so I think I'll run along to bed."

Now I *had* to get up from the table, a move I'd been delaying because of the bump in my lap. I waited for Neil to step to Todd, offering a good-night hug; then I rose, hiding my condition behind him.

Todd took more than a hug, kissing Neil on the lips, telling him, "Thanks for everything—your friendship, the job here, opening your home to me . . ."

Neil readily accepted the kiss, telling Todd, "Our pleasure. Have a good night's sleep."

When Neil stepped away, Todd offered his arms to me. I clapped my arms around him, saying something inane, waiting for the kiss, and bang, there it was. It wasn't quite passionate, but it was no peck, lingering a few seconds, perfectly enjoyable. "Night, Todd," I said when he finally broke away and headed out to the hall and up the stairs.

Neil and I watched him leave, then cleared the dessert things from the table. From the side of his mouth, Neil said, "Cocktails . . . wine with dinner . . . must've been those last few drops of Cointreau."

Meaning, Todd was drunk.

Meaning, he wouldn't have otherwise made such a suggestion.

But to my eye, Todd hadn't looked drunk at all.

PART THREE

Due Diligence

FATAL FALL

Paper-mill executive found dead at her new Dumont home

by CHARLES OAKLAND
Staff Reporter, Dumont Daily Register

OCT. 23, DUMONT, WI—Gillian Reece, chairman and CEO of Ashton Mills, was found dead of an apparent fall from a ladder on Wednesday. The fatal incident took place in the new home that she and husband Esmond Reece had just finished building in rural Dumont County, east of the city. She was 52.

A Wisconsin native, Gillian Reece studied business and accounting at college in Madison, then began her career in Milwaukee. She would later join the financial team at Ashton Mills, then headquartered near Harper. Her stellar rise at the paper manufacturer culminated in the top executive positions just over a year ago.

In anticipation of a friendly merger with Quatro Press, Mrs. Reece moved the corporate headquarters of Ashton Mills, as well as her home, to Dumont.

The merger with Quatro, which was to be finalized at a ceremonial signing today, is in jeopardy. Perry Schield, CEO of Quatro Press, told the *Register,* "Serious issues have recently been raised regarding the wisdom of merging with Ashton. The agreement could be validated by my signature alone, but I'm no longer willing to proceed. As far as I'm concerned, the deal is off."

The timing of Mrs. Reece's death vis-à-vis the failure of the merger appears coincidental. The body was discovered around noon yesterday, and Dumont County coroner Dr. Vernon Formhals made an initial estimate of 11:00 A.M. as the time of death.

Sheriff Douglas Pierce, noting no apparent signs of foul play, told a reporter at the scene, "For now, I'm working on the theory that this death was an accident."

An autopsy is being conducted, results of which are still pending. ❏

Chapter Fifteen

Neil and I had trouble falling asleep that night. The day's events at the Reece house had been exhausting, leaving us emotionally drained, but they also kept the mind active, reliving the episodes we had witnessed, pondering those we had not. What's more, the evening had ended on such an unexpected note—Todd Draper's explicit suggestion of a three-way—it was impossible simply to kiss good night, roll over, and drift off to peaceful slumber.

It was equally impossible, at least for me, to discuss what had happened, despite my nagging desire to explore with Neil the possibility Todd had raised. When Todd had made his overture, it would have taken only the slightest nudge from Neil, a wink of approval, to lure me into an untried adventure. But with the passing of time—a mere hour, perhaps—Todd's proposal had lost not only its immediacy, but its heat.

Had Neil been quicker than I to grasp the risks of welcoming Todd to our bed? Or was he, as I had then speculated, buying time, keeping Todd's pitch on the back burner long enough to weigh with me the ins and outs of experimenting with the bounds of our relationship? If the latter, there was no better time than right then for Neil to roll onto his side, facing me, and to ask, Say, Mark? What'd you make of Todd's come-on tonight? Think he was serious? Have you ever considered . . . ?

But Neil asked none of that. In fact, although he was restless, he said nothing at all. I found this silence not awkward, but oddly comforting, as it demonstrated he was struggling with Todd's proposition as much as I was. Not that I hoped he would reconsider and give in to this lusty temptation (by now I wasn't sure *what* I wanted—after all, I was the guy who was such a stickler for the rules). Still, I was heartened to know we were on the same page, neither prudish nor prurient, neither condemning nor condoning. Somewhere in the middle, we were searching for our comfort zone, our reality, our truth.

Lying there in the dark, I greeted Neil's tossing as a sign that I could relax. And finally, secure in his sleeplessness, I slept.

Later, I was visited by dreams. From these evanescent shadow plays, most of them the mere nonsense of my sleeping mind, two dreams were sufficiently congealed to moor in the crags of my memory upon waking. One was a juiced-up replay of what had happened at our dining-room table that night.

Neil and I are sitting across from Todd when he leans forward, elbows on the table, and begins to explain how we could help him out of his dry spell. He further explains how he could spice up our quiet life in central Wisconsin. Neil and I turn to each other, shrug a why-not, and rise from our chairs. Circling the table in opposite directions, we meet behind Todd's chair and lift him to his feet. With a loving smile, he stands perfectly still as we undress him. Then the *real* fun begins, right there, down on the floor.

This dream was decidedly pleasurable. The other was not.

In it, I am watching television, an old rerun of a *Dynasty* episode in which Joan Collins as Alexis is gearing up for a catfight with Linda Evans as Krystle. But as the confrontation heats up, Joan Collins is transformed into Joan Crawford, as portrayed by Faye Dunaway in *Mommie Dearest*, with Dumont's own Glee Savage done up in spit curls as the cowering daughter Christina. Then Faye morphs into none other than Gillian Reece, and the fireworks begin. Gillian and Glee exchange a sizzling round of bitch slaps, which I find hilarious, so I start to laugh. Hearing me, Gillian hisses and looks out from the screen, which instantly disappears, and all three of us are transported to her two-story living room. "Tina," says Gillian with a snarl, "bring me the ax." Glee pulls an ax from a tangle of wire hangers and hands it to Gillian, who comes after me. Sensing mortal danger, I stop laughing and try to run, only to be tripped by the same wire hangers, which skitter and spin about the limestone floor. As Gillian takes aim, I fall, hitting my head on the floor. Upon impact, I awake.

We had gone to bed on the early side, so in spite of the restlessness that preceded sleep and the dreams that interrupted it, I awoke uncommonly refreshed, ready to take on the uncertainties of the day. Neil was also up and at it early. We showered and dressed, then went downstairs together, finding Todd waiting for us in the kitchen. He had started the coffee and now sat at the table reading my front-page report of Gillian's death.

Since the story wasn't news to him, he looked up at us with a cheery smile, unaffected by the grim emotions that had gripped all of us the previous evening while discussing the tragedy. "Hi, guys! Sleep tight?" No doubt about it—he was one handsome man.

"Not so bad," said Neil. "How about you?" Stepping to the counter to pour coffee, he paused to give Todd's shoulder a squeeze.

"Like a baby," he replied. "A big, fat, happy, *drunk* baby."

"You're anything but fat," I told him, sitting in the chair next to his, "and I *don't* think you were drunk last night."

"You're right, Mark," he said, looking me in the eye with a steady gaze. "I was sober as a proverbial judge."

"Oh, really?" asked Neil, bringing three mugs of coffee to the table. "I've rarely heard a judge discuss group sex over dessert." His breezy tone suggested not the least discomfort with the topic, nor did he seem to be scolding Todd for anything inappropriate.

Good God, it didn't take much—already I felt the prod of arousal. Just where, I wondered, did Neil stand on all this?

Todd told him, "It seems you've been hanging out with the wrong judges."

"Perhaps I have," agreed Neil, mussing Todd's hair as he joined us at the table.

I was tempted to do the same, to run my hand through Todd's sandy hair (which looked so much like Neil's), to give a physical sign that his touch was welcome in return. But this was *breakfast,* the start of a busy day, hardly the time to be flirting with the emotional whirlwind of a possible threesome. Besides, there was no plausibly innocent manner in which I could feel Todd's hair as Neil had just done. Coming from me—an observer of their patter, not a participant in it—such a gesture would be transparently suggestive, flirtatious, and needy. Or was I over-analyzing the situation? Fusty, fussy, prissy me. If Neil could tousle Todd's hair, why couldn't I? Because, it occurred to me, I had simply waited too long. The moment had passed.

I blinked, realizing Todd was staring at me.

"Wow," he said. "Must be the morning light, Mark. I didn't notice before, but you have the most striking—and gorgeous—green eyes."

Neil laughed. "He hears that all the time."

"Now and then," I allowed. "Thanks, Todd."

"Hey," he said, "do you want eggs or something? I'd be happy to cook."

"Nah, don't bother," said Neil, sounding a bit distracted. "Doug should be here soon. He usually brings pastry on his way from the gym."

"Doug?"

"Sheriff Douglas Pierce," I reminded him. "He's a close friend."

"Let me get this straight. The sheriff, a gym hound, delivers your breakfast every morning. What's up with that?" quipped Todd. "Is he gay?"

"Matter of fact, he is. But he's not stopping by today. I think he had an early dentist's appointment. I'm meeting him downtown at the coroner's office."

Todd mused, "There's nothing quite like a visit to the morgue to get one's day going, is there?"

"That's appetizing," said Neil. "Still up for eggs?"

"No, thanks. Never touch 'em."

"They're an excellent source of protein," I noted, not intending to sound suggestive.

"Wouldn't want to run low on *that*." Todd gave us a wink.

Even so, there were no takers for eggs, so we settled on toast and day-old kringle.

Then Neil and Todd headed over to the Reece house.

And I went downtown to meet Doug.

Dumont's public-safety building housed not only the sheriff's department and jail, but also various department offices, including that of the coroner. The facility was open at all hours, but as I walked into the dispatch area that morning, there was the unmistakable bustle of beginning a new day, as if someone had just unlocked the front door for business. A shift was changing, coffee was perking, and a scratchy radio gave the local weather forecast—sunny skies again, still cool.

I paused to ask a dispatcher at the window, "Is the sheriff in yet?"

"Yes, Mr. Manning"—they all seemed to know me—"he just arrived. Said you could find him with Dr. Formhals."

"Thanks. I know the way." As I headed down the hallway that led to his office, terrazzo flooring clicked underfoot, fluorescent lighting hummed overhead.

The coroner's door was marked with an inelegant plastic sign, and I knew from previous experience that there was no need to knock. Walking in, I heard conversation on the other side of a partition that separated a small waiting room from the doctor's office space.

"That you, Mark?" called Doug.

"Yes, it's I." The response slipped out naturally from the grammarian within, but even as I said it, I knew how pedantic I sounded. With a cough, I added, "It's me, I'm here."

"Morning, Mark," said Dr. Formhals, stepping around the partition to shake my hand. His brown skin looked inky black against a starched white lab coat. "Always a pleasure to welcome you to these sad surroundings." He was referring not only to the morgue itself, which lay beyond his offices, but to the utilitarian decorating, the artificial light, the plastic plants, and the shabby, county-issued metal furniture. Only his desk of ornately carved wood, far too big for the space it occupied, showed any sign of personality or character.

I greeted the doctor, then reached to shake hands with Doug, who was seated, trapped at the far end of the ungainly desk.

Doug said, "Vernon was just sharing with me some of his initial findings."

"Mind if I sit in?"

Doug grinned. "That's why I asked you here." He felt compelled to explain to the doctor, "Mark's perspective on mysterious death has always been useful to me."

"Of course, Douglas. Of course." Formhals sat behind his desk, gesturing that I should take the remaining chair, next to Doug. "I hate to disappoint either of you, but in the case of *this* death, there's very little mystery."

I asked, "Testing confirms your initial theory of an accidental fall?"

"Largely, yes."

"What has me puzzled," I said, putting on my glasses, taking out my pen and notebook, "is why the fall proved fatal. Even if Gillian was at the top of the ladder, up on the balcony, she was no more than ten feet or so above the floor. I've heard of people surviving much higher falls—several stories, in fact."

"You're correct, Mark, but there are two types of fall, known as either 'controlled' or 'uncontrolled.' In a controlled, vertical fall, a person lands upright, on the feet. Upon impact, energy is absorbed by the feet and legs, which can cause great injury but still spare the vital organs. Falls of more than a hundred feet have been survived in this manner."

"From the look of things," said Doug, "I'm guessing Gillian didn't land on her feet."

"Correct. And that's exactly what defines an uncontrolled fall, which can be fatal from even a short distance, as from a stepladder. Compounding the problem for Mrs. Reece, she landed on a stone floor, which is extremely unforgiving."

I asked, "What did the autopsy show?"

"Massive head injury, shearing of the aorta, and most significantly, a snapped cervix—she broke her neck. Death came very quickly, if not instantly. I doubt that she suffered."

I recalled, "She didn't even bleed."

"I assure you, Mark, she bled a great deal internally."

Doug asked, "Were you able to establish a more precise time of death?"

Formhals opened a folder on his desk and glanced at the top page inside. "My original estimate of eleven o'clock proved quite accurate. The victim died some thirty to sixty minutes prior to the time when Mark and his associate found her."

Although the coroner seemed satisfied Gillian's death had been accidental, I was nonetheless grateful that Lucille Haring and I had been working in a crowded newsroom at the time of death. If the investigation were to take an unexpected turn, it might be handy to have a clear-cut alibi.

I asked Doug, "What about your examination of physical evidence at the scene? Any developments?"

He shook his head. "Nothing unexpected. There were fingerprints all *over* the place—very predictable at a construction site with numerous workers present. The *absence* of fingerprints on the ladder or the balcony railing would have triggered my suspicions, but there were so many sets of prints, they're impossible to sort out. Nor was there any other evidence of foul play—no faulty ladder rungs, no ripped buttons or torn clothing, no fistfuls of hair."

"What's more," Formhals added, "there was no flesh or blood under the victim's fingernails, which would have indicated a struggle. Similarly, there were no bruises or wounds, no signs of external trauma other than those directly attributable to the fall."

I wondered, "What about that welt on her left cheek?"

With a pensive nod, Formhals acknowledged, "I keep coming back to that. It's intriguing, Mark, to say the least, especially given the bizarre bout of slapping you witnessed earlier that morning. The problem is, the welt on the victim's cheek cannot be conclusively identified as the result of a slap. More likely, it was an abrasion sustained in the fall; in other words, the welt was the result of the fall, not the cause of it."

Doug said, "It sounds as if you're ready to render an opinion, Vernon."

"I'm zeroing in on it." Formhals pinched the knot of his necktie. "I'll continue to review the evidence while awaiting results of toxicology and other routine testing, but at this point, I can give you a fairly accurate idea of the main points to be covered in the final autopsy report."

I poised my pen as the coroner referred to his file.

He continued, "The *time* of death has been established as eleven o'clock Wednesday morning. The *cause* of death was an uncontrolled fall from a ladder. The *mechanism* of death was bleeding into the brain and cardiac arrest, both resulting from massive internal injury. Which leaves only the *manner* of the victim's death." He tapped his notes.

"Accidental?" asked Doug.

Dr. Formhals reviewed, "There are only four possible manners of death: natural, accidental, suicide, and homicide. We *know* the victim didn't die of natural causes, such as illness or old age, and we *assume* she didn't take her own life, as neither the circumstances nor her personal history pointed to suicide."

"That's an understatement," I said. "Say what you will about Gillian Reece, but I have no doubt she had a strong will to live."

"The manner of her death, therefore, was either accident or homicide, and I am strongly leaning toward a final ruling that her death was accidental. Lacking any additional evidence, it would be difficult—indeed, impossible—to prove foul play."

With that, the doctor closed his file.

I capped my pen.

Chapter Sixteen

L unch promised to restore a welcome sense of normalcy to my life, which had been disrupted over the past two days by the arrival of Todd Draper and the departure of Gillian Reece. In the case of Todd, this disruption was not altogether unpleasant, quite the contrary, at least in regard to the effect he'd had on my fantasies. In the case of Gillian, her death might have been accidental, but it was nonetheless disturbing, and I still couldn't shake the uneasy feeling that the timing of her fatal fall had coincided too neatly with too many other people's interests.

So when I learned that morning that Neil would be joining me as usual for lunch at First Avenue Grill (he had missed the day before) and that Todd would *not* be joining us (he needed to keep an eye on the curtain installation at the Reece house), I was grateful for the return to a familiar and pleasing routine—even if it would last only an hour. I could ogle Todd later, and I could postpone my search for answers, if answers were to be had, in the perplexing circumstances of Gillian's death. For the moment, I just wanted everything back the way it had been prior to Tuesday.

Walking along First Avenue from the *Register* to Neil's office, I felt a rush of anticipation, as if I hadn't seen him in years and we were about to reunite. In a sense, I realized, my flirtation with Todd's proposed ménage had created an unintended distance in my relationship with Neil, and I doubted if Neil was even aware of it. Our lunch date presented a promising chance to assess whether damage had been done, and if so, an immediate opportunity to fix it.

When I walked through the front door of Neil's office, he was busy on the phone at his desk, sounding hassled. I stepped behind him, gave his shoulders a hug, and kissed the top of his head. He patted my hand as he talked, twisting his head to kiss my fingers when the other party began gabbing back at him.

Waiting for him to finish, I strolled about the office, studying some perspective drawings of various projects he had on display, then sat at the conference table, watching passersby on the street.

"Sorry," he said, hanging up the phone. "I was at the Reece house longer than I'd planned. Just got in—need to catch up on a few calls." He picked up the phone again.

"No problem, no rush. How's everything going with the curtains?"

He grinned. "I'd like to tell you they're drop-dead gorgeous, which they are, but that description might seem insensitive, under the circumstances." He dialed.

"And, uh . . . how's Todd doing?"

"Fine." Then he spoke to the person he'd called, a supplier who was behind on something. Neil's tone was not quite rude—never, not Neil—but he did sound stressed. I wished I hadn't mentioned Todd, which was clearly the source of his distraction. Still, I now understood that his instant dismissal of Todd's proposition the night before had been a cover for his confused reaction to it. He had been as tempted as I had been to consider intimacy with Todd, and he was now struggling, as I was, to sort out two conflicting emotions—guilt, for feeling attracted to Todd, and disappointment, for turning him down. We really did need to talk this out.

"Let's get going," he said, hanging up the phone and standing. "We're running late, and I'm starved. How about you?" He switched off his desk lamp and grabbed a jacket.

Sensing this was not the best time for a heart-to-heart, I stood, answering, "You know me—always ready for lunch."

Meeting him at the door, I patted his back as we stepped outside. He locked up; then we walked the block or so to the Grill.

"Nancy's got a good crowd today," I noted as we passed one of the restaurant's front windows.

Since we were later than usual, we were the last of the lunch customers to be seated. The prim, well-dressed owner, Nancy Sanderson, had saved my prime table for us, seating us in a corner between the fireplace and the windows, where we could see the whole dining room, which was packed. Berta, our usual waitress, didn't need to ask—she brought iced tea for me and iced coffee for Neil—then recited a few specials, from which we chose without opening our menus.

I had brought a newspaper from the office, that morning's *Chicago Journal*, and shared a few sections of it with Neil during the lull as we waited for our lunch to arrive. Although we were both reading, he seemed conspicuously quiet, lost in his thoughts. I was itching to broach with him our predicament with Todd, but I was deterred both by the public setting of the restaurant and by my own unsure feelings. Why rush, I reasoned, to open a discussion that offered little likelihood of being resolved then and there?

Immersed in these thoughts, I reacted with a start to the sound of Neil's voice when he asked me something. "What's that?" I said, setting down the paper and slipping off my glasses.

"The coroner," he repeated. "How did your meeting go this morning?"

"Ah!" I responded with an eager smile, grateful for a topic other than Todd Draper. "Doug and I met with him as planned. The long and the short of it is, Vernon thinks Gillian's death was an accident."

"Hngh." Neil set his section of the paper on the table; a splashy decorating feature covered the front page. "I'm sort of surprised. Gillian had trouble brewing on so many fronts—not that I think any of those people would stoop to kill her."

I nodded. "That's exactly the dilemma I've been tussling with. Given all the enmity associated with Gillian, coupled with the timing of her death, I'd say the circumstances are highly suspicious. Still, we *know* all these people, some better than others, and none of them strike me as the type who would resort to murder."

"So where does that leave the investigation?"

"I guess it's dead-ended. Vernon is still waiting for the results of some routine testing, but he doesn't expect them to reveal anything. Barring the arrival of stunning new evidence, the death will be ruled accidental. At this point, in effect, there *is* no investigation."

"Well, I suppose that's good news." With a sigh, Neil added, "One less thing to worry about." If his other worry was Todd Draper, he quickly dismissed it, as his spirits seemed to lighten when he saw Berta approaching. "Make way," he said, clearing our papers from the table. "Here's lunch."

As always, it was excellent. Nancy, who not only owned the Grill but also provided its culinary vision, never failed to amaze me. Working out of a storefront in a small town, she had contributed greatly to our contentment there, raising our perception of Dumont's quality of life. The turkey-and-corn fritters she served us that day, perfectly attuned to the chillier weather and the season of harvest, would have done anyone proud, even some snooty "name chef" in a trendy metropolis. Nancy kept hinting at retirement, but I hoped the day would never come.

Savoring our meal, finishing our fritters, and conversing of nothing momentous—the food, the weather, the purely mundane—we managed to set aside the vexing issues that had recently intruded on our lives, simply enjoying each other's company. At one point, Neil took my hand and quietly mentioned that he loved me. "Ditto, kiddo," I told him.

Because of our late start, the crowd in the dining room had thinned some. When Berta picked up our plates and moved from the table, it seemed as if most of the other patrons had been swept out the door.

"Hey," said Neil, "isn't that Glee?"

Sure enough, there was my features editor, Glee Savage, sitting with another woman at a table across the room. Even with her back to us, there was no mistaking the big floppy-brimmed hat of shocking scarlet silk—who *else* in Dumont would make such a statement? I asked Neil, "Can you see who's with her?"

He leaned for a better view. "I think . . . yeah, that's Tamra Thaine."

"Oh?" I leaned as well, confirming with my own eyes that Glee was lunching with Esmond Reece's yoga teacher, who wore an all-white outfit of pleated slacks and bulky sweater—pin a big orange mum on her chest, and she'd have looked like an escapee from some middle-aged pep squad.

"Nothing against either woman," said Neil, "but they seem an unlikely pair. I wonder how they even know each other."

"Simple. I introduced them—well, indirectly. The *Register* is doing a story on Tamra's hoodoo institute, and I assigned it to Glee."

Neil smirked. "Try to keep an open mind, Mark."

"Sorry. It should make an interesting feature, if Glee can sort it all out. I wish her luck; Tamra's lingo was way beyond me."

Other patrons got up and left, affording Neil and me a better view of Glee and Tamra's table. I could now see that their lunch had ended. Dessert dishes had been cleared, and the two women were lingering over coffee. In fact, their cups were empty, as evidenced when Glee lifted hers for another sip, but finding none, set it down again. Deep in conversation, they seemed oblivious to their surroundings.

"It seems they've hit it off," noted Neil. "They're yakking like schoolgirls."

Berta returned to our table with coffee and offered dessert, which we declined. When she left, we sat back with our coffee, spoke of this and that, and kept an eye on Glee and Tamra.

Their conversation seemed mostly whispered—and intense. They leaned close to each other, speaking and nodding. Glee had a steno pad on the table, but she wasn't writing notes, and in fact, the pad's cover was closed.

Voicing my own thoughts, Neil said, "It doesn't *look* like an interview."

"I admit, it seems odd for a business lunch. And Glee's not the gossipy type."

With a grin, Neil reminded me, "She's a reporter."

"Touché. But you know what I mean. She's as professional as they come. Maybe Glee is just trying to . . . to draw Tamra out. Maybe she's trying to dig for some background because she feels Tamra is holding back. This so-called institute struck me as nutty from the get-go. Maybe Glee drew the same conclusion and is sniffing around for an exposé."

"Maybe," said Neil, sounding unconvinced.

His skepticism was warranted. While my theory sounded reasonable, it didn't quite account for what I saw. In their whispered conversation, Glee didn't appear to be needling Tamra for information that Tamra, in turn, was trying to withhold. Rather, the two women seemed mutually engaged, and I couldn't help characterizing their shared attitude as furtive, scheming, and—just possibly—guilty.

"I hate to interrupt all this delicious intrigue," said Neil, setting his cup on the table, "but I need to get back to the office."

I glanced at my watch. "So do I." Standing, I hailed Berta, who stood at the ready with our check.

She brought it to the table and waited while I signed; the amount would be added to an account I ran there. Neil stood, slipping his jacket on while thanking Berta and wishing her well. Berta returned these courtesies, then bustled off to another table.

As she moved away, I realized that Glee and Tamra had just risen from their chairs with a flourish of napkins, a popping of breath mints, and a snapping of purses. They had not yet noticed us, but would soon encounter us as we all made our way to the door.

"Glee!" I said. "What a pleasant surprise." Though I had been eyeing her every move for some minutes, it seemed far more gracious to let her believe I had spotted her just that moment.

"Mark! Neil!" She beelined toward us with Tamra in tow, meeting us near the hostess stand at the door. "I didn't see you when we came in."

"My fault," said Neil. "I made Mark late—catching up on some phone calls."

"Ugh." She leaned close to Neil. "Don't you sometimes feel like pulling the cord out of the wall?"

"In fact, I do—sometimes."

I asked, "Is that Tamra?" The woman was not only slow catching up with Glee, but she seemed to hide behind her, as if wanting to disappear into the crowd. But there was no crowd left in the room, and her white outfit was conspicuous anyway—Labor Day was nearly two months past.

She mumbled, "Hello, Mr. Manning," but remained at several steps' distance.

"You know my partner, Neil, of course." I gestured to him.

She nodded, but did not step forward to greet him or shake hands. She said nothing, as if embarrassed and tongue-tied.

Hoping Glee would offer some explanation for their meeting, I asked obliquely, "Nice lunch?"

"As always." Chipper as ever, Glee turned to Nancy at the hostess stand, telling her, "The fritters were marvelous."

Nancy gave a deferential bob of her head. "Thank you, Miss Savage."

I made no move to go, telegraphing to Glee, I'm waiting . . .

She got the message. "Thanks for the lead on that story, Mark. It ought to be a good one. I asked Tamra to lunch in order to get some background on her new, uh . . . yoga parlor." Glee's awkward phraseology indicated that she had not even scratched the surface with Tamra regarding the intended scope of the institute.

"In that case," I said, "let me take your tab—it'll save you the trouble of an expense report."

"You're the boss," said Glee, bright-eyed. She handed over the leather folder that contained her check.

"I'll square up with Nancy. Will I see you back at the office?"

"Sure thing, Mark. Thanks for lunch." And she opened the door. Tamra slunk past all of us without a word. Glee followed her out to the street, and they walked away together, huddled in conversation again.

Under his breath, Neil told me, "Very strange," as I stood at Nancy's podium, signing the second lunch check.

"Thank you, Mr. Manning," said Nancy. "I hope everything was to your liking today."

"It's always to our liking, but today was exceptional. Thank *you*." I closed the folder and handed it to her.

"My pleasure." As I checked my pockets, preparing to leave, Nancy added, "I'll look forward to seeing you again this evening at seven."

"Oh?" I turned to Neil with a blank expression. "Do we have plans? Fine with me, but I don't recall—"

Nancy tapped her pencil on a line of the ledger spread out before her. "Sheriff Pierce made the reservation. Party of three."

Neil reminded me, "It's one of Doug's payback dinners—for breakfast every day."

"He shouldn't do that."

"But he likes to."

"I mean, what 'breakfast'? We make coffee; he brings kringle."

Nancy struggled to conceal her grimace with a tight smile.

Neil told her, "We'll be here, and we're looking forward to it."

I added, "But we may be four instead of three."

Neil nodded, thinking aloud, "We can't very well abandon Todd."

"No problem at all," Nancy assured us.

Then she turned her pencil on end and went to work with the eraser, neatly amending the reservation.

Chapter Seventeen

When I arrived back at the *Register,* Connie yoo-hooed me from behind the receptionist's window in the lobby. "Mr. Manning? Glee came in about two minutes ago. She said to let you know she'd like to talk to you."

"Thanks, Connie." I gave her a wave and climbed the stairs to the editorial floor, taking them by twos.

Activity in the newsroom was at its midday high—phones rang, editors called from desk to desk, writers rushed to and from assignments—but I had no trouble spotting Glee, as she hadn't yet had time to remove her big red hat. She was standing with our senior photographer, choosing from a series of digital pictures that flashed on a monitor. Even from a distance, I recognized on the screen the copper saucepan I'd seen her carrying on Tuesday. In the photos, it was brimming with a colorful, seasonal assortment of squashes and gourds, far too pretty to eat (for all I knew, they might have been plastic).

Glancing up from the monitor, Glee saw me and gave a high sign. I returned the signal and pointed to my office, then headed in that direction, working my way around the city desk.

I had just entered my inner office and removed my sport coat when

Glee rapped on the glass wall. Standing in the doorway, she asked, "Got a minute?"

"Sure, Glee. What's on your mind?" I sat at my desk.

She sat across from me, removing a huge pin from her hat. "I suppose you're *itching* to know what's up with Tamra Thaine."

"That's putting it mildly." I grinned.

"*Well*"—Glee removed the hat and set it in her lap, shaking her hair—"as I told you, I set up the lunch date in order to do some initial research for the story."

"On the yoga parlor?"

"Whatever it is." Glee stuck the pin into the crown of her hat. "Point is, Mark, we never got that far. I intended to conduct a structured background interview, but Tamra just wanted to . . . *talk*."

"She didn't have much to say when we ran into you at the door."

"Trust me—she had plenty to say at the table, and she started in again as soon as we were out on the street. She'd *still* be talking if I hadn't fibbed about a pressing deadline."

I laughed, sitting back in my chair. "I've used that one myself."

"*You*, Mark? Nonsense. You're far too principled."

I blinked. Now that Glee mentioned it, I couldn't recall that I had ever used the reporter's classic white lie: Can't talk now, I'm on deadline. I had doubtless said those words, but I would have spoken them honestly, while in the middle of filing a story.

Glee continued, "I'd prepared some background questions, but since my knowledge of Eastern studies is so scant—heck, it's nil—I merely wanted to prime the pump and let Tamra take the lead."

"Your plan must have worked. You said she talked her head off."

"She did, but it had nothing to do with my prepared questions. In fact, she never even gave me a chance to open my notebook. She just plunged in and kept going. Honest to God, I don't know how she managed to eat." Glee paused in thought before adding, "She *is* a vegan. I guess eating doesn't really matter."

Trying to keep Glee on track, I asked, "If Tamra wasn't telling you about the institute, what was she blabbing about?"

Glee sat back. Her slick red lips stretched with a smile. "Esmond. She was talking about Esmond Reece."

"Gillian, too?" I leaned forward with interest.

"Uh-huh. Though the purpose of our luncheon was to discuss business, Tamra used our meeting as an opportunity to vent decidedly more personal matters. I know you've been wondering whether Tamra and Esmond's relationship is based on anything more than a shared interest in Eastern studies. Well"—Glee leaned forward over my desk, her face only a foot or so from mine—"I have at least half of the answer for you."

With a wry smile, I asked, "Should I be taking notes?"

"They're all up here." She tapped her noggin. "Here's the gist of Tamra's gabfest: From the beginning, she and Esmond recognized each other as soul mates, but Tamra confided to me that her feelings run deeper. She has long harbored a romantic interest in Esmond. She's quite certain, though, that his interest in *her* is only platonic."

"So they've never been intimate?"

Glee shook her head. "Tamra was blunt on that point—she regrets that it's never happened. I *suppose* she could've been lying to me, but my instincts tell me she was sincere." Reading something in my face, Glee asked, "What's wrong?"

"I suspected all along there was some romantic chemistry between them, but if it was a one-way crush, I'd have thought their roles would be reversed. After all, Esmond was the one living with a harpy. It's easy to imagine that Tamra's serene manner and mind-set would appeal to him."

"That's what Tamra thought, too. She couldn't *imagine* why Esmond stayed with Gillian—other than the obvious financial considerations. Now, though, with Gillian dead and Esmond in control of a considerable fortune, Tamra seems obsessed with taking their relationship to the next level." Glee exhaled noisily, concluding, "I heard *way* more than I was planning on, Mark. Who does she think I am—Dear Abby?"

I laughed. "Did she want your advice, or was she just dumping?"

"Dumping, mainly, but that didn't stop me from *offering* advice."

"Yes, Abigail? What'd you tell her?"

She flipped her hands, as if the answer were self-evident. "I warned her against pursuing Esmond."

"Why? He's a free man."

Glee countered flatly, "He's a nut. He showed the supreme misjudgment to marry Gillian in the first place—enough said." Having made her point, Glee stood.

I stood as well. There was no purpose to be served in defending either Esmond *or* Gillian, as Glee's attitude stemmed from emotional wounds too deep to allow reasoning. I simply noted, "If Tamra intends to make her feelings known to Esmond, she should at least give it some time. Gillian isn't even buried yet."

"I suppose you're right." Glee's tone conveyed that she couldn't care less about social proprieties insofar as they applied to Gillian Reece— dead or alive. Getting back to business, she asked, "Do you want me to stay on the story? Regarding Tamra's institute, I mean."

"Sure, it's worth pursuing." Stepping with Glee to my outer office, I suggested a tack or two she might take in following up with Tamra. We both acknowledged that we were stumped as to whether Tamra's venture was on the level, so Glee's first priority was to determine whether she was writing an informational piece or an exposé.

While discussing these particulars with Glee, however, my mind was focused not on the legitimacy of Tamra's institute, but on another thought, one regarding a motive that might have been relevant to a suspicious death currently deemed accidental. I now had confirmation that there was an element of sizzle to the relationship between Tamra and Esmond, and this provided a clear, plausible motive for Gillian's demise. What's more, if Tamra was correct that Esmond had not previously been inclined to explore romance with her, she was naming herself as the most likely suspect.

"I'll set up another meeting with her," Glee was saying, moving to the door.

"Try it on her own turf this time. A drive out to the 'compound' might prove enlightening."

"Good idea. I'll let you know—"

"*Mark*," said Lucille Haring, rushing in, "sorry to interrupt, but—"

"I was just leaving," said Glee, stepping behind Lucy at the door. "Next!" And she disappeared into the crowded newsroom beyond my glass wall.

"Sorry to barge in," said Lucy, sounding breathless, "but I thought you'd want to see this." She carried a sheet of paper, holding it by the corner with her thumb and index finger—a dainty gesture that looked ridiculously out of character for Lucy, whose drab green pantsuit never failed to remind me of a Texaco uniform.

"What is it?" I asked, stepping toward her and reaching for the paper.

"Uh-uh-uh," she clucked. "Don't touch." She moved to the round conference table and, setting down the paper, suggested, "Better get your glasses."

Ducking into my inner office, I grabbed the glasses from my desk, put them on, and joined Lucy at the table, sitting next to her.

"It's a letter," she said, "that came in today's mail, postmarked late yesterday in Dumont. The envelope has been on my desk since this morning. I just got around to reading it."

Leaning over the table, I saw at a glance that the single-page missive, folded in thirds to fit in an envelope, had not been signed. It had been typewritten, single-spaced, on an old machine with a worn cloth ribbon. The individual letters were not only fuzzy, but misaligned, forcing me to adjust my glasses on the bridge of my nose. The letter said:

Wednesday, October 22

To the editor:

The death of Gillian Reece today was the direct result of actions she herself had taken. She was guilty of a one-woman conspiracy that would have had devastating consequences for Dumont.

The planned merger between Ashton Mills and Quatro Press was never intended to be an equal partnership benefitting both companies. Rather, Mrs. Reece had carefully concocted a hidden scheme to take control of Quatro, then establish a competing printing plant offshore. Quatro's assets, technology, and customers would be transferred to the other plant, wholly owned by Ashton/Quatro Corporation.

The net effect of this trickery would be to greatly enrich Mrs. Reece and AQC while destroying Dumont's principal industry, Quatro Press. More than a thousand local families would lose their livelihoods. The resulting high unemployment in Dumont would further benefit Ashton Mills by allowing the company to pay less for labor in a deflated market.

Gillian Reece deserved her fall from power and her fall to death. For obvious reasons, this letter must remain . . .

Unsigned

Looking up from the typewritten page, I found Lucy's eyes staring into mine. "Unless I'm mistaken," she said, "this puts an entirely new spin on things."

Still trying to absorb the full meaning of what I'd read, I said, "She meant to bleed Quatro Press . . . bleed it, gut it, then trash it. I just can't believe it."

Lucy, at the moment, was more objective than I. "That's assuming the letter writer knew what he—or she—was talking about. The letter accuses a woman who's not here to explain herself."

I slowly shook my head, appalled by the magnitude of Gillian's scheme. "After what I've learned of the woman in the last few days, I shouldn't be surprised she would stoop to such betrayal."

"Betrayal?" asked Lucy. "You're not the type, Mark, to take business dealings so personally."

"I *backed* this merger from my position on both boards, Lucy. I put my own reputation on the line. What's more, my uncle *founded* Quatro

Press, and I inherited a good deal of interest in that company, as did Thad—my kid's financial future rests on Quatro's corporate well-being."

She grimaced. "I hadn't thought of that."

"If the merger had gone through today, my Quatro stock would be replaced with new AQC shares. My ownership of the *Register* is highly leveraged by that stock. Even if the stock retained its value, there's a booby trap, and it's deadly. Sudden, astronomical unemployment in Dumont would have a devastating ripple effect throughout the local economy. For starters, our advertising and circulation revenues would plunge. *Then* where would we be?"

"Up a creek?"

"Big time. But there's more. If the *Register* started losing money, I'd be forced to sell my stock in order to keep the paper afloat—for a while. But a continued decline would ultimately force the paper to fold, leaving me with squat."

Lucy gave a pensive whistle. Then she jerked her head toward the letter on the table. "Even though it's addressed 'To the editor,' I assume you don't plan to run it on tomorrow morning's op-ed page."

"No," I replied, mustering a half laugh, "I think this one qualifies as physical evidence. Doug Pierce will surely find it of interest."

Lucy stood. "I'll find a plastic sleeve for it."

"Good idea. And I'll call Doug."

Though there was a sprawling, many-buttoned speakerphone right there on the table, I reached inside my pocket, pulled out my cell phone, and punched in the sheriff's direct number.

Twenty minutes later, Lucy escorted Sheriff Douglas Pierce into my office, and the three of us sat around the table, where the letter was sandwiched between gleaming sheets of acrylic. After reading it, Doug asked, "Who's handled it?"

"I'm the only one," said Lucy. "I opened it." The torn envelope was on the table as well, protected by a second plastic sleeve.

"Good. The envelope may have been handled by dozens of people, but chances are, the letter itself was handled only by you and the writer." He took the letter from the table and held it up to a fluorescent fixture in the ceiling.

"Is there a watermark?" I asked.

"Yup. Ashton Classic Bond—twenty-five percent cotton."

I recalled the slogan " 'The sterling standard of serious stationers.' "

Lucy wondered, "Do you suppose someone from Ashton Mills sent it?"

I paused in thought. "Ashton's stationery is available everywhere, especially around here. I wouldn't make too much of the paper. Besides, why would someone at Ashton tattle on Gillian? They had everything to *gain* from her scheme."

Doug noted, "Not *everyone* at Ashton was involved in Gillian's plot. It may have been her doing alone."

"True," I allowed. "We don't even know if the letter is trustworthy."

" 'Trustworthy,' " Doug repeated with a chuckle. "It's an odd description for a document that may have been written by a killer." He put the letter on the table.

Lucy asked him, "You're thinking Gillian's death may not have been an accident?"

"The circumstances of her death were suspicious from the outset, but there was no physical evidence suggesting otherwise. This"—he tapped the letter with his finger—"is more than a subtle suggestion. It's safe to say this investigation has just entered a new phase. Gillian's death may well have been a homicide."

I surmised, "You think the letter is credible."

"This is conjecture, and the investigation will have to sort through it item by item, but here's my current take on the letter." Doug sat back, explaining, "The central contention of the letter, that Gillian was plotting to destroy Quatro Press, strongly suggests that her death was tied to the merger. The writer, of course, may have fabricated this to conceal some other motive for Gillian's death, but the fact that the letter was written at all is a clear indication of foul play—if Gillian had died accidentally, why would the writer stir the waters? Bottom line: regardless of motive, the writer of the letter may well be the killer."

Lucy had begun taking notes. The familiar grid had appeared on her pad—her method of visual logic. Swirling her pencil in one of the squares, she said, "So the best way to identify the killer is to identify the writer of the letter. And the best way to identify the writer is to identify his or her motive."

Picking up on her reasoning, I added, "The motive to explore first is the one the writer implies, that Gillian was killed to prevent the merger from proceeding."

"Exactly," said Doug.

I recalled, "Tyler Pennell, the accountant performing due diligence, expressed growing reservations about various aspects of the merger. Maybe he was on to something."

Lucy suggested, "Maybe he wrote the letter."

Doug frowned. "I worked with Tyler on a recent case, and he really knows his stuff—but he doesn't strike me as the murderous sort."

"Hardly," I agreed. "Besides, he had no direct interest in the merger, as far as we know. His role was that of an impartial outsider, an auditor."

Doug concluded, "He's the first person we need to see."

Lucy offered, "Want me to track him down?" She stood.

I told her, "Sure, Lucy, thanks," and she went to her desk in the newsroom.

Doug leaned forward, picked up the letter, and studied it for a moment. "We'll check this for fingerprints and send it out for typewriter forensics, but we don't need an expert to figure out this was written on an old clunker—maybe a piece of junk from somebody's basement."

"Or maybe it was written by an old person, someone who never got modern. The wording seems intelligent enough, with a firm grip on business terminology."

Doug nodded. "I noticed that. It must have been written quickly after the murder. The wording makes reference to Gillian's fall yesterday, and the envelope was postmarked the same afternoon."

Dropping my head back, I breathed a sigh to the ceiling. "It's outrageous," I muttered.

"What?" asked Doug. "The merger plot? Or the murder?"

"Both." I stood, sorting through my thoughts, which I now realized were highly conflicted. "On the one hand, if what the letter says is true, Gillian's actions were indefensible. She planned to victimize the whole town—bad enough—but she was also shrewd enough to understand that I would be victimized as well."

Doug agreed, "It's awful. Maybe the letter writer wasn't far off base—she got what she deserved."

Through a troubled squint, I said, "That sounds pretty strange, Doug, coming from you."

"Hey, look," he said, rising to speak to me face-to-face. "As a cop, I'm sworn to track this down and, if a crime has been committed, bring the wrongdoer to justice. And I'll do precisely that. But the point is, if Gillian had wrecked your life, Mark, I'd be tempted to throttle her myself."

I couldn't hide my smile. "Doug, you're a good friend—as well as a great cop."

With a modest shrug, he said, "Thanks," then stepped to the glass wall and looked out into the newsroom.

I continued, "The point I was driving at, though, is this: There can be no justification for murder, certainly not as a means of settling a business dispute. Two wrongs don't make a right. I mean, why did the killer take such an extreme measure to quash the deal? Couldn't he have simply blown the whistle? The merger would have collapsed as soon as Gillian's true agenda was revealed."

Doug said to the window, "We'll have to talk to the killer about that. Right now, we know nothing."

Lucy popped back inside my office. "I managed to locate Tyler Pennell. He just headed over to Quatro Press—has an appointment with Perry Schield."

Doug glanced at me. "Then we'd better get going."

"We?"

He grinned. "I know you're as hot as I am to get to the bottom of this. Besides, you're fully acquainted with the terms of the merger. I'm clueless on this stuff—I wouldn't even know what questions to ask."

"Great. Count me in." I stepped to my inner office and grabbed my jacket. Returning, checking my pockets for notebook and pen, I told

Lucy, "By the way, put a hold on tomorrow morning's editorial page, will you?"

"You're the boss."

"I'll dash off something after I get back from Quatro. I'm afraid when news of the letter hits—and speculation begins concerning the presumed murder—a lot of people will think of the killer as a hero. We need to keep this in perspective. This wasn't just a matter of payback. A deadly crime has been committed."

Lucy nodded. "I'll hold the space for you."

Chapter Eighteen

D oug drove. We considered phoning ahead, both as a courtesy to Perry Schield and to make sure we wouldn't miss Tyler Pennell, but Doug decided, "Nah, let's keep our visit a surprise."

To describe Quatro Press as a "printing plant" wouldn't begin to give an accurate picture of the sprawling facility. Located north of town not far from the interstate, Quatro might be mistaken by a passing motorist for a large industrial park, which would be a close guess, except that Quatro was the sole occupant of this veritable village, served by a grid of roadways and its own rail spur.

When Doug flashed his badge to the guard at the main gate, he got an awkward salute from the gal in uniform, who welcomed him, "Afternoon, Sheriff."

As we rolled onto the grounds, Doug turned to me, noting, "It's been a while since I've been out here. I hardly recognize the place."

I explained, "Quatro was in a phase of almost perpetual expansion during the last decade or so, until recently, when the manufacturing segment of the economy went flat and Chinese competition, with its dirt-cheap labor, began making inroads in both the printing and the paper industries."

"And that's what the merger was all about?"

"Yup. Vertical integration and consolidation of resources—that's one way to stay lean. At least that's what we *thought* Gillian had in mind."

Pierce didn't recognize the place not only because it had grown, but because Neil had been on retainer the last few years and had given a face-lift to the existing facilities while designing new buildings from the ground up. The result was a tasteful, cohesive whole that had won plaudits in several urban-planning journals. An office tower contained the executive headquarters on its top floor, the sixth, highest in all Dumont (it even sported a winking red beacon on its roof to ward off errant, low-flying aircraft, which struck me as an exaggerated precaution). The tower had been built some thirty years earlier, but Neil's artful rehab of both interior and exterior had energized the glass-and-steel box with a gleaming new look of up-to-the-minute industrial chic.

Doug parked in a visitor's space near the front entrance. As we got out of the car and walked to the building, he said, "I know Tyler Pennell fairly well, but I've never met Perry Schield. Anything I should know about him?"

I paused on the sidewalk. "He's sixty-two and, frankly, not the most dynamic CEO that Quatro's had at the helm. He's really not the right person to lead the company through the challenges it's facing in a brutal business climate. That's why I found it so appealing to bring Gillian into Quatro's management team."

"It sounds as if you were planning to push Schield aside."

"We were," I admitted. "I think Perry understood that, and I don't think it bothered him much. He would end up retiring a few years early. Cashing in a heap of Quatro stock, he'd walk away with millions."

"Except," noted Doug, "that Quatro stock would have become AQC stock, and there was no way to predict its worth."

I gave Doug a knowing grin. "That's an intriguing wrinkle, isn't it?"

I opened the door for him, and we walked through the lobby. The receptionist flashed me a smile, saying, "Good afternoon, Mr. Manning," then returned her attention to a crossword puzzle. I led Doug into a waiting elevator and pushed the top button.

When the doors slid open again, we found ourselves in the hushed, smaller lobby of the executive suite.

"Ah! Mr. Manning. So nice to see you," said Janet, the woman behind the desk. The senior member of Quatro's secretarial pool, Janet had a mound of perfectly coiffed pewter-colored hair, which coordinated nicely with a nubby wool suit of mouse gray. "Had we known you were coming, I'd have posted your name on the welcome board." She adjusted her glasses and peeped at a list on her desk to make sure she hadn't missed something.

"Sorry to pop in unexpected, but I wonder if Perry has a few free minutes."

"Mr. Schield is always pleased to see *you*, Mr. Manning." She knew me as both a board member and a major stockholder. "But I'm afraid he's tied up in a meeting right now."

Doug ventured, "Does he happen to be with Tyler Pennell?"

Janet's eyes popped, as if Doug had performed a psychic feat. "Why, *yes*, in fact, he is."

"Actually," I told her, "we're here to see both of them. Do you suppose we could interrupt? It's important."

She paused a moment to consider my request. "Certainly, sir. They're not in Mr. Schield's office, or I'd announce you. They went to the library." She gestured down a hall.

"I know the way, thanks." I stepped away with Doug.

"Uh, Mr. Manning?" said Janet, penciling something on a log sheet. "Your guest is . . . ?"

"This is Sheriff Pierce."

"Oh." She nodded an uncertain welcome, then glanced down to log him in.

Leading Doug through the hall, I asked, "Did you bring a copy of the letter?" The original was safely stashed in his briefcase, in the car. Lucy had made copies for us, but I hadn't noticed where he'd put his.

He patted the chest of his sport coat. "All set."

Approaching the closed door to the library, a small meeting room decorated with a few books, I lifted my hand, prepared to knock. But Doug gave a tiny shake of his head. "Like I said"—he lowered his voice—"let's surprise them."

So I turned the knob and walked right in with Doug on my heels.

Tyler and Perry were huddled at the end of a long table, comparing notes, (*literally* comparing notes, hunched over files spread open before them). Their silent tableau projected an unmistakably conspiratorial air, and when they saw us enter the room, they appeared not only surprised, but shaken. "Oh, gosh, sorry," I told them. "I must have misunderstood Janet. I thought she said you were in the conference room, but there was no one there, so I just started opening doors."

"No problem, Mark," Perry said awkwardly, rising. "What can I do for you?" He struggled to suppress a cough.

"Doug," said Tyler, also flustered as he rose, "it's been a while. Good to see you again." He crossed the room to shake hands.

"Perry," I said to the older man, "have you met Sheriff Douglas Pierce?"

"Uh, no, I don't believe I've had the honor." He stepped forward, extending his hand.

When we had finished with introductions and some strained pleasantries, Perry, playing host, suggested, "Why don't we all sit down." Then he and Tyler resumed their seats at the end of the table, closing their folders as they sat. They were similarly dressed again, as when I'd met with them in my office on Tuesday morning. Today their business suits were gray, pin-striped, instead of solid navy blue. They really could have passed for father and son.

Doug and I joined them at the table, putting several chairs' distance between us and them. I asked good-naturedly, "Why the meeting, fellas? Due diligence is now moot, isn't it? The merger is off."

Perry nodded gravely. "I just wanted to make my intentions *explicit* to Tyler. With neither my signature nor Gillian's, the deal's off, and that's fine by me."

"He could have read that in this morning's paper." I grinned.

"I did, in fact," said Tyler. "Perry and I still felt the need to touch base on a few issues. Anything wrong with that?" His breezy tone could not fully mask the defensiveness of his words.

"Nothing at all," I told him.

"Mark," said Perry, "I can't believe how close we came to making a colossal blunder." He tapped the thick folder in front of him. "Gillian was up to no good, and I hate to say it, but we were damn lucky she fell from that ladder yesterday. If a fatal accident ever had a silver lining, this is it."

Doug's brow arched; I'm sure mine did as well.

Perry told us, "I'm sorry to sound insensitive, but that's how I feel." Something gurgled in his throat. He covered a cough with his hand, then swallowed.

"Under the circumstances," said Doug, "I can't say I blame you. But I'm surprised to hear you refer to Mrs. Reece's death as a 'fatal accident.' Surely you've heard by now." Doug knew very well that the existence of the letter he was carrying was not yet public knowledge. By implying that it was, he hoped to trip Perry or Tyler into acknowledging that they were aware of the letter, which would be tantamount to confessing to having written it.

But the ploy didn't work. Either Perry and Tyler had rehearsed their shared look of guiltless ignorance, or they were genuinely in the dark.

"Heard about what?" asked Tyler.

Perry added, "Why wouldn't I refer to her death as an accident?"

I explained, "We received an anonymous letter at the *Register* today. The sheriff believes, and I concur, that the letter is compelling evidence that Gillian didn't die by accident. Rather, Gillian may have been pushed from that ladder, and at issue"—I paused for effect—"at issue was the merger."

Predictably, Perry and Tyler reacted to this news with stunned silence.

Notching up the drama of the moment, Doug added, "The writer of the letter was probably the killer."

"Good God," said Perry, running a hand through what was left of his silver hair, "this nightmare just gets worse and worse."

With no apparent emotion other than curiosity, Tyler asked me, "What makes you think the issue behind Gillian's death was the merger?"

"The letter makes it plain that someone didn't want the merger to happen—and with very good reason."

Perry interjected, "A *lot* of us were getting cold feet." Then he swung his head away from us, indulging in a deep, hacking cough.

"According to the letter," said Doug, producing the folded copy from his inside pocket, "Mrs. Reece was less than forthright with her intentions regarding several key aspects of the merger." Both Tyler and Perry craned for a look as Doug unfolded the letter and skimmed through it for a moment in silence. He continued, "If these allegations are true, Mrs. Reece was guilty of attempting some extremely serious business shenanigans, and the big loser"—he paused, folding the letter and returning it to his jacket—"the loser would have been Quatro Press."

Perry whipped the linen handkerchief from his breast pocket and worked up a ball of phlegm.

Tyler asked, "What, exactly, was she up to?"

"That's what I was hoping *you* could explain," said Doug. "I'm a dunce when it comes to the intricacies of business and high finance."

"Me? What would I know about it?"

I answered, "You were performing due diligence, Tyler, and you claimed several times to have discovered 'blips' and 'inconsistencies' in Ashton's books."

"Those were accounting matters—concerning some odd travel expenses and such. It sounds as if *you're* referring to issues deeply embedded in the contractual language."

"That was under your purview as well, wasn't it?"

"It was, but I generally defer those matters to legal counsel. Both Ashton and Quatro were well represented."

I nodded. "Still, it seems strange that with all this talent and all these safeguards, *someone* didn't see through Gillian's scheme. What, you ask, was she up to? Nothing less than the total demise of Quatro Press. She planned to siphon off our assets, technology, and customers, transferring them to another plant offshore. Very quickly, Dumont would be faced with a monumental unemployment problem."

I had assumed, by laying these details bare, I would elicit cries of surprise and outrage, if not from Tyler, certainly from Perry. Instead, they turned to face each other, looking not stricken, but smug.

"You see?" said Perry. "Our worst fears have been realized."

Tyler corrected him, "Our worst fears were *almost* realized."

"I suppose we should be thankful."

"Thankful, sir?"

"The deal's dead." With a snort of laughter, Perry added, "And *so* is Gillian."

"Yes, sir. Thank God."

Eyeing each other, Doug and I decided there was no purpose in prolonging our visit. We stood. Doug said, "Thanks for your time, gentlemen. I'm sorry for the interruption, but we thought you should be made aware of these developments."

"Certainly, Sheriff," said Perry, also standing. "We appreciate the courtesy."

"We do," echoed Tyler, rising. "Thank you, Doug." They shook hands.

I added my good-byes; then Doug and I left. Closing the library door behind us, I heard Perry clear his throat. Tyler said something, but I couldn't make it out.

Doug and I walked the hallway in silence, then wished Janet a terse farewell before stepping into the elevator.

When the doors slid shut, I said, "It's funny, isn't it? Tyler had expressed reservations about vaguely described 'issues' pertaining to the merger, and he managed to raise Perry's concerns as well. But just now, he played dumb when questioned about the extent of his knowledge of Gillian's plan. Why would he claim not to have seen the red flags that were the very object of his due diligence?"

"Good question." Doug furrowed his brow in thought. "One thing's for sure—Tyler Pennell deserves some additional scrutiny."

With a *ding*, the elevator stopped at the ground floor.

"Right," I said. "Something doesn't add up."

Chapter Nineteen

B ack in the car, driving downtown, Doug reminded me that we had dinner plans that evening.

"Do you mind if we include a fourth?" I asked. "We have a houseguest, the curtain guy from Chicago."

"No problem. The more the merrier." After a moment's thought, Doug asked, "A curtain guy, huh? Is he sort of . . . you know?" Doug dangled a limp wrist, a gesture unnatural to him, wondering if our guest was the nellie sort.

"In fact"—I laughed—"he's not."

"Just curious."

Back at the office, I got to work on my editorial for the next morning's paper, but I had trouble pulling it together because of repeated interruptions questioning the makeup of page one. Clearly, receipt of the anonymous letter was big news in Dumont, and since it had been sent directly to the paper, the *Register* could claim a proprietary interest in the matter—we found ourselves sitting on an enviable exclusive. At the same time, however, the letter was in police hands as evidence in a probable homicide case. In the public interest, we felt obligated to play down our treatment of the story, revealing nothing of the specific motive implied by the letter. After several phone conversations with Doug, we reached a consensus regarding the extent of our coverage.

Everyone was satisfied, but I still hadn't finished my editorial for the opinion page.

Realizing I would need to stay late at the office, I phoned Neil and, getting his voice mail, told him that Todd was welcome to join us for dinner and that I would meet them at the restaurant at seven.

I needed every minute. After five, I was able to wrap up my own column handily, but the ongoing modification of the news story itself required repeated tweaking of the front page. When I finally signed off on both the story and the layout, I had a scant two minutes remaining to get to the restaurant. Compulsively prompt (exacting, meticulous me), I dashed through the lobby and decided to drive the few blocks down First Avenue, relieved beyond measure to find a parking space within a few yards of the door. Spotting Neil's car already parked at the curb, I trotted up the sidewalk, ducked under the awning, burst into the restaurant, and checked my watch—seven on the dot.

Flushed with self-satisfaction, I hailed the owner, "Evening, Nancy."

"Good evening, Mr. Manning. My, you seem winded." She eyed me askance, not quite approving. "Mr. Waite and his friend are here, but Sheriff Pierce phoned to say he was running a few minutes late."

"No problem. I'm flexible," I lied as Nancy led me to our table.

Neil and Todd rose to greet me, each of them clapping me in a hug, kissing my cheek. I told them, "Hope you weren't waiting long."

"Just got here," said one of them. "Have a drink," said the other.

I nodded to Nancy, who bobbed her head and went off to pour my usual aperitif, a chilled glass of Lillet.

As we settled at the table, I noted how different the Grill looked at night, especially with autumn well upon us and the sky outside the windows now completely black. Indoors, the lights had been dimmed some, and votive candles flickered at each table, where white linen had replaced the lunchtime butcher paper. Not far from our table, a few logs burned lazily in the fireplace, which lent a note of warmth and approaching winter. Outside on First Avenue, cars zipped by, only their headlights visible. If you squinted, you might have thought you were seated in a faddish bistro on some side street in Chicago (well, maybe Wilmette).

Neil asked, "And how was your day?"

"Eventful." Unfurling my napkin and placing it in my lap, I added, "I'll fill you in later." If we were to discuss details of the Gillian Reece case, now a murder case, I wanted Doug present to set the limits. Turning to Todd, I asked, "How are things going at the house?"

"Moving along nicely—now that you-know-who is out of the picture. We ought to wrap it up sometime this weekend."

"Pleased with the results?"

Neil answered for Todd, "They're *gorgeous*—some of the finest window treatments I've ever seen—not only in Dumont, not only in Wisconsin, but anywhere. They're truly world-class."

"Thanks, Neil." Todd, seated between us, reached for Neil's hand and gave it a friendly squeeze. No doubt about it, they would make a nice-looking couple. Not only did they have similar hair, features, and builds, but that night they had even dressed similarly, in corduroy blazers with leather buttons, perfect for the nippy night. Try as I might, I couldn't squelch the fantasy of bedding both of them.

They rose together, all smiles, leaving me at a momentary loss— were they taking off, ditching me?

"Doug!" said Neil. "Join the party."

Feeling foolish for having missed Doug's entrance, engrossed in thoughts of the corduroy twins, I rose from my chair and joined in the round of hellos.

"Long time, no see," Doug told me, patting my back.

Neil made the formal introduction: "Doug, I'd like you to meet our friend Todd Draper from Chicago."

"Pleased to meet you, Todd." Doug extended his hand.

Neil continued, "Todd, this is Doug Pierce, sheriff of all the land."

Todd shook Doug's hand, growling, "Oooh, a lawman. Are you packing heat?"

"Not tonight." Doug flapped open the side of his sport coat. He wasn't wearing the shoulder holster I sometimes glimpsed by day, but both his phone and his badge were clipped to his belt. He added, "Why do you ask? Expecting trouble?" His tone was beyond congenial; he sounded downright playful. Was it just my imagination, or was some chemistry happening?

"Let's get you a drink, Doug," said Neil, signaling Berta, who was approaching just then with my Lillet. She wore the same stiff white uniform and white hose she wore by day, looking like a plump nurse of yore, replete with a starched white headband bobby-pinned to the front of her hair like a tiara.

Doug asked for Scotch as we settled at the table. Doug sat facing Todd; I faced Neil.

Todd told Doug, "I understand this is your party. Sorry to intrude."

"It's no intrusion at all. Mark and Neil are probably my best friends, so I'm happy to meet *any* friend of theirs."

Neil asked him, "How was your day?"

"Eventful." Doug gave me a knowing glance.

Neil noted, "That's the very word Mark used. What's up?"

I told Doug, "I thought I'd better wait till you got here. I haven't said a thing."

It was now Todd and Neil's turn to exchange a glance. "Good grief," said Todd. "What'd we miss?"

With a quizzical look, Doug said to me, "I appreciate your sense of discretion, but why so hush-hush? I mean, here, among *us?*"

I hesitated. "There's no delicate way to put this, but Todd was among those who had an ax to grind with Gillian."

Todd suddenly looked ashen. Neil looked confused. Doug chuckled. "Okay," he said to me, "I get it. You never bought into the theory that Gillian died accidentally, and prior to this afternoon, you suspected *everyone* who'd recently had a run-in with her."

"Almost everyone," I allowed. I had never seriously considered that Glee Savage might have killed her college foe, but the others were too numerous to sort out—or dismiss.

"Perk up, Todd," said Doug. "The investigation took a surprising turn this afternoon. We now have every reason to believe that Gillian was indeed murdered. And we have *no* reason to believe it had anything to do with draperies."

"Uh," I corrected him, "they're called curtains."

Doug flashed me a puzzled look.

"Murder?" said Neil, cutting to the meat of Doug's story.

Just then, Berta arrived with Doug's Scotch and a set of menus. She prattled through a list of the evening's specials, but none of us listened, wishing either to drink or to continue our discussion. First things first. When Berta had waddled away, I lifted my glass to the others, saying, "To the pleasure of your company."

"The pleasure of *our* company," Todd seconded.

Doug and Neil added toasts of their own; then we drank.

Quickly setting down his glass, Neil repeated, "Murder, Doug? You were saying . . . ?" Todd, also eager to hear details, leaned forward on his elbows.

Doug took another swallow, swirling his drink before telling them, "An anonymous letter arrived at the *Register* today. It contained some disturbing allegations regarding Mrs. Reece's background motives for entering into the merger, and it suggested she was killed to prevent the deal from being finalized." He leaned forward to assure Todd, "It made no mention of curtains."

"God, I *hope* not." Todd flumped back in his chair with a comic sigh of relief.

With a tone of concern, Neil asked, "What did the letter say about Gillian's background motives?"

Turning, Doug deferred the question to me, so I explained what I understood of Gillian's plans to destroy Quatro Press. "Had she succeeded, Dumont's economy would end up in a tailspin. Many jobs would've disappeared, and lots of investors could've lost lots of money."

Todd asked, "Doesn't that mean there are lots of potential suspects?"

I nodded. "In a sense, I'm glad I myself didn't know about Gillian's plot, or I'd have to be considered a logical suspect. My ownership of the *Register* is heavily leveraged with Quatro stock, so I could have lost everything."

"Mark," said Neil, "don't even think such things—let alone say them."

"Fortunately, I have an airtight alibi. I was in a crowded newsroom at the time of Gillian's death."

Neil continued, "I meant, don't say such things about 'losing everything.' Good God, talk about instant devastation. I'm truly stunned by the scope of Gillian's plan."

"Not I," said Todd, shaking his head. "*Nothing* would surprise me about that woman. If you ask me, she got what she deserved."

Neil admitted, "I'm inclined to agree with you."

"Now, hold on," I said. "We're talking about murder, which is *never* justified." Sensing that my righteous words were falling on deaf ears, I decided to take a more pragmatic approach. "Besides, we don't know for a fact that Gillian was plotting all that. The letter's allegations are just that—unproven accusations."

"Actually," said Doug, raising a finger, "we know a bit more than we did earlier. We've checked both the letter and its envelope for fingerprints. As expected, the envelope contains a mess of prints—it tells us nothing."

"But the letter itself?" asked Neil.

"The letter bears the fingerprints of only one person, Lucille Haring, who opened the envelope at the *Register* and was first to read the letter."

Todd looked confused. "So . . . ?"

"The fingerprints don't tell us *who* wrote the letter," Doug explained, "but the absence of prints on the letter does tell us that the writer took considerable caution to conceal his or her identity. It's one thing to sign a letter 'Anonymous,' as any two-bit prankster would do, but to take pains to handle the letter with gloves, that shows real intent—and unless I'm way off base, it also shows guilt. So I think we can take the letter at face value. The writer knew what Gillian was up to, and the writer killed her to thwart her plan."

We sat in silence for a moment. "Hmm," said Todd. "That's fairly sobering." Then he downed a strong slug of his drink.

Berta reappeared, asking if we were ready to order. As none of us had looked at our menus, we asked for more time and ordered another round of drinks.

Trying to puzzle through what Doug had told us, Todd asked, "Can you learn anything by analyzing the letter's handwriting, or was it written on a computer?"

Doug shook his head. "It was neither handwritten nor word processed. The letter was written on a typewriter."

"A *typewriter?*" said Todd. "Nobody uses a typewriter anymore."

With mock defensiveness, Neil informed him, "*I* do."

I laughed. "This was a far cry from your slick Selectric, Neil. The print was so bad, it must have been pecked out on a clunkety manual from Ye Olde Typewriter Museum. The ribbon was so worn, you could barely read the text."

Neil cocked his head. "I wonder if they still make cloth ribbons."

"Beats me," said Doug, "but we've already identified the machine."

"You *have?*" I asked. Todd and Neil looked equally surprised.

Doug clarified, "We've identified the model, not the particular machine. Even in the computer age, typewriter forensics comes in handy now and then. On the basis of the type and a precise measurement of its spacing, we know the machine was a Royal manual from the 1940s. The specific model is rare enough that we stand a chance of tracking it down—unless, of course, it's stashed in the culprit's attic. It'll be a challenge, but we're working on it."

I recalled another instance of a letter typewritten by a killer. Shortly after my arrival in Dumont, my cousin Joey Quatrain had found a portable Smith-Corona from his youth stored with some other junk at the house on Prairie Street. Its cloth ribbon was meant to print either black or red, but because the toggle above the keyboard was faulty, it printed both colors at once; the tops of the letters were black, the bottoms red. That machine, deemed useless, was eventually hauled away in a Goodwill truck with boxloads of other refuse, but not before it had left a crucial clue in helping us determine who had slain Joey's sister, my cousin Suzanne, mother of Thad Quatrain—who was consequently entrusted to my care.

Lost in these memories for a few moments, I hadn't realized that our conversation at the table had shifted topics. Doug was saying, "Sure, sometimes it's lonely, but I knew what I was getting into when I chose this career. Law enforcement is a full-time job."

Todd eyed him skeptically. "We all have full-time jobs, Doug. And plenty of cops have wives or lovers. Where's that special person in your life?"

I knew from experience that questioning along these lines always made Doug squirm, so I fully expected him to skirt the issue of his love life, or lack of it, by steering the discussion down some other course, far less personal. Instead, he exhaled a pensive sigh, answering, "Maybe it's just that tired old excuse—maybe the right man hasn't come along."

"Maybe he hasn't." Todd paused meaningfully. "Or maybe he has."

Neil and I looked at each other wide-eyed. The napkin in his hands was twisted in a knot.

"Suppose I turn the tables," said Doug. "Where's the special person in *your* life—back in Chicago?" I regretted not having filled him in before dinner.

Todd shook his head gently. "There's no one."

I thought Neil would jump in, saving Todd the discomfort of explaining that his lover had died. But Neil was curiously mute, looking distracted, as earlier that day, at lunch, when our conversation had touched on Todd and I had wanted to explore our inhibitions about Todd's come-on.

"There's *no one?*" asked Doug, incredulous. With a broad smile, he added, "What—or who—are you saving yourself for?"

Todd raised both palms. "Let me back up. There *was* someone, named Geoff. But he died in a car wreck a couple of years ago."

"Oh, jeez, Todd, I'm sorry. God, that was clumsy of me. I didn't know—"

"It's okay, Doug. Of *course* you didn't know about it. And guess what. In spite of what happened, your question is no less valid. What *am* I saving myself for?"

Doug reached across the table and touched Todd's hand. "You're just giving yourself some time. I understand." As Doug withdrew his hand, I heard a snap, a spark. Though it was tempting to attribute the sound to the electricity of physical attraction, it had probably emanated from the nearby fireplace.

"I've already given myself some time, Doug." With a soft laugh, Todd recounted, "I had this very discussion with Mark and Neil when I arrived on Tuesday. I explained to them that night, and it's no less true now, that I'm finished grieving. It's time to find someone—or at least have a fling." Todd sat back and crossed his arms with a smug grin. "In fact"—his eyes darted first to me, then to Neil—"I think I shocked our friends here when I suggested last night that a recreational tumble might be in order. It seems they weren't interested."

"No kiddin'?" asked Doug, amused beyond measure.

"No kiddin'. They just weren't interested." Todd leaned forward, asking quietly, "How about you, Doug?"

In the years since I had met Doug, I had known him to connect with another man, physically, only once. It was a fleeting encounter, and it damn near cost him the next election. Since then, he had kept his nose to the grindstone, a single-minded public servant, celibate as a priest (well, bad metaphor). Now here he sat, being openly proposi-tioned by a handsome man—a curtain designer—in the chatty con-fines of the town's best restaurant. I expected him to freak, to flee, or at the very least, to decline Todd's offer in stammering confusion.

But no. He paused in thought, then told Todd, "Stranger things have happened. Time will tell."

Neil's jaw sagged.

As Berta passed by, I caught her eye.

"Yes, Mr. Manning?"

"I think we'd better order now."

Todd reminded her, "And don't forget that second round of drinks."

Chapter Twenty

Dinner was leisurely and, for a weeknight in Dumont, ran much later than our habit. Todd and Doug did most of the talking, and while their conversation was occasionally laced with innuendo, it was less heated than their initial flirtation. Neil and I didn't say much, eating our food without tasting it, speaking when questioned, doing our best to maintain a spirit of conviviality.

My mood had soured, and I wasn't sure why, not exactly. By all appearances, Todd and Doug were hitting it off, and I knew I should feel happy for Doug. Other than Neil, he was my closest friend in Dumont, and I had always felt he was much too wed to his work, that he deserved some love in his life, a touch of romance. While his prospects with Todd were uncertain, they had shared an evident spark of interest, which I knew I should encourage. Todd, after all, was well known to Neil, and I too had come to think of him as a friend, so it was not as if Doug was trifling with a suspicious or unknown character.

Poking at my food, I realized what was troubling me. And this discovery, far from lifting my spirits, only made me more vexed. My uneasiness, I was ashamed to admit, stemmed from base jealousy. The night before, Todd had made a sexual overture to Neil and me, a proposal in which I still found a fitful appeal. Now, before Neil and I had had the opportunity to discuss what had happened and to reach a mutual, honest, reasoned response to this come-on, Todd had shifted gears and made his pitch to Doug Pierce, my best friend.

Compounding my distress was the latent attraction I had always felt for Doug, since the moment when we had met, on Christmas Day nearly four years earlier. I had never allowed expression of this attraction, cloaking it in the bounded intimacy of friendship, but the torch still fluttered, and I still carried it.

So the two guys making goo-goo eyes at each other over the table were the very two guys who had played a role in my fantasies, one of them for years, the other for a day or two. And now they were shutting me out.

The fourth guy at the table I had lived with and loved for nearly six years. Neil was my bedrock, my ultimate fantasy, and my friend. My life, my sense of self, had been redefined in terms of "us." Day-to-day existence was unimaginable without him, so I knew that these other notions—experimenting with the bounds of our relationship—were inherently dangerous. What's more, I felt ashamed for even entertaining the thought that someone else could spice up our sex life. Eight years younger than I, Neil was no slouch in that department, and most men (that is, most sane, gay men) would be blissfully content to be known as his exclusive property in bed.

But he too was troubled. Having been so close to him for so long, I could easily decode his distracted manner, his minimal conversation, his indifference to Nancy's wonderful meal. All of these symptoms mirrored my own, so I knew that he too was struggling with the interplay between Todd and Doug. I was reasonably certain that he had never thought of Doug in any context other than that of friendship. Doug wasn't Neil's type; I was. But so was Todd, and now Neil clearly regretted having dismissed Todd's proposition so quickly and reflexively the night before. The result of all this emotional dithering was that Neil and I were both stuck in a thick stew of doubt. We needed to talk.

At meal's end, when Berta presented the check, Todd made a show of grabbing it and thrusting a credit card into Berta's palm.

"Hey," said Doug, "that's mine."

Todd said firmly, "I want to do this."

"But that's too generous," Doug persisted. "I hardly know you."

"Sure you do. Any friend of Mark and Neil's is a friend of mine."

Doug relented, "Then I owe you one."

"Yeah. I guess you do." Todd's double entendre was none too subtle.

We were last to leave the Grill that night. It was well past nine, and Dumont's main drag was dead. Doug and Todd draggled on the sidewalk for a minute or two, protracting their shared evening with small talk, at last saying good night with a hug; then Doug walked away to his car. Todd had ridden with Neil, and I had brought my own car from the *Register*, so we drove home separately, Neil leading.

Following, I noticed Todd in Neil's passenger seat, his head turned in profile, gabbing away. I reasoned he was asking Neil about Doug, wanting to know *everything*. Neil's head remained aimed straight ahead, eyes on the road. It seemed he had very little to say.

By the time we arrived home, set up the coffeemaker for the next morning, glanced at the day's mail, and locked up the house, it was just past ten. Still on a buzz from meeting Doug, Todd decided to stay up reading awhile.

Pleading fatigue—true enough—Neil and I went upstairs to our room.

We undressed without saying much, then stood together in the bathroom, brushing and flossing. Neil was naked; I always wore a loose pair of old cotton gym shorts during the transitions from daytime dress to bedtime nudity and back again (my sense of propriety, I guess).

After spitting mouthwash into the sink, Neil looked up at me in the mirror, saying, "In case you didn't get the message at the Grill, Todd's got the hots for Doug. I got an earful in the car. Think Doug's really interested?"

"He can be pretty hard to read."

"Yeah." Neil breathed a feeble laugh. "Especially in regard to *that* stuff."

"What stuff?"

With a dramatic swoon and a fluttering of his eyelids, he amplified, "Affairs of the heart."

Happy to see a touch of his old humor, I took him in my arms. "It's awkward for Doug. It seems so difficult for him. I hope he finds some happiness—in regard to *that* stuff."

"What stuff?" With a sly grin, Neil slid his hand down my back, hooking his thumbs under the waistband of my shorts.

Nuzzling the side of his head, I whispered, "Affairs of the heart." I kissed his ear, then slid my tongue into it.

With a groan, Neil went limp in my arms (my tried-and-true mode of foreplay, which seemed at once both simple and daring, never failed). "It's been a busy week," he said, lolling his head on my shoulder.

"Meaning?" I took his head in my hands and brought his lips to mine, indulging in a deep kiss, intensely tasty—cinnamon and mint, our mingled mouthwash flavors.

"Meaning"—he pushed the waistband of my shorts beneath my buttocks—"we've been neglecting each other."

"We've had a lot on our minds." I didn't need to explain that I was referring to Todd Draper.

"*I'll* say." Neil's thumbs circled to the front of my shorts, then nudged them past my penis, which bobbed free, making hot contact with his.

Letting my shorts drop to the floor, I stepped out of them and pulled Neil into a full-body embrace. "This is exactly where we belong."

"Not exactly," he said coyly.

"Hmm?" What, I wondered, did he have in mind? Was he thinking of Todd, downstairs, curled up with a book?

He clarified, "We belong in *bed*." With an exaggerated wink, he reached to switch off the bathroom lights, then led me into the bedroom.

From either side of the bed, we pulled back the comforter and top sheet, dropping them to the floor, giving us a clean canvas, as it were, on which to perform. Neil switched off his bedside lamp; I checked the alarm on the clock radio before switching off mine. Then we both lay down, rolling to the center of the bed.

As our bodies met and we enjoyed another long, probing kiss, I realized that neither of us was erect; somewhere between our first and second kiss, between the bathroom and the bed, we had both lost the prong of arousal. Perhaps the fussing with the bedding and the clock had blindsided our mission. Perhaps the cold sheets had taken a momentary toll. They would soon be heated up, I reasoned, and I was confident that both Neil and I would quickly be sporting an embarrassment of turgid riches, raring to go.

But after some prolonged snuggling, frenching, and general carrying-on, neither one of us had mustered much to work with. I then entertained Neil with another bout of ear-probing, but even that failed to produce the intended effect.

So we both hunkered down for some reciprocal oral stimulation. When we finally abandoned that effort, we were not only limp, but also wet, cold, and hopelessly shriveled. Hell, we even tried basic, old-fashioned hand jobs, both on ourselves and on each other—but still, no go.

What, I wondered, was going on? Deep inside, I already knew the answer. Without budging an inch from his book, Todd Draper had invaded our bed. The time, I sensed, was finally right for the heart-to-heart Neil and I had been postponing.

I let go of his penis and framed his face with my hands. With a smile I hoped he could read in the darkness, I said, "It seems we're both a bit distracted tonight."

"Sorry. I hate to let you down."

"Don't be nuts. It's a mutual thing." After a moment's hesitation, I added, "I know what's on your mind, Neil. Let's talk about this."

There was silence, then an airy sigh. Touching my lips, he said, "I'm so lucky to have you—and so grateful we don't need to keep secrets from each other."

"That's what we're about. It's 'us,' remember? We need to clear the air."

"You're right, Mark"—I sensed him smiling back at me—"and so perceptive. Of *course* I killed Gillian. How did you piece it together?" Rolling away from me, he reached to switch on his lamp.

My eyes crackled at the assault of light.

My brain was spinning.

My heart, I swore, had stopped.

Neil hadn't said much all day, but the floodgates were now open. "You can't imagine what a relief it is to know we can finally *talk*," he was saying as he reached from the foot of the bed and lugged the comforter up from the floor. By then I was sitting up, glassy-eyed and numb. Neil scrunched next to me, sitting with his legs crossed Indian-style, and wrapped us both in the downy duvet. Like kids huddled in a tent, camping in the backyard, I already felt terrified by the ghoulish story I would be told, sure of its outcome without knowing the particulars. Neil said, "I suppose you're wondering exactly how it happened."

"Uh, yeah . . . ," I managed to say, nodding uncertainly.

"Okay, I'll start at the beginning—well, the beginning of the part you don't know, after we both left the Reece house yesterday morning. We'd seen all those blowups with Gillian; then, around nine, you went to the paper. I went looking for Todd to see if I could get him back on the job."

"Todd said you spotted his car at some coffee shop on the edge of town."

"Right. A big Mercedes with Illinois plates—that was a no-brainer. But I didn't think the rest would be so easy. I mean, Gillian had *slapped* him, and frankly, I wouldn't have blamed him if he decided to pull his crew, dump the boxes on Gillian's lawn, send her a bill, and tell her to fuck herself. She deserved no better. But I was in a bind, and Todd— God love him—understood my predicament and took pity. He said he'd finish the job, but *only* if Gillian stayed out of the way till all the curtains were up and the photos were taken. I promised him she would cooperate, then returned to the house to lay down the law. That was sometime after ten."

"Was Glee still there?" My features editor had arrived as we were leaving, and I recalled her telling me later that Gillian had kept her waiting for an hour while rushing the workers to finish their jobs.

Neil shook his head. "Glee's car was gone, and so were all the trucks. But Gillian's Bentley was still parked outside, along with one other car, which I didn't recognize. So I went inside to see what was going on. As far as I was concerned, the job wasn't finished, so I walked through the front door unannounced, hoping to underscore that I still held a measure of authority on the premises. I wasn't two steps inside the foyer, though, when I realized Gillian was at it again."

Warily, I asked, "At what?"

"At someone's throat, bitching up a storm in the living room. She was shrieking at some guy, who was yelling right back. I didn't know his voice, but they were arguing about the merger, and then, when Gillian derided him has 'Twinky Tyler,' I realized he was the guy who's been looking over the agreements."

I nodded. "Tyler Pennell. He was also at the Reece house on Tuesday afternoon, when you first took Glee and me on the tour. It was Tyler who was arguing with Gillian in the living room that day; I broke it up so Gillian could keep her appointment with Glee."

"Ah," said Neil. "Glee and I never saw him; I was showing her around the house. In any event, Tyler returned Wednesday morning, and I heard plenty. Standing in the hall, I wasn't intentionally eavesdropping. They were so loud, it was impossible not to hear them, and their argument was so bitter, it seemed wrong to intrude. So I just stood there and listened. Once I got the gist of their fight, I was so shocked I could barely breathe, let alone move."

"What was it about?" I asked, though I sensed the answer.

"It turns out, Tyler's earlier uneasiness about the merger had motivated him to keep digging, and yesterday morning, he determined that Gillian had been sending some of her people to China on repeated trips, but the travel expenses were apparently disguised somehow. Digging deeper, he found evidence of capital expenditures to a Chinese company that's building a printing plant there. Everything fell together for him, so he returned to confront Gillian with his discovery of her plot. He described it in detail, accusing her of not only bad faith in her dealings with Quatro, but also, probably, criminal intent. The technicalities of their discussion were beyond me, but I heard enough to realize that *your* fortune was in jeopardy, as was the whole way of life we've established here." Neil paused, wrapping an arm around me under the comforter.

"I'll bet Gillian went ballistic."

"Actually, at that point, she seemed to calm down. She must have understood that Tyler knew enough to crush the deal, so—get this— she offered to buy his silence. He laughed at her, but when she named a nice, round six-digit figure, he froze. She told him, 'I see I've caught your attention, Twink. Scruples be damned, huh?' Tyler grumbled that he'd have to think about it, then left. I heard him coming, so I stepped behind one of the double doors as he shot through the foyer. He was so agitated, I'm sure he didn't see me."

"And he said he'd 'have to think about' Gillian's offer of hush money?"

"Those were his very words." Neil continued, "Well, I waited a minute or so for the tension to ease, debating whether I should confront Gillian myself or leave and fill you in. I had just decided to go and find you when I heard Gillian fussing around inside—she was ripping the curtains. *That* got me moving, and I ran into the living room. She was up on the balcony, trying to tear the fringe off the top of the one panel that'd been installed. I shouted up to her that we had to talk, but she said she was busy and told me to leave. Like hell. I climbed the ladder, joining her on the balcony. Grabbing her hand, I told her to leave the curtains alone.

"She said, 'I paid for them, dammit—and I'll trash them if I want.'

"I asked, 'The same way you plan to trash Quatro Press?' She froze, and I repeated the same line she'd used on Tyler: 'I see I've caught your attention.' Then I went on to explain that I'd overheard everything Tyler had discovered, concluding, 'If Tyler doesn't blow the whistle, let me assure you, Gillian—I will.'"

I asked Neil, "*Then* she went ballistic?"

"Nope. Same deal. Cool as can be, she tried to buy *my* silence. I laughed at her offer, telling her there was no amount of money that could entice me to betray the man I'd built my life with. Realizing she couldn't bribe me, she decided to try another tack and threatened to put into effect a backup plan she'd devised. She informed me that she'd planted language in the merger agreement that could be construed in such a way that Perry Schield and Quatro's board members—namely you, Mark—would be seen as parties to a scheme of price-fixing and insider trading, with serious punitive consequences. This sounded like gibberish to me, and I accused Gillian of bluffing. *Then* she went ballistic. Enraged, she hauled off and gave me a bitch slap, a doozy, then backed off, stepping from the balcony to the top rung of the ladder. But I wasn't going to let her leave without a taste of her own medicine. I'd indulged her far too long already. So . . . I slapped her."

"With your right hand? On her left cheek?"

"I guess so. Point is, I must have hit her harder than I intended. She lost her footing *and* her grip, toppling backward. I grabbed for her, but missed. I expected her to scream on her way down, but instead, she used her last breath to call me an asshole. A split second later, she hit the stone floor."

"Good God," I said with a soft gasp.

Neil paused, collecting his thoughts. "I tore down the ladder, calling her name, then gave her body a shake. It was awful, how her head sagged from her neck. Clearly, she was dead. And I was equally convinced that I needed to get out of there—fast. I'm still not sure what the consequences might be if I owned up to what happened, but it would be sticky at best, and I don't want to be hassled with it."

"*Hassled?*" I asked. "A woman died."

"I understand." He nodded resolutely, signaling that he'd thought this through, over and over. "But it's just too hard to untangle. I mean, I didn't go there intending to kill Gillian, so it certainly wasn't murder. When I got there, I learned things that understandably angered me, and we had a confrontation. Her bitchiness and her threats escalated, and finally, she hit me. I hate to sound childish, but it's true—she started it. Then I hit her back. Was it self-defense? I'm not sure. Did I mean to kill her? Of course not. Might I have reasonably predicted she would fall from the ladder as the result of my slap? I just don't know because I didn't have time to think about it before I reacted. Did my slap play some role in her death? Sure. So where does that leave me—in the eyes of the law?"

"I'm not a lawyer," I told him. "I can't sort that out."

"Well, neither could I. So I fled. Do I feel bad about what happened?

Absolutely. On the other hand, I feel no guilt—at least no deep-down, I-was-at-fault sort of guilt. If I can live with it, and no one's the wiser, that's that."

I wanted to tell him, But there are *procedures*. I wanted to lecture, We're a society of *laws*.

"I had that appointment in Green Bay," he continued, "and I was already running late, so I took off. The ninety-minute drive gave me plenty of time to think. What worried me most was not that Gillian had died—there was no fixing that now—but that her scheme was still in place, unexposed. Based on what I'd heard, I had no idea whether Tyler Pennell could be depended on to blow the whistle, and the signing, which needed only one signature for validation, was scheduled for the next day. I myself couldn't expose Gillian's plot without raising suspicions, so I hit upon the idea of sending an anonymous letter to the *Register*. I could spell out exactly what I knew, and I was reasonably sure it would end up in your hands in time to halt the merger.

"Turns out, my meeting with the cabinetmaker was a breeze; I was in and out within thirty minutes. He's located on the outskirts of the city, so I drove downtown and found a used-office-equipment store, where I bought an old typewriter, the Royal, for practically nothing. Then I went to a supermarket and bought stationery and envelopes. Next, I stopped at a drugstore and bought latex gloves. Finally, I found a quiet park, where I wrote the letter at a picnic table.

"Driving back from Green Bay, I tossed the typewriter into a weedy ditch along an empty stretch of rural highway. Arriving back in Dumont shortly before five, I mailed the letter at the post office, confident you'd receive it the next morning. Then I came home—and helped you and Todd fix dinner." With his story told, Neil flopped back on the bed, nesting in the pile of pillows that had been disarrayed by our foiled attempt at lovemaking.

Wryly, I noted, "You were quite the busy boy yesterday." Though I was dismayed and shaken by my knowledge of what had happened, I had to admit that he'd planned his strategy well and executed it deftly—the merger had come to a crashing halt, and I'd been clueless to his role in it.

He locked his hands behind his head, grinning up at me. "Proud of me?"

"Neil," I reminded him, "Gillian died."

"I mean, the rest—the letter and all."

"It's all kind of . . . complicated." Sitting there like a baby wrapped in a blanket, I couldn't find a more explicit word, an expression sufficiently neutral, to convey the maelstrom of concerns and emotions that cluttered my mind.

"The important thing is"—he pulled me down next to him—"we're back on the same page again. You were so right, Mark. We *did* need to clear the air." He gave me a kiss.

"Talking is good," I agreed vaguely, feeling inane.

He pulled the covers up around us, tucking us in for the night. "You haven't answered my original question. So tell me: How did you piece it together?" Reaching over to his nightstand, he turned off the light.

I felt eerily adrift in the blackened room, as if bobbing on a dark, vast sea. Clearing my throat, I attempted a casual laugh, asking, "What makes you think I was able to piece it together?"

"Well," he recalled, "when the sex didn't happen, you said it didn't matter because you knew what was on my mind. You encouraged me to talk about it."

"Neil"—I turned to face him in the dark, resting my hand on his chest—"it seems we both had our signals crossed. I'm ashamed to admit this, but I thought you were upset that Todd came on to Doug at dinner tonight."

"Why would *that* bother me?"

I didn't want to explain that I'd been laboring under the mistaken notion that Neil had been considering Todd's proposed three-way—clearly, I'd been off by a mile—so I simply told him, "When Todd got flirtatious with Doug tonight, that's when *you* became quiet and withdrawn."

"Ohhh. No, Mark, I barely noticed what was going on between Todd and Doug. Just before that, Doug had been talking about the anonymous letter. He said he'd concluded that it was written by the killer. He said they'd determined the exact model of Royal typewriter the killer had used. And he expressed his intention to track down the actual machine. *That's* why I clammed up. I'd been having those worries all day."

It all made sense. Feeling foolish, I rolled onto my back, staring up toward the ceiling I couldn't see. The issue of Todd Draper's bedtime inclinations, which had weighed so heavily on my mind, now struck me as very minor indeed.

"Hey . . . ," said Neil, sounding suddenly wary. "Then you really *didn't* know—about Gillian, about me."

I swallowed. "No, Neil. I had no idea."

"But you do understand, don't you?" He sat up.

"Understand what?"

"Why I did what I did—you understand that, right?"

I didn't have an answer.

"Mark"—he leaned over me, grasping my shoulders—"tell me I can count on you to keep the writer of that letter anonymous. I *can* trust you, can't I?"

I didn't have an answer.

PART FOUR

Controlling Interest

JUSTICE ON TRIAL

Executive's death must not be dismissed as payback for deceit

by MARK MANNING
Publisher, Dumont Daily Register

OCT. 24, DUMONT, WI—Disturbing developments of the last two days have taken a toll on Dumont's business community, stretching our emotions in opposing directions.

On Wednesday, the untimely death of Ashton Mills executive Gillian Reece, killed in an apparent accident at her new home, sent shock waves through corporate offices throughout the county. Not only had a major local industry lost its shining star, but a long-awaited merger between Ashton Mills and Quatro Press was dashed.

Then, on Thursday, receipt of an anonymous letter (as reported on the front page of today's *Register*), revealed that Mrs. Reece had concocted a heinously greedy scheme that would effectively destroy Quatro Press and a significant portion of Dumont's economy. Further, the letter persuaded Sheriff Douglas Pierce that Mrs. Reece's death was anything but accidental, and he is now in the midst of a murder investigation.

The temptation might be great to shift Wednesday's sympathies for the deceased Mrs. Reece to the author of the letter received Thursday. Some might perceive the anonymous writer as a hero, a contemporary Robin Hood who has exposed and slain an enemy of the community.

To lionize a killer, however, is to abandon every notion of law and due process, which must remain cornerstones of any society deemed civilized. The taking of human life is the greatest of wrongs.

Gillian Reece is to be memorialized today in a private service for family and close business associates. In laying her to rest, it must be remembered that her failings do not justify her tragic end.

The age-old maxim has never rung truer: two wrongs don't make a right. ❏

Chapter Twenty-one

During my quarter century of practice as a professional journalist, I'd had my fair share of brushes with unexplained death. Working on the assumption—or the knowledge—that a wrong had been committed, I had understood that my role as a communicator was to work in tandem with law enforcement, but apart from it, assisting the investigation in any way possible while taking pains not to intrude upon it. In that way, the public's "right to know" has always been best served. Such is the traditional function of the press, the so-called fourth estate.

From a journalist's perspective, my career had been inordinately fruitful in that I had often landed news assignments whose outcomes carried a measure of social import. Like so many other eager students pursuing journalism in college, I had been inspired by the intrinsic romance of the profession. My goal had not been simply to be involved with reporting, but to be challenged by reporting that matters. Few news stories capture the public interest more readily than an unsolved murder. I'd been lucky—many such mysteries had carried my byline.

By most accounts, I had handled those stories well, both in their writing and in the background research that had brought them to print. I had quickly learned that stories of mysterious death follow a predictable pattern. It begins when a body is discovered, and it ends only after a laborious process of interviews, digging, and deduction, when the culprit is finally named. There had been little variation to this routine.

Sometimes the killer had been identified on the basis of hard evidence, with no wriggle room. At other times, when the evidence had been compelling but sketchy, I had coaxed or even tricked the suspect into a flummoxed admission of guilt. Never, though, had the responsible party taken *me* unawares by gushing a spontaneous, detailed account of the victim's death, as Neil had done on Thursday night. His confession was all the more remarkable because he had delivered it while lying naked with me in bed.

There is indeed a first time for everything.

Now, Friday morning, as I walked downstairs from our bedroom, I struggled to reconcile my future course of action with my new knowledge of what had happened to Gillian Reece. For me, suddenly, the central question of the case was no longer whodunit, but how to deal with it.

My every instinct told me Neil was bound by principle to come clean, but he had flatly rejected that option, arguing that the expediency of remaining silent far outweighed the ethical niceties of submitting his tangled circumstances to the scrutiny of blind justice. Though I could understand his reasoning, I found it difficult to accept. So the great, looming question was this: If Neil was not inclined to go public with his admission, and if I failed to convince him otherwise, would I be morally compelled to take matters into my own hands? In other words: Would I rat on my own lover?

I, after all, was the guy who played by the book and followed the rules. Not two days earlier, I had scolded the local sheriff for driving ten miles over the limit. Just a day ago, my features editor had chided me for being too principled to tell a white lie about being on deadline. My sense of decorum would not allow me to stand naked in my own bathroom—proper, priggish me. And now, this morning, the entire town was reading my high-minded words demanding that Gillian Reece's killer be brought to justice.

There was a moral in there somewhere, but as I crossed the front hall toward the kitchen, I was damned if I could see it.

"Hey, Mark! Morning!" said Doug as I entered the kitchen. He looked chipper and freshly showered, sitting at the table with a big, gooey kringle he had picked up on his way from the gym. Next to the pastry was the latest edition of the *Register*, folded open to my editorial. Tapping the paper with one hand (the other held a flaky wedge of kringle, bleeding raspberry jam from its edge), he told me, "Strong stuff. You didn't mince words. Well said." With a nod of approval, he chomped the tip off his Danish.

Neil turned from the counter, where he was pouring coffee, and gave me a smirk—he'd read the paper.

"Well," I waffled, "it may have been a bit heavy-handed. I wrote it late yesterday in the heat of the moment." For Neil's benefit, I added, "Didn't mean to come across as such a hard-liner."

Doug squinted at the paper, then at me. "Nothing wrong with a hard line—especially when you're dealing with murder."

It wasn't murder, I wanted to tell him. I didn't even think it was manslaughter. But I couldn't tell Doug such things without telling him the rest, and although I had given Neil no absolute assurance that his secrets were safe with me, he could reasonably assume my loyalty, so I said nothing. Besides, I hadn't had my coffee yet. If I was going to tussle with a moral dilemma in my kitchen that morning, I needed to have all cylinders firing.

Neil brought three mugs of coffee to the table. Adroitly shifting topics, he asked me, "Any stirrings upstairs?"

"Not yet." Joining them at the table, I told Doug, "Todd stayed up late last night, reading."

At the mention of Todd's name, Doug's face brightened. "What a great guy—but I wish he hadn't paid for dinner. Thanks for introducing us."

Neil grinned. "It seems you two . . . hit it off."

"Oh?" asked Doug, trying not to sound too eager. "Did he say anything?"

"Not much," Neil fibbed. "But I think he had a good time."

"Know what? So did I. Todd's so . . . *interesting.* I mean, a *curtain* designer. Who'd have thought?"

Dryly, I answered, "Surely not I."

Neil flashed me a dirty look, then told Doug, "Sometimes people just click. There's no predicting when you might fall for someone—or who it might be."

Doug nearly choked on his coffee. "Hey," he said, setting down the mug, "who said anything about 'falling for' anyone?" His embarrassed smile admitted the very assertion he sought to deny.

"Oh, brother." Neil reached for a slice of kringle, telling Doug, "Your bluffing skills could use a little work."

"Well," he admitted, sounding a tad giddy (this was totally out of character for our butch local lawman), "let's just say Todd took me by surprise. I was expecting dinner with friends, which is always pleasant, but nothing unusual. I wasn't quite prepared for what . . . 'happened.'"

Good God, I realized, something had indeed "happened"—something like unforeseen chemistry.

As Doug and Neil pattered on in this vein, it was apparent that Neil was not the least bit troubled by Doug's interest in Todd; in fact, he was actively encouraging it. Now that I knew I'd been ridiculously off base in interpreting Neil's recent distracted behavior, I reminded myself that the Todd issue was resolved. Neil had no interest in him sexually, so it was time for me to dismiss those thoughts as well.

But it wasn't that simple or logical. I was dealing with other emotions that Neil didn't share. Namely, my years of unspoken attraction to Doug had provided an agreeable fantasy that still bubbled at a slow simmer just below the surface of our friendship. In a sense, Neil's friendship with Doug was purer than mine, untainted by that whiff of lust, so he could easily—eagerly—step into the role of matchmaker. I, on the other hand, found myself egotistically peeved that Doug's affections were being boxed up, bound in ribbons, and handed over to the hunky, sandy-haired curtain maker from Chicago.

These feelings were shameful, I knew. Rationally, they couldn't be justified, but emotionally, I couldn't shake them. I was still dealing with Neil's revelations of the previous night, so my unresolved concerns about death and culpability merited far more brain space than my niggling hots for either Todd *or* Doug. I could deal with them later.

For the moment, I decided, our breakfast conversation would serve a more pressing purpose if it focused more on Doug's investigation and less on his swooning.

"So, Doug," I said, moving my coffee aside and leaning forward on the table, "where are we with regard to Gillian Reece?"

Both Doug and Neil were instantly sobered. Neil got up and stepped to the counter to get the coffeepot. Doug said, "We're making some progress on the typewriter front."

"Oh?" asked Neil, returning to the table, pouring for each of us.

"Maybe 'progress' is an overstatement, but now, at least, we have a solid plan for pursuing that aspect of the case."

"Last night you said the typewriter was probably stashed in the culprit's attic." Neil set the pot on the table and sat again.

"That's still a good possibility, and if so, we'll never find it—I can't get a search warrant for every attic and basement in town. But there's another possibility. Suppose the killer got hold of an old typewriter for the specific purpose of creating an 'untraceable' letter. Where would he get it, if not from his own attic? A garage sale, maybe. Or an antique shop. Or a store that sells used office equipment."

Neil glanced at me.

Doug continued, "We know the letter was written sometime Wednesday between eleven, when the victim was killed, and five, when the letter was postmarked. We determined there were no garage sales in Dumont on Wednesday, so we checked local shops that might carry old typewriters. Not only had no one *sold* a typewriter in Dumont lately, but no one had even had one in the store."

Neil noted, "It sounds as if you've hit a dead end."

"Probably, but think about it—just because Gillian was *killed* in Dumont and the letter was *mailed* in Dumont doesn't necessarily mean the letter was *written* in Dumont. There was a six-hour window during which the killer could have easily left town. The way I figure, he could have driven anywhere within a two-hour radius, leaving plenty of time to buy the typewriter, write the letter, and drive back to mail it. The only cities of any size within that radius are Appleton and Green Bay, so it's worth making a check of shops in those towns." Doug swirled the coffee in his mug, then took a swallow.

Neil looked dazed and ashen.

Through a ticklish cough, I told Doug, "Sounds like a long shot."

"It is, but if anyone sold a forties-model Royal two days ago, they're sure to remember it and can probably give a good description of the buyer. That alone wouldn't stand up as hard evidence, but I think we could build a strong circumstantial case around it."

Neil was speechless as Doug detailed his plans to identify both the machine and the person who had written the letter that said Gillian Reece deserved to die.

I felt tongue-tied myself, at once both sympathetic to Neil's dilemma and annoyed that he had let it mushroom out of control. It was upsetting enough that he had played a role, unwitting or not, in Gillian's death. But it was worse that he had not immediately owned up to it—and worse still that he had concocted a cloak-and-dagger scheme to justify the incident through an anonymous letter, a ploy that Doug seemed poised to blow wide open. I was tempted, then and there, to halt the discussion and to prod Neil, point-blank, to tell Doug everything he knew. I reasoned, however, that Neil's interests would be far better served if he arrived at that conclusion himself and voluntarily came clean with Doug.

So I waited. But so did Neil, saying not a word.

I was getting antsy, squirming in my chair. What's more, I had begun to feel dizzy and light-headed—I was probably hyperventilating—either that, or I'd had too much caffeine. I *had* to say something. If Neil wasn't going to straighten out this mess, I felt ethically compelled to do so myself. At what point, I tried to decide, did my civic duty take precedence over my loyalty to Neil? Did my silence not make me as guilty as he? And what exactly, I wondered, was he guilty of? Slapping a woman? Not signing his mail?

Doug was saying, "But that's not the only development."

Now what? My shoulders slumped.

"Hmm?" said Neil, emerging from his own thoughts.

"After leaving the restaurant last night, I was a little keyed up, so I decided to go down to the department and check my desk. Turns out, Tyler Pennell had left me a message saying he needed to talk to me. When I called him back, he said he wanted to see me and offered to come to the station. Then, when he arrived, he announced he was prepared to make a statement and get something off his chest."

"He *confessed?*" asked Neil. Wishful thinking—both Neil and I already knew the forensic accountant had played no role in Gillian's death.

"Tyler was feeling guilty, all right, but not about the murder. He just needed to do some soul-baring. According to his statement, Tyler had indeed discovered all the details of Gillian's plot to enrich Ashton Mills—and herself—at the expense of Quatro Press and its workers."

I recalled, "That wasn't his story when we talked to him at Quatro headquarters yesterday afternoon. He claimed to know no particulars of Gillian's plan."

"And that's what he was feeling guilty about. He told me he'd gotten scared and had lied to us Thursday."

Neil asked, "What was he scared of?"

"The appearance of deeper guilt. Here's his version of what happened: Tyler's due diligence had revealed the full extent of Gillian's intended shenanigans, so he went to her new home on Wednesday morning to confront her with his discovery. That was around ten-thirty, after all the workers left. He found her in the living room, and they talked. Then they argued, and it got pretty heated. Tyler threatened to kill the deal. Gillian must've known he had the goods on her—she offered to buy him off. The sum was interesting enough that Tyler said he'd have to think about it, then left. He insists that Gillian was alive and well when he walked out of the house, sometime before eleven."

Neil asked, "And there was no one else around?"

"Tyler wishes there *had* been a witness to corroborate his story, but he was agitated and left in a hurry, seeing no one. When the news broke that Gillian had been killed around eleven that morning, Tyler knew this would cast suspicion on his visit, so he simply clammed up about it. Even stickier, to his way of thinking, was his consideration of the bribe, which could ruin his career as an impartial auditor of corporate finances. Unfortunately for Tyler, the bribe is crucial to his story—it provides the explanation of why he left when he did. When he learned yesterday about the letter and its contents, he feared, logically enough, that this aspect of the case would eventually lead back to him, so he decided his best course of action was to correct his earlier lie and tell me everything."

Eyeing Neil, I told Doug, "Wise move."

Doug nodded. "It was. Tyler's story doesn't conclusively clear him of being at the house when Gillian was killed, but it's a plausible, consistent scenario, and it's a reasonable explanation for his suspicious behavior yesterday. Most important, he *volunteered* his statement last night, so I'm inclined to believe him. He's still a potential suspect, but my instincts now lead me away from him. Someone *else* must have arrived at the house after he left—or while he was there, overhearing details of Gillian's scheme. With any luck, we'll track'm down." Sitting back, Doug concluded, "I'm working on it."

This, I hoped, would give Neil the nudge he needed to tell Doug what had happened. Instead, he got up from the table, went to the sink, and rinsed his cup.

Doug pushed back his chair and stood. "I'd better get going. Busy day ahead. Will I see you guys at the memorial?"

I stood. "Sure, Doug. Esmond invited us. We'll be there."

Turning from the sink, Neil added, "It's the least we can do. Not only was Gillian a wonderful client, but I thought of her as a friend."

Doug said, "From everything I've heard about the woman, she was lucky to have even *one* good friend in the world. It'll be interesting to see who shows up." He moved to the back door.

"See you there, Doug. And thanks for the kringle."

"Anytime, guys." Saluting us with a thumbs-up, he opened the door and left.

Taking Doug's and my coffee mugs from the table, I stepped behind Neil and, reaching around him, poured the cold coffee into the sink.

Setting down the cups, I wrapped my arms around Neil's waist. Softly, I said into his ear, "If you give Doug a few minutes, you can probably reach him in his office."

"Why would I do that?"

"He was willing to give Tyler the benefit of the doubt because he volunteered his story. Connect the dots, Neil."

He turned to me. "Tyler's situation was *nothing* like mine. He decided to talk because he *hadn't* been in the house when Gillian was killed; he was trying to prove his innocence. Exactly what do you think I have to gain from opening up to Doug? I was *there*, Mark, arguing with Gillian when she fell and died. If some hotshot prosecutor put the right spin on this, he could decide that I had not only witnessed Gillian's death, but caused it. Is that what you want?"

"Of course not."

"Then why in hell should I say a word about this to Doug?"

I couldn't think of a convincing answer.

But I knew I was right.

Chapter Twenty-two

Gillian Reece's private memorial service was scheduled for eleven o'clock at, of all places, the Dumont Institute for Eastern Studies. The day before, when Esmond Reece had phoned me at my office to invite Neil and me to attend, I had asked, dismayed, "Couldn't you find a . . . a church or something?"—this from a man who had even less interest in churches than in Eastern studies.

Esmond had replied, "I realize, Mark, that the institute may not seem the most appropriate setting for Gillian's memorial, considering her recent hostility toward the project. But it's often been noted that funerals are more for the benefit of the living than the dead, and the grounds of the institute are where I'm most comfortable. Besides, Gillian won't even *be* there. The coroner hasn't released her body yet. When he does, I'll have it cremated."

Neat and simple.

Sometime after ten-thirty, I swung past Neil's office, picked him up, and drove out beyond the west side of town. We didn't say much, each of us lost in thought.

Heavily on my mind was Doug's intention to investigate typewriter sales in Green Bay and Appleton. I recalled that Glee Savage had gone to Appleton after visiting Gillian on Wednesday, intending to interview a woman about a hospital fund-raiser, but they had never connected.

Glee, of course, had delivered the first bitch slap—an opening salvo that would escalate into a nasty little war—on Tuesday afternoon. Might these circumstances be sufficient, I wondered, to deflect suspicion from Neil, who was not generally known to have fought with Gillian on Wednesday or to have traveled to Green Bay that same afternoon?

The road blurred, and I slowed the car as I was overcome with disgrace. How could I possibly be scheming to pin responsibility for Gillian's death on my perky, loyal features editor? Besides, the other facts of the case didn't fit. Doug would have a tough time proving that Glee had bought a typewriter in Appleton—because it simply never happened.

Shaking these thoughts from my head, I saw the institute's twiggy sign come into view. There were quite a few vehicles parked on the roadway, indicating that the gravel parking court within the compound was already filled.

"Wow," said Neil, "I didn't realize there'd be such a crowd."

"Me neither." Braking the car and pulling over to the shoulder, I added, "When Esmond phoned yesterday, he was still working on the guest list. I assume there'll be a lot of the higher-ups from Ashton Mills. Beyond that, who knows?"

We got out of the car, stretched our legs, and began walking along the row of parked cars toward the driveway. Neil noted, "It's strange that Esmond would invite Todd and Glee." Our houseguest's Mercedes and my editor's eye-popping fuchsia hatchback were among the vehicles at the side of the road. Neil continued, "They've both had recent blowups with Gillian. That's pretty perverse, almost as if Esmond is taking pleasure in inviting his wife's 'enemies' to her own memorial."

Entering the grounds of the institute, we walked the pine-lined drive toward the clearing near the main building. The crisp fall day felt even chillier in the shadows of the dense, pungent trees. Arriving in the parking court, we found that it was indeed already filled with cars—smells of petroleum mixed with the scent of pine, a combination I found surprisingly pleasant.

Despite the plenitude of cars, we saw no people, so we assumed everyone was indoors somewhere. Then Neil spotted a carelessly scrawled sign, posted near the door of the main building. He read aloud, "Memorial in drumming circle." An arrow pointed to the path I had walked during my visit on Tuesday afternoon.

Neil asked, "What's a drumming circle?"

Slinging an arm across his shoulders, leading him around the building, I answered, "A circle in which one drums."

"Oh." He knew there was no point in pressing me for details.

We followed the narrow path of matted pine needles, ducking occasionally beneath errant, low-hanging limbs. Nearing the circular clearing, we could hear the muffled sound of many voices engaged in quiet conversation.

Entering the circle from the dim pathway, I was momentarily blinded. Though the sun had begun its autumnal decline, it was high enough in the midday sky to enter the surrounding chimney of trees in a brilliant oblique shaft. The trees it touched were radiantly green; the others, in contrast, looked inky black.

The fire pit at the center of the circle contained the remnants of more charred logs than on Tuesday. Had Esmond and Tamra spent their nights here—watching the moon, planning their future, celebrating the demise of a woman who had obligingly stepped out of their lives? Esmond and Tamra stood across from the pit, at the far side of the circle, dressed as I had always seen them, she in white, he in a dark shade of gray. Since neither Gillian's body nor ashes would be present, I expected a photo of the deceased, perhaps on an easel, but there was nothing to represent the woman we gathered to remember.

The mourners (the usual term, though it seemed not entirely apt) were loosely assembled around the pit in a crescent. The crowd was deepest where we entered from the path, thinnest at the tips of the crescent, leaving plenty of room for Esmond and Tamra, who stood without speaking, wearing benign smiles.

Working our way into the crowd, I noticed Tyler Pennell and Perry Schield, two of the "enemies" Neil had referred to. They stood together in their matching business suits, looking uncomfortable among the many Ashton Mills executives and board members who were present. A day earlier, Perry and Quatro Press had been scheduled to join ranks with these people, but now, as the result of Tyler's discovery, there was nothing but bitterness between the two corporations. Perry dabbed at his mouth with a wadded white handkerchief, looking flushed and feverish in the cool, woodsy air.

"This is fine," I told Neil, preferring to stand at the outer edge of the circle, near the trees, about halfway in. If Esmond and Tamra's position in the circle were deemed twelve o'clock, the path would be at six and we at nine.

Because of my seat on the Ashton board, I knew almost everyone present, while Neil knew very few of them. We spotted Glee Savage near one of the crescent's tips (eleven o'clock). She discreetly waved her steno pad, indicating she intended to bring back a story. Directly across the fire pit from us (three o'clock) stood Todd Draper, who also acknowledged us with a wave. He tapped his watch and bobbed his head from side to side, indicating he wished they'd get on with it—he wanted to get back to the Reece house and the curtain-installation project.

I mimicked Todd's head-bobbing, indicating that I sympathized—I would rather have been just about anywhere but there. Checking my watch, I realized that our impatience was warranted. It was a few minutes past eleven.

As if on cue (maybe their Eastern studies had honed their psychic skills), Esmond and Tamra stepped in unison toward the pit of charred rubble. Sensing that the service had begun, the crowd instinctively hushed.

"I want to thank you all for coming," said Esmond. His voice was clear, strong, and confident, not that of a man in mourning, but that of a man who had been liberated. "While the recent passing of my wife, Gillian, was both unexpected and untimely, we can take comfort in the knowledge that all events—inscrutable as they may seem—are part of a plan." He then repeated a statement he'd made on the afternoon when he'd learned of the fall that had killed his wife: "Her death has restored a certain harmony to the absolute."

No one present could mistake the tone of Esmond's words—he was happy to chalk off Gillian's sudden death as a twist of fate, a mere quirk of cosmic energies. He ignored the developments of the previous day, the anonymous letter that seemingly proved his wife's death was no accident. While I found a measure of relief in this omission (the writer of the letter stood at my side), I was nonetheless disquieted by Esmond's singular lack of interest in the details of how his wife had died. For all he cared, she could have been struck by a lightning bolt or a falling safe—she was simply gone, which suited him fine, and that was all that mattered.

As Esmond spoke, my attention drifted and my eye wandered. Glancing toward the path (six o'clock), I saw Doug Pierce enter the drumming circle and pause to get his bearings. Giving him a high sign, I caught his attention, and he began making his way toward us, around the back of the crowd.

Joining Neil and me, he shook hands with us and asked, under his breath, "Did I miss much?"

"Not a thing," I answered. "It's the damnedest 'funeral' *I've* ever seen."

Neil added, "Esmond hasn't even mentioned the suspicious nature of Gillian's death. If only for the sake of appearances, he ought to fake some remorse."

Doug arched his brows. "Do you think Esmond has something to hide?"

Neil instantly backed off. "No, I have no reason to think that."

"Well, *someone* has something to hide. Gatherings like this always make you wonder: Is the killer here among us?"

Near the fire pit, Esmond was saying, ". . . which is why it's so comforting to have friends at a time like this. In recent years, I have had no greater friend than Tamra Thaine, founder and director of the Dumont Institute for Eastern Studies. In the coming weeks and months, you'll be hearing far more about this wonderful new addition to the social— and spiritual—fabric of our community. Today, you'll have the opportunity to meet Tamra for yourselves and to hear her inspiring words. It's my pleasure to introduce Tamra Thaine, who will preside over the remainder of this memorial."

Esmond stepped back, and the woman in white leotards and tunic stepped forward, as if trading places in front of a microphone that wasn't there.

"Good morning," she said in a flat tone that was neither inviting nor off-putting, warm nor cool. "Esmond has asked me to contribute a few thoughts to this gathering. While I did not know Gillian Reece all that well, I can say without hesitation that her greatest fortune in life was her relationship with Esmond Reece." Tamra turned to flash him a timid but loving smile, then continued, "It is through the good heart and generous spirit of people like Esmond that we come to know the divine consciousness of this world. In fact, Esmond has recently committed to underwrite fully the development of this institute as a gift to all of Dumont . . ." Tamra had plenty more to say, but she did not again mention Gillian, even once.

As she yammered on, the crowd began to get restless, like kids squirming in church. Neil nudged Doug, saying quietly, "Todd's here. Did you see him?"

Doug asked too loudly, "*Where?*" Then he hushed himself. "No, I didn't see Todd. Where is he?"

Neil directed Doug's gaze across the fire pit to the three o'clock position, where Todd craned his neck to peer back at us, giving Doug a subtle but eager wave.

Doug's face brightened as he mouthed silent, unintelligible greetings to Todd across the gap that separated them. They began an exchange of looks, shrugs, and smiles that simulated conversation but communicated only that they were glad to have established a sense of connection, however remote or tenuous.

"It's rare in life," Tamra was saying, "that we encounter a person who so perfectly embodies both the intuitive and intellectual polarities of our existence. Esmond Reece, however, is truly at one with the universe, possessing an essential nature and an internal heat that harmonize with the dynamic aspect of consciousness . . ."

Yeah, maybe, I thought, but he won't eat meat.

Someone's cell phone went off.

Tamra continued with her tribute, undaunted but annoyed, as the insistent chirp sent a wave of distraction through the crowd. Purses snapped; men dug in their pockets; various mourners turned away from the sunlight, attempting to read the displays on their phones. I double-checked my own phone, confirming that I had switched it off, when I realized the ringing came from Doug's belt. So engrossed had he become in his mimed colloquy with Todd, he hadn't even heard the offending warble.

I jabbed him with my elbow. "Your phone."

"Oh, jeez. Sorry." He unclipped the phone from his belt, checked the display, and said, "Excuse me. I need to take this." Answering the phone, he made his way behind the crowd and left the drumming circle, following the path to the parking area.

Tamra droned on, ". . . through the extraordinary generosity of Esmond Reece. This ashram will become a place of retreat for seekers wishing to escape the fatigue of worldliness. By engaging in spiritual practices . . ."

I nudged Neil. "Heard enough?"

"I'll say."

Jerking my head toward the pathway, I said, "Let's get out of here." We skirted the crowd as Doug had done, then left the circle.

Tramping along the shady path, Neil said, "What'd you think of Tamra's 'tribute' to Gillian?"

"It was good of her to mention the woman's name—once."

"You'd think she and Esmond would be smarter than that. I mean, neither of them cared for Gillian, and I suppose their reasons for resenting her were justified, but today, they all but trashed her. Don't they realize their tacky performance is bound to cast *them* in a suspicious light?"

"Apparently not." Then I added, meaningfully, "They know *they* weren't involved with Gillian's death."

I wanted to engage Neil in a discussion of *his* involvement, not to mention my own growing complicity in the cover-up, but we were reaching the end of the path. A bright patch of sunlight lay just ahead, made all the more dazzling by the glint of chrome from cars parked in the courtyard.

Emerging from the pines, we spotted Doug in the clearing among the cars, phone to his ear, nodding in conversation. As we approached, he flipped the phone shut and returned it to his belt, asking us, "Did Tamra wrap it up already?"

I shook my head. "Still hard at it. We lost interest."

Neil asked him, "Going back in?"

"Nah, why bother?"

Tentatively, I asked Doug, "Didn't you find the memorial . . . peculiar? Esmond and Tamra couldn't come up with a single kind word about Gillian."

He shrugged. "I guess they hated her, but I doubt they killed her—not unless one of them bought a typewriter in Green Bay."

Neil and I exchanged a glance. One of us asked, "What do you mean, Doug?"

He grinned. "Just heard from one of my deputies; that long shot paid off. He was phoning around Green Bay and Appleton, and he found a store in Green Bay that sold an old Royal on Wednesday afternoon. I'm driving over there today to question the clerk myself." Doug had risen through the ranks of his department as a detective, and he still liked to step in when a case caught his interest.

Neil and I were dumbstruck. Fortunately, Doug's attention was diverted just then by Todd Draper, who emerged from the pines whisking needles from his hair and his clothes.

"Doug!" said Todd. "There you are—I was hoping to bump into you today."

Doug crossed the parking lot, not quite running (but almost), meeting Todd near the entrance to the main building. They shook hands awkwardly, then leaned together for a brief, stiff hug.

As Neil and I approached them, Doug told Todd, "Thanks again for dinner last night. I wish you hadn't—"

"Stop that." Todd laughed. "I enjoyed it."

"Well, point is, I owe you one. Not sure how long you plan to be in town, so how 'bout tonight? Can I take you to dinner?"

"Of *course*." As a not-so-subtle aside, Todd told Neil and me, "I was hoping he'd ask."

Doug told him, "I have business in Green Bay this afternoon, so I don't know when I'll be back, but seven should be safe. Suppose I meet you somewhere?"

"Sounds great."

Doug's invitation had pointedly been addressed to Todd solo. Nonetheless, I piped in, "Why don't we have dinner at the house? You've already eaten at the Grill, the best place in town, so anything else would be a letdown. We'll cook for you guys. That way, it won't matter if Doug runs early or late in Green Bay."

"You don't need to do that," Doug said pleasantly, with no apparent disappointment.

"We insist," said Neil, ever the cordial host.

Todd told Doug, "Fine with me."

Doug raised his hands in surrender. "Okay—but let me bring the wine—I can at *least* do that."

I patted his back. "Fine, Doug. You bring wine. Dinner for four, seven o'clock on Prairie Street."

With that settled, the four of us left the courtyard, walking the long drive toward the road, where our cars were parked. Todd and Doug led the way, gabbing with each other, getting chummier by the minute. Neil and I brought up the rear, saying little.

Neil, I was sure, was fretting over Doug's trip to Green Bay. That was troubling me as well, but at the moment, I was still pondering our dinner plans for that evening and my impromptu invitation to the house. Neil had seconded my suggestion out of a pure sense of hospitality; that was his way. My own motives, however, had been less genteel. I knew in my heart of hearts that I had extended the invitation only because I was reluctant to let Doug spend the evening alone with Todd. I felt bitter disappointment in myself for harboring this petty jealousy, but I was unable to set aside that emotion and deal with it just then. There was something else looming, much bigger and more insidious—namely, whatever information Doug might glean from his trip to Green Bay.

Arriving at the road, we said a round of farewells, confirming our plan to meet again that evening. Todd got into his Mercedes and headed back to the Reece house. Doug got into his tan, county-issued sedan and headed east, back toward town—and Green Bay beyond. Neil and I got into my car, thumping both doors closed. I fired up the engine and switched off the radio.

"Neil," I said, turning to him, "you can reach Doug in his car. Don't you think you'd better talk to him—right now?"

He shook his head with resolve. "I had no idea they'd be able to trace where the typewriter came from, and I admit, that has me worried."

"It *should*. It has *me* worried—plenty."

Calmly, Neil continued, "The shopkeeper was this really old guy, Angus Maas. He seemed confused, possibly senile. I had to remind him to charge sales tax, and then he didn't know how to calculate it. I paid with cash and never gave him my name. I just don't think he'll be able to give Doug anything to work with. My best approach, I'm sure, is silence. If the investigation comes up with nothing solid, Gillian's death will be ruled accidental, and this whole mess will simply go away."

He was banking on a big "if."

And I had a hunch he would soon regret his risky supposition.

Chapter Twenty-three

Though I have never approved of nail biting, viewing it as a dark character flaw on a level not much higher than beer drinking or (God forbid) gum chewing, the tensions of that afternoon had me gnawing away. Once I got started, I didn't stop till I bled.

Sitting at my desk checking proofs and shuffling mail, I kept waiting for the phone to ring, jumping every time it did. There were only two people I expected to hear from—Doug or Neil—dreading that either of them would call with regard to the other, bearing exceptionally bad news. Whenever anyone else phoned (a frequent occurrence in a newspaper office), I brusquely rang off, informing my none-the-wiser caller that I was on deadline. Glee would have been proud to hear me stoop to such chicanery.

Watching the clock, I tried to calculate the progress of Doug's afternoon. Not knowing if he had checked his desk or stopped for lunch, I reasoned he would arrive in Green Bay sometime between one-thirty and two-thirty, locating Angus Maas at the office-equipment store no later than three. How long would they talk? And what would Doug learn? If he made a damning discovery, would he phone me or Neil? Probably not. Would he alert the sheriff's department in Dumont and send a deputy to do his duty at Neil's office? Possibly. Or would Doug drive back to Dumont to question Neil himself? I simply didn't know.

Around three-thirty, having heard nothing, but figuring that Doug had by now learned whatever he would learn, I began to feel light-headed again and decided I needed some fresh air. Rising from my desk, I put on my sport coat, checking pockets for pen, notebook, and phone. Leaving my office, I spotted Lucy in the newsroom and told her I would be out for a while.

"Something up?" she asked. It was a logical question, as I rarely left the building in the late afternoon, when deadlines were approaching. Still, I couldn't help feeling that her simple query was laced with suspicion. Clearly, I was in a foul state of mind.

"Just need some air," I told her. "Keep an eye on things. I shouldn't be long."

Traipsing down the stairs and through the lobby, I waved to Connie, telling her, "Back in a few minutes."

"Oh, Mr. Manning?" she warbled through the hole in her glass cage. "Do you have your cell phone?"

"Yes, Connie." And I slipped out the door to First Avenue.

Given my mind-set, I half expected the sky to be roiling with black clouds, a portent of powerful storms and general mayhem, but the week's lovely weather continued unabated. Birds sang, the breeze rustled through gold-and-crimson foliage up and down the parkway, and the sun, already low in the cool autumn sky, warmed my face as I looked westward. I instinctively headed in the direction of Neil's office and, beyond that, First Avenue Grill, as they were my usual destinations when walking this street. But I didn't want to encounter Neil on this trek—not now, with everything so uncertain and with the outcome of Doug's investigation hanging over us like a razor-edged pendulum—so I simply crossed the street, where Neil would be less likely to see me if he happened to glance from his windows as I passed.

Trying to clear my mind, trying to breathe easier (which never works), I ceased to notice my surroundings for a minute or two, as if walking through a daydream. When I snapped out of it, I was standing at an intersection, waiting for the traffic light to turn (at least I'd been sentient enough not to cross on red—there was little traffic, but still, it was a matter of principle as well as safety). Beyond the intersection lay the little downtown park where I had stopped on Tuesday to talk to Roxanne, who had phoned me from Chicago during my stroll to meet Neil for lunch. My lawyer friend, I realized, might be able to offer a more lucid picture of the confusing legal thicket in which both Neil and I now found ourselves.

When the light turned green, I crossed the street and made my way through the patch of turf that marked the center of town, navigating around beds of bright chrysanthemums and low hedges of juniper. The bench under the cannon was vacant—it generally was—so I settled there and slipped the cell phone out of my pocket. Though I'd been careful to bring pen and pad, I'd neglected to bring my reading glasses, a newer habit that was not yet fully ingrained. Flipping the phone open, I found that I could make out the buttons clearly enough in the direct sunlight, so I punched in the number that I still recalled with ease.

"Mark!" said Roxanne as she answered her direct line; apparently her phone had learned to recognize my cell number. Without skipping a beat, she added, "So it *was* murder, huh?" When I had spoken to her from my office on Wednesday, Gillian's death was deemed accidental, but I presumed Roxanne had read this morning's story from the *Register*, distributed overnight by wire service. Because of my long tenure at the *Chicago Journal*, that paper now kept tabs on some of the juicier events reported from central Wisconsin.

"It wasn't murder," I assured her, "though it wasn't entirely accidental, either."

"But the anonymous letter," she said, sounding skeptical. "The writer had the dirt on Gillian, had something to lose if the merger went through, and stopped the deal by stopping Gillian—dead in her tracks. Right?"

"Each of your points is true, Roxanne, but you've missed the all-important issue of intent." I repeated, "It wasn't murder."

She paused, digesting this. "You sound awfully sure of yourself."

I paused. "I know more than I wish I did."

"Hmm, that's really something, coming from *you*—Mr. Nose for News."

Her comment was more astute than glib. Under normal circumstances, I'd be itching for insights that would allow me to report an important local story with such intimate knowledge. But these circumstances were anything but normal—and far too intimate. I told Roxanne, "Let's just say this case has hit uncomfortably close to home."

"Uh-oh. Don't tell me—Glee Savage *did* exact her ultimate revenge on Gillian. Poor Glee. It's hard to imagine a sweet woman like that . . . snapping. But it happens. I'm sorry, Mark. You must really have a mess on your hands at the paper."

"If only it were that simple."

"It's *worse?*"

"Much, I'm afraid."

With a tone of genuine concern, she asked, "Do you need a lawyer?"

"I honestly don't know. That's why I called. I hoped you could help me sort this out."

"Tell you what—I'll be happy to help any way I can, but since I'm not representing you at the moment, we're not protected by attorney-client privilege, so tell me what you can in hypotheticals."

I asked, "Like 'a friend of a friend'?"

"You're such a clever lad. Okay, Mark—spill it."

As I paused to gather my thoughts, I noticed a tan sedan cruise by on First Avenue. The glare of sunlight on the windshield masked the driver. I wondered for a moment if it was Doug Pierce—on his way to Neil's office. But then I realized the timing was off; Doug could not have returned from Green Bay so quickly. Then again, I mused, the way *he* drives . . .

Dismissing these thoughts, I told Roxanne, "A friend of mine—"

"A friend of a friend," she corrected.

"Whatever. This friend was involved with building the Reeces' new house."

"How involved? The draperies, for instance?"

"They're called curtains, not draperies. But no, he was much more involved than that." Then the bombshell: "He designed the whole house."

"Oh, Christ . . . ," Roxanne muttered.

"So this friend had occasion to be at the house often, especially during the final stages of the project. He came and went as he pleased, checking on various contractors. Late Wednesday morning, he went to the house to discuss a sticky issue with Gillian—curtains, in fact."

Speaking in terms of "this friend," I continued to detail for Roxanne exactly what had happened when Neil confronted Gillian on the library balcony. I concluded, "This friend raced down the ladder and determined that the fall to the stone floor had killed Gillian on the spot. Fearing that the truth was his word against anyone's, he fled."

Roxanne breathed a long, thoughtful sigh, which rattled through the earpiece of my phone. "What was this letter all about?"

I explained how "this friend" had driven to Green Bay to meet a cabinetmaker, deciding along the way to write an anonymous letter exposing Gillian's plot. I detailed how he had bought the typewriter, ensured that the letter carried no fingerprints, disposed of the typewriter, then mailed the letter upon returning to Dumont.

Considering all this, Roxanne said, "No witnesses, no prints—objectively speaking, I'd say this friend has no problem."

"Ah, but he does. Working on a hunch, Doug Pierce determined that an old typewriter of the correct make and vintage had been sold in Green Bay on Wednesday. He's over there right now interviewing the shopkeeper, whom my friend describes as addled."

"Oops. Did your friend have sense enough to pay cash?"

"He did. But still, I think he's in big trouble. I've been pushing him to come clean with Doug, but he's afraid of being accused of something far worse than what he actually did."

Without hesitation, Roxanne said, "I don't blame him."

"Roxanne," I insisted, "ethical dilemmas are *always* best served by the truth."

"Tell that to Harley Kaiser."

I caught my breath, nearly choking.

"Don't tell me you've forgotten about Dumont's intrepid district attorney. Your DA is not only a hot dog, but a chauvinist, right-wing, *homophobic* hot dog. He'd have a field day with this."

Good God, dealing with Doug was one thing, but Harley Kaiser was another entirely. I'd had many run-ins with him at the paper regarding our reporting of breaking stories. Worse, this arrogant prosecutor seemed hell-bent on making trouble for my household. Just a year earlier, he had nearly charged Roxanne with murder while she was visiting my home. Shortly after my arrival in Dumont, he'd had *me* arrested, though briefly. And he'd unsuccessfully sided with that harpy feminist, Miriam Westerman, in attempting to steal my nephew, Thad, from his home with Neil and me. With all those strikeouts, Harley Kaiser would be frothing at the mouth to score a solid hit against Neil.

Roxanne was saying, "So the worst-case scenario is that Doug will get a description of Neil from the shopkeeper. Even if that happens, he may be willing to look the other way."

"That *won't* happen, Roxanne. Trust me, I know Doug far better than you do. Sure, he's become a close friend, but he's a cop first—a point he's articulated to me on several occasions."

"Then what do you suggest?"

"*You're* the lawyer." I instantly regretted my testy tone.

"Mark"—her tone was consoling—"this is Neil's issue, and it sounds as if he's already decided how to deal with it." I noticed we had dropped the hypotheticals; "this friend" was now openly "Neil."

"But it's my issue, too. I *know* the facts of the case, and I've been withholding them from Doug. That's complicity, isn't it?"

"Not if no one knows about it."

"Roxanne, listen. As a journalist, I'm committed to a certain code of ethics—"

"As a lawyer, so am I. But I don't believe my ears, Mark. Are you actually telling me you're on the *fence* as to whether your love for Neil outweighs your duties as a journalist? Get a *life*, pal. I may be a sworn member of the bar, but my advice to *you* is decidedly pragmatic: do whatever is necessary to preserve your happy home."

"I don't believe *my* ears," I countered. "Are you saying the end justifies the means?"

"Of course not. I'm saying that Neil occupies a special position in your life. If you were *married*, you couldn't be compelled to testify against him, nor would you even consider doing so."

"But we're *not* married, not technically."

"In your *hearts* you are. It's not *your* fault public policy hasn't yet adjusted itself to the reality of your lives. What do you want to do—hang Neil on a technicality?"

Though I knew Roxanne's reference to "hanging" Neil was figurative, it was nonetheless sobering. I thanked her for her counsel and good intentions. Then, after exchanging promises to keep each other posted, we said good-bye.

Returning the cell phone to my pocket, I realized she had spoken the very words I had hoped to hear: "Preserve your happy home." Though I valued her advice, I understood that my decisions and my actions would be my own. Ultimately, I had to answer to myself.

Mulling my predicament, I sat and watched the traffic, scanning the avenue for tan sedans.

It seemed I was there for hours.

Chapter Twenty-four

The imagined hours on the park bench were no more than fifteen or twenty minutes. The amount of time I sat there was irrelevant—it brought me no nearer to solving my quandary. Though Roxanne had seconded Neil's decision to remain mum, I simply didn't agree with either of them.

Neil had played a role in Gillian Reece's death, and although that role was not intended, he was nonetheless accountable for his actions. The extent of his responsibility for Gillian's death was a complicated matter of law and public interest. It was *not* a matter for Neil or Roxanne to dismiss as a hassle best avoided. And while the consequences of Neil's actions were *his* dilemma, complicity in the cover-up was mine. It was apparent I could not convince him to level with Doug Pierce. Failing that, was it then *my* responsibility to set things right—and tattle on my own lover? The very notion sickened me. My instincts told me to play along and hope for the best. But my intellect told me that I could not abandon my principles and integrity—the very benchmarks that had defined not only my career, but even my sense of self.

These onerous thoughts dominated the remainder of the afternoon, which I spent at my desk behind a closed door, insulated from the newsroom and from the world beyond. I had asked Connie to screen my calls, fending off all but Doug or Neil. When it was nearly five, I had heard from neither of them, so I lifted the receiver and dialed Neil at his office.

"Oh, Mark," he answered, "I was just about to call you."

Unable to judge the tone of his voice, I asked, "You've, uh, heard from Doug?"

"No. I heard from *Todd*, about dinner. He finished at the Reece house for the day and offered to make a run for groceries."

"Oh, jeez, I nearly forgot—and *I'm* the one who was so quick with the invitation. Too much on my mind, I guess."

"*Tell* me. Anyway, he's shopping as we speak."

"The perfect houseguest." With a touch of humor, I added, "If the curtain biz falls flat, maybe he'd be interested in a . . . position. With Barb gone, we could use some extra help."

Neil laughed. "Fat chance. Todd's got a waiting list of clients *this* long."

"Good for him." I laughed as well, and it felt good. My spectrum of emotions that day had ranged from anxiety at the one end to depression at the other.

"Uh, Mark?" asked Neil. "Have *you* heard from Doug?"

I exhaled loudly. "Not a peep. He's surely finished in Green Bay by now if he intends to be at the house by seven."

"Then no news is good news, I guess."

"I guess." But I knew it wasn't that simple. If the old shopkeeper had provided a dead-on description of Neil as the buyer of the vintage Royal, I doubted if Doug would phone to say, Brace yourself, Mark— I'm locking up your boyfriend. No, he'd deliver such news in person, and by my calculation, he was now in his car, speeding our way.

Neil asked, "What time will you be home?"

"I've had a tough time clearing my desk, but I'll be there by six. This 'party' was my idea—I ought to pitch in in the kitchen."

"We'll be waiting for you." Before ringing off, Neil added, "But if you hear anything from Doug, let me know."

"Count on it."

———

Around six, I arrived home, still having heard nothing from Doug. Parking in the garage, I entered the house through the back door, finding Neil and Todd already hard at work, preparing dinner. Something hissed in a skillet, filling the room with warm, inviting smells. I felt instantly hungry as I closed the door on the chilly dusk.

"Hey, Mark! Welcome home," said Todd, turning from the countertop where he was mincing vegetables—onions, I think—on a cutting board. He sounded chipper with anticipation of the night that lay ahead.

"Hi, Mark," echoed Neil, sounding not at all chipper as he wiped his hands and stepped to the door to give me a kiss.

Slipping out of my sport coat, I offered, "Need an extra pair of hands?"

Todd and Neil looked at each other and exchanged a shrug. "Nah," said Neil, "everything's under control. Relax." Easier said than done, I thought.

Todd said, "I bought some oranges, Mark. If you're looking for something to do, how 'bout a drink? I don't know about you guys, but I could sure use something."

Neither Neil nor I needed convincing. We too needed a drink, though our nervousness was rooted in something decidedly more ponderous than Todd's date jitters. Without further prompting, I set about pouring us a round of our usual evening cocktail—Japanese vodka on ice, twist of orange peel.

Todd and Neil were so busy with their culinary chores, they barely paused to skoal with me. "Wish me luck tonight," said Todd, raising his glass.

Under his breath, Neil said, "Wish *me* luck tonight."

"Hm?" asked Todd.

I fudged, "Neil always tenses up before dinner guests arrive."

Neil and Todd turned to resume their preparations. Neil was so distracted, he didn't even protest when I offered to set the table, a task in which he took particular pride, not normally entrusting it to me.

I was glad to have something to do. Moving to the dining room, I worked on the table like a man on a mission. Napery, cutlery, china, crystal—I set each item with dogged, eyeball precision, resisting (but just barely) the temptation to get a ruler. Candles were already placed on the table, and I moved from the sideboard a bowl of flowers that Todd had arranged.

Finishing my task, feeling mentally exhausted by it (to say nothing of the accumulated strains of the day), I dashed upstairs, took off my tie, splashed water on my face, and changed into a fresh shirt—starched, of course—rolling up the sleeves a couple of turns for an evening at home. By the time I returned downstairs, it was seven o'clock.

Strolling into the kitchen, checking my watch, I asked, "No sign of our guest?"

Neil gave a feeble shake of his head while chomping an ice cube from the bottom of his cocktail glass.

"Not yet," said Todd. "Wonder what he's up to."

My thought exactly.

Neil whirled a hand, asking me, "Do you suppose we should call him?"

"No point in *asking* for trouble."

"Huh?" said Todd.

"I mean, he'd let us know if his plans got fouled up. Let's give him a few minutes." Then we all fell silent, busying ourselves with tasks already done. I returned to the dining room and refolded the napkins—just so.

Several minutes later, while I was making a mess of the flowers Todd had so artfully arranged, headlights flashed through the windows of the front hall. "He's here!" I called.

Todd and Neil rushed from the kitchen, and we all made our way to the door. Switching on the porch light, Todd peeked from the curtain at a side window like a high school princess awaiting the football hero to pick her up for the prom. A car door slammed. "Oooh," said Todd, "he's wearing a tweedy green blazer tonight—I *love* that on him."

I agreed, "I've always liked that jacket."

Neil gave me a quizzical look. I wondered how he could possibly have never noticed how attractive Doug looked in that coat. And posing the question seemed to supply the answer—Neil simply didn't harbor sexual feelings for Doug.

Footfalls sounded on the porch steps, and a moment later, the doorbell chimed, just as Todd swung the door open, admitting a cold gust of October night air along with our local sheriff. "Hi, everyone," he greeted us, closing the door behind him. "Getting nippy out there."

"Almost Halloween," I noted, feeling inane.

"Everything okay, Doug?" Neil tapped his watch. "We were ready to send out the dogs."

"Sorry. I know how picky you guys are about wine, so I took my time shopping for it." Handing me the bag he carried, he added, "Hope it measures up."

Barely glancing inside—I couldn't even read the labels—I said, "Aww, you shouldn't have, Doug. You're too generous."

"I didn't know what you'd be serving, so I brought a red and a white."

"Perfect." I handed the bag to Neil, who took it to the kitchen.

Todd offered, "Drink, Doug?"

He thought a moment. "Sure, why not? Scotch, rocks."

"Comin' right up." Todd darted to the kitchen.

Alone with Doug in the hall, I asked, pointedly, "Not on duty tonight?"

With a wry expression I couldn't interpret, he answered, "I'm *always* on duty, Mark, but a man needs a drink now and then."

Cutting the small talk, I leaned close to ask, "What happened in Green Bay?"

He blew a silent whistle. "Soon enough, Mark."

"Hey, Doug," called Neil from the kitchen doorway. "Todd wants to know if you want a twist with your Scotch."

"If it's handy." Doug went to the kitchen, but paused in the doorway, turning back to me. "Join the party, Mark."

Though wary of where the party was headed, I didn't want to miss anything, so I scampered through the dining room and joined the others in the kitchen.

"Fresh one, Mark?" asked Neil as I entered, hoisting an empty cocktail glass.

"Uh, sure."

As Neil poured another round of vodka, Todd handed Doug his Scotch. It was a stiff one—the ice didn't take up much room in the glass.

When all four of us had a glass in hand, we made a toast to friendship. Doug added, "Life's not much without it—friendship—especially when the going gets rough."

What did *that* mean? I slurped the vodka, watching Doug over the rim of my glass. He looked as troubled as his words had sounded.

"Hey," said Neil, "let's not stand around the kitchen. Let's get civilized—in the living room."

"How about the den?" I suggested, preferring the more intimate setting.

"Fine," everyone agreed. "Sure." Then we gathered a few plates of appetizers and trekked across the hall together to my uncle Edwin's woody lair.

I offered, "Care for a fire?" Silly question. So I went to work at the hearth while the others seated themselves around the low table. Neil made sure Doug and Todd ended up together, facing the fireplace from the chesterfield love seat. Its leather squeaked as they settled in, practically hip to hip.

When I had the fire going, I took the remaining chair, across from Neil's, near Todd's end of the love seat. Reaching to lift my glass from the table, I breathed a weary sigh. "Long day."

Doug, who didn't look at all fatigued, turned to face Todd, telling him, "Long *week*. I guess you found more than you bargained for in Dumont."

"*I'll* say." The lilt of Todd's voice was clear enough—what he hadn't expected to find in Dumont was Douglas Pierce.

Doug laughed. "I meant, your curtain job at the Reece house didn't go exactly as planned."

"The curtains did," Todd assured him. "The client didn't."

Neil said, "Yeah, poor Gillian. *Her* week didn't go as planned."

"Under the circumstances," said Todd, "you're more sympathetic to the woman than *I'd* be. After all, she could have screwed you and Mark out of a fortune, so it's a good thing her week did get fouled up."

Flatly, Doug noted, "All a matter of perspective."

Todd swirled his drink, nodding. He asked idly, "Any news on the case?"

Neil and I both went on alert. Too eagerly, I asked, "Yeah, Doug—Green Bay?"

With a tiny shake of his head, he told me, "Not now, Mark. Let's try to enjoy the evening." Patting Todd's knee, he added, "With such pleasant company, why dwell on disappointing topics?"

What, I wondered, was his plan? Did he want to eat first—*then* lower the boom?

Neil gave me a questioning look that seemed to ask, Now what?

I wanted to take him aside and tell him, This is your last chance. Do what needs to be done. Don't force me into the god-awful position of making the right decision *for* you.

"Uh," said Doug, clearing his throat, "this is sort of awkward, but there's something I really need to say."

Through a skeptical squint, Todd said, "I thought you didn't want to dwell on the heavy stuff."

Doug's face brightened as he explained, "This has nothing to do with what happened in Green Bay, but it *is* sort of heavy—at least for me."

Neil said, "You've captured our attention, Doug. What's on your mind?"

"Well, I want to thank you and Mark for introducing me to Todd." Doug turned to the man next to him on the sofa. Looking him in the eye, he continued, "Todd, we've known each other . . . how long? About twenty-four hours. We've had the chance to really talk only once, last night at dinner. By any reasonable measure, we've barely met, so the things I'm trying to say will sound premature. But you won't be here for long, and I don't know when I might see you again."

Todd opened his mouth to speak, but Doug forged ahead, telling him, "And that's the point, Todd—I *want* to see you again. I want to see you often. I know the logistics seem impossible, but we can deal with the thorny details later. For now, I just want you to know—" He broke off, wiping his brow with the back of his hand. "Christ, I'm no good at this. Lack of practice, I guess."

Todd said, "You're doing fine. You were saying?"

Doug swallowed. "For now, I just want you to know that . . . (a) I find you highly attractive . . . and (b) I'm already very fond of you . . . and (c) . . . well, (c) I think I could grow to love you." Doug blinked, looking stunned, as if he couldn't believe his own words.

Todd eyed him sternly for a moment. "Sheriff?" he asked through a scowl. "Do you have any idea what you're getting into?" Then he broke into a wide grin, flung his arms around Doug, and pulled him forward for a deep, long kiss—which was eagerly accepted. It was as if they were two starving men, grateful to be nourished by each other.

Neil and I exchanged an astonished look, not only because the love scene on our love seat was so unexpected, but because it involved *Doug*. Our friend the sheriff was easily the most circumspect and strait-laced gay man we knew. Though publicly "out" and, by all appearances, comfortable with himself, he never lost sight of the proprieties of his office. Discretion was his watchword, so this sudden display of affection was nothing shy of nuclear. The foundation of the house seemed to rumble beneath us.

A loud *ding* carried from across the hall.

Coming up for air, Todd announced, "Supper's ready."

We all had a good laugh, then paused to lift our glasses.

Doug told Neil and me, "Thanks again, gentlemen."

"I'll second that," said Todd, swooning next to Doug.

"Glad to help," said Neil.

"Sincerely," I told them, "we never expected to share such a moment with you, but thanks for including us."

We drank to their happiness, to their first blush of romance, ignoring the geographic obstacle they faced, to say nothing of the unknown developments in Green Bay, a cruel uncertainty that still hung over the night.

Before long we had left the den and gone to the kitchen, where we all pitched in—making up plates, opening wine, soaking a few pans—before moving our party to the dining room. The oblong table was set for two on one side, two on the other. There was now no question as to the seating arrangement; Doug and Todd sat together as a couple.

When we had settled into our meal, having complimented each other on the food and the wine, our conversation hit a lull. Neil noted, "Everyone's kinda quiet."

The others may have been quiet because they were savoring their dinner, but I wasn't even aware of what was on my plate, grappling with so many questions that focused on Green Bay. What had Doug learned there? When would he reveal those findings? What action would he take? How would the outcome affect my life with Neil? Would Neil avert all this anxious doubt and come clean with Doug? If not, would my own scruples seize the moment and force me to speak up, leading Neil to conclude that I had betrayed him and that our love had meant nothing? My stomach twisted with a painful knot as I tried to swallow.

"I was just thinking," said Doug, setting down his fork.

"About what?" Todd asked.

Doug turned in his chair to face Todd. "About us."

"We're 'us' already? I like it."

"Good, so do I. But I hardly need to tell you—we've got some issues ahead of us."

Todd chortled. "The four-hour drive?"

"Mainly. And all it represents. You're a city boy; I'm not. I'm a cop; you're not."

"Uh-uh-uh," clucked Todd. "Don't you get it? That's what makes our attraction so pure, so genuine—there is *nothing* superficial or convenient or predictable about it. It's so offbeat, who knows, it just may be the real thing. Time will tell, and we've got plenty of that. I've been out of circulation for a while, and unless I'm mistaken, you've never been *in* circulation. So we can take this slow and easy. If you think you might be able to handle a long-distance relationship, so can I."

Doug traced his fingertips across Todd's cheek. Smiling, he affirmed, "I can handle it." Then he turned to Neil and me. "Sorry, guys. Hope I'm not embarrassing you. Truth is, until last night, I'd almost forgotten that I've needed another man's love." With a soft chuckle, he shook his head. "God, I don't believe the way I've been tossing that word around tonight."

Todd slung his arm around Doug's shoulders. "Sheriff, you can toss that word in my direction anytime you like."

Neil told both of them, "We're not the least bit embarrassed. We couldn't be happier for you." Smiling, he took my hand.

I mirrored his smile, but said nothing. I wanted to feel happy for Doug—in fact, I *did* feel happy for him—but mostly I felt the knot in my stomach. It was difficult to share Doug's joy while wondering if he had already been on the phone to Harley Kaiser, informing our intrepid prosecutor of Neil's role in Gillian's death.

"I think we could use some dessert," said Neil, pushing back his chair. When someone groaned in protest, he added, "Tonight's a special occasion. Besides, it's ready to serve."

"Sure," said Todd, standing. "Let me help." Then he and Neil cleared our dinner plates, carrying them to the kitchen.

A few quiet moments passed. Then Doug leaned toward me over the table, asking quietly, "Are you okay, Mark? You haven't said much tonight."

"*Doug*," I said, hunching forward on my elbows, "I'm a nervous wreck. I realize you're trying to have a pleasant evening, and I'm glad you and Todd are making such headway, but I don't know how you can be so cool about the investigation. When I asked you about it in the den, you said, 'Why dwell on disappointing topics?' "

Doug said flatly, "The time didn't seem right."

Getting flustered, I stammered, "Well, why not? I mean, when? And what did you mean—'disappointing topics'?"

He sat back. "I meant just what I said—what I learned was disappointing."

Todd and Neil were whisking into the room with dessert and coffee. Neil asked, "What was disappointing, Doug? Not the meal, I hope." He plopped a plate in front of me; I have no idea what was on it.

"No, the meal was great." Doug explained, "We were talking about my trip to Green Bay this afternoon. I met with the shopkeeper who sold that old Royal typewriter on Wednesday. The results of the interview were disappointing." Eyeing Neil, he emphasized, "*Very* disappointing."

Speechless, Neil slid into his chair.

I felt my heart pounding in my neck.

Todd set the coffeepot on the table and took his seat next to Doug, asking, "Disappointing? How so?"

Doug drummed his fingers on the table. "The man who runs this used-office-equipment store is a nice old guy named Angus Maas, and—"

"*Angus?*" asked Todd.

Doug nodded. "That's his name. It looked as if the business hadn't seen much action lately, and he wanted to be helpful—I think he just appreciated the attention. He had no trouble recalling the transaction, probably the only sale he made all week. The buyer helped him figure out the sales tax . . ."

Oh, God. It was all lining up, all the circumstantial evidence that would point directly to the man seated at my side. Neil sat listening with a blank expression as Doug related the events of that afternoon, drawing nearer to the moment when Neil would be named the author of the anonymous letter. Mentally, I tried nudging Neil to the admission that could help him salvage a shred of credibility. But I've never had much faith in telepathy, so I wasn't very good at it. Neil sat stone-faced as the story unraveled. My only remaining option, I now realized, was to take matters into my own hands. Tasting bile in my throat, I waited for a pause in the story, then began, "Doug—"

"But he never got the guy's *name*," Doug continued. "The customer paid cash, and the description Angus gave me was vague at best, so the bottom line is, I've got *nothing* to go on. The entire afternoon was just a wild-goose chase—and *that's* what I call disappointing results." He crossed his arms over his chest, shaking his head.

Neil and I dared to glimpse at each other. I'm sure my numb, bug-eyed relief was even more transparent than his was. Fortunately, Doug wasn't watching.

Todd asked him, "Isn't there some other way to trace the typewriter?"

"Nah, I don't think so. And you know, driving back today, it occurred to me that I'd taken the wrong tack altogether. I mean, whoever bought the typewriter was honest enough to help the old guy compute his own sales tax, and that doesn't sound like a homicidal sociopath.

Even if it *was* the killer, I doubt if he still has the typewriter. So even if I found him, I'd have no hard evidence to link him to the letter. Tomorrow morning, the death of Gillian Reece will be ruled accidental."

Todd circled a finger around Doug's ear. "Tomorrow morning's a long way off. Got any plans tonight?"

Doug paused to consider Todd's suggestion, but not long, before replying, "I thought you'd never ask. My place?"

I was tempted to offer, Just use the guest room. You're already here. And Todd's all settled.

But I bit my tongue, vowing never again to indulge in fantasies of tinkering with the sleeping arrangements upstairs on Prairie Street. Go with my blessing, Doug. Take Todd. And have a ball.

Todd pushed back his chair and stood, telling Doug, "Your place—it's a deal. Give me two minutes to throw a few things together." He kissed the top of Doug's head, flashed Neil and me a cagey grin, then tore across the front hall and shot up the stairs.

Neil sat back and laughed with sheer delight.

"What's so funny?" asked Doug. "My dating skills may be a little rusty—hell, they're nonexistent—but I made a prize catch tonight."

"You sure did. You *both* did." Neil's old sparkle was back. The grim pall of the last two days had lifted. "I wasn't laughing at *you*, Doug. It's the irony of your trip to Green Bay—Gillian's death was just an accident after all."

I tried to telegraph, Don't press your luck.

"If not, *I'll* never be able to prove it." Doug reached for the coffeepot. "Coffee, guys?"

"Why not?" I said. "I'm already keyed up. I have an inkling I won't get much sleep tonight"

"Funny," said Doug, rising and moving around the table, "I've got that same inkling myself." He rested a hand on my shoulder while pouring my coffee.

Neil mused, "So the kindly old shopkeeper wasn't much help . . ."

Doug stepped to Neil and poured coffee for him. "No, Angus Maas was pretty hazy in his recollections—said something about sandy blond hair—a few other details, not much else."

Neil's eyes slid in my direction.

Doug put the coffeepot on the table. Then he fingered the amethyst stud that glinted from Neil's earlobe. "You know?" he said. "If I were you, I'd put that in a drawer somewhere. Purple's not your color at all."

Neil's eyes froze on the badge clipped to Doug's belt.

"Well, I'm gonna see if Todd needs a hand. He's taking way too long up there." Doug grinned, turned, and strolled from the dining room.

He crossed the hall, then started up the stairs.

When Neil could breathe again, he fumbled to remove the stud.

Though a bit shaky myself, I offered, "Let me do that."

Standing, I stepped behind Neil's chair, rested his head against my hip, and unfastened the stud, which I plucked from his ear. Slipping the amethyst into my pocket, I knelt beside him, brought my lips to his ear, and kissed the tiny pink wound.

Epilogue

Was it mere friendship that compelled Doug Pierce to look the other way, exactly as Roxanne had predicted? Somehow, I find it hard to believe that just because we're pals of the sheriff, Neil was entitled to one free "Get Out of Jail" card. Or was it the love bug that prompted Doug, freshly bitten, to ignore the unsavory entanglements of police work so he could focus on recreational entanglements with Todd Draper? I find it equally hard to believe that Doug's commitment to duty was that shallow.

A more likely answer is that I had simply been blind to an aspect of Doug Pierce that was more flexible, more human, than I was willing to acknowledge. Had I been projecting my own inflexibility upon a man I admired, assuming he was like me in every respect? Someday—maybe, I'm not sure when—I'll have to ask him about that.

One thing's for sure. I'm grateful that Doug did what he did. And I'm ashamed that both he and Roxanne were able to grasp "the big picture" with such expediency, while I myself struggled to find a foothold in a miasma of doubts, a whirlpool of technicalities, and a quicksand of conflicting ethics. I'm all the more ashamed that this pothering brought me to the brink of a betrayal cloaked in rectitude.

With the distance of time, I'm now able to look back at what happened and to understand that the main issue was always clear to me—

Neil did not murder Gillian Reece. While he was involved in the circumstances that led to her death, his conscience was clean, and I should have accepted the logic of his determination that he had not been responsible for the tragedy.

Ultimately, that responsibility traced back to Gillian herself. She had plotted against many people, deceiving business associates as well as the entire town, and she did not hesitate to resort to physical abuse when her scheming and her verbal bullying failed. As Neil wrote in his letter, she deserved not only her fall from power, but her fall to death—simply because it was she who had instigated each vicious volley in a chain of events that led to inevitable reactions and a fatal conclusion.

If Neil was able to grasp so succinctly the significance of what had happened, why couldn't I as well? Why did my conscientiousness stray into obstinacy? Because, as Gillian herself had informed me in no uncertain terms, I was a tight-ass. What's more, she had taken no small pleasure in informing me of my reputation as a prissy snob. Though it stung to hear such blunt assessments, I now understand that I had needed to hear them. So it's ironic that I owe Gillian a debt of gratitude for confronting me with observations that my friends wouldn't voice, but apparently felt.

Have I changed? I hope so. I'm trying. Not only have I learned a valuable lesson regarding my own rigid views, but I've also felt a measure of liberation in adopting this previously foreign mind-set. If I feel like biting my nails, I bite them. If a friend finds some latitude in the speed limit, I keep my mouth shut. I've even learned to stand naked in my own bathroom. These concessions, while admittedly shallow, are an encouraging sign of deeper roots. How successfully I nurture them, only time will tell.

Time has already brought developments on other fronts.

Our friend Doug Pierce did indeed find love with Todd Draper. The small-town sheriff and the big-city curtain designer discovered, after spending their first night together, that they were not only physically compatible, but true soul mates, the real deal. Working so far apart, they came to find their long weekend drives increasingly taxing, so they've now bought a little place in Lake Geneva, near the Illinois state line, which allows them less time on the road and more time together. Todd is even talking about opening a workroom in Milwaukee, which would further close the gap.

When I saw that Doug and Todd were truly in love, my lingering designs on Doug at last ceased, and I happily abandoned the fleeting erotic interest I'd had in Todd. With those distractions aside, I have confirmed my contentment to be alone with Neil. We look forward to growing old together.

As for Thad Quatrain, our inherited son, he looks forward to a promising career in theater while continuing his study in California with the noted director Claire Gray. (Contrary to the instincts of some—and the wishful thinking of others—I'm quite sure Thad is not latently gay.)

As for Roxanne Exner, also known as Mrs. Carl Creighton, she and her husband have permanently retreated from the political arena and are solidly focused on their roles as two of the most influential attorneys in Chicago. We don't see them as often as we once did, but friendships like that are not threatened by time or distance. Roxanne and I know we can always count on each other, lean on each other, depend on each other. We're only a phone call away.

As for cell phones, I use mine all the time now and never think twice about it.

As for Esmond Reece, the man who helped make cell phones possible, he and Tamra Thaine discovered that the good people of Dumont had little interest in Eastern studies—in fact, none—so the two of them rolled up their sticky-mats and moved to Sedona, where the harmonic convergence is said to be lovely this season.

As for Perry Schield, the Quatro Press executive retired shortly after the fateful merger with Ashton Mills was averted. Perry's decision to leave the company surprised no one. His younger clone, Tyler Pennell, surprised everyone, however, when he abandoned forensic accounting and moved away with Perry to a secluded cabin in the wooded northern region of the state. Neil and I received a single Christmas card signed by both of them, but we haven't heard a peep from either of them since.

As for Glee Savage, now in her later fifties, she shows no sign of slowing down, and her eventual retirement from the *Register* has never been discussed. She still carries big purses, still wears big hats, and still drives the fuchsia hatchback. She has not again slapped another woman, at least not publicly, at least not to my knowledge. At an editorial meeting one afternoon, Glee noted my relaxed attitudes with a cautious measure of approval, wondering aloud, "What's next, Mark? Don't tell me you'll now allow us to occasionally split an infinitive." I was forced to remind her that there are certain lines one simply does not cross.

As for Lucille Haring, she is still my second-in-command at the paper, and I'm glad, as always, to have her. She still wears her hair too short, and while it's still carrot red, it's beginning to show some gray at the temples. Though she may still pine for Roxanne, she rarely speaks of her, for she has begun keeping company with Nancy Sanderson, the widow restaurateur, who is some twenty years Lucy's senior. Tongues, most assuredly, are wagging.

As for mysterious death—enough. My days at the *Register* have seen far too much of it, certainly for a town of this size. It's inevitable, I suppose, that deadly mischief will again visit Dumont. Sooner or later, it's bound to happen. But when it does, I'll resist the temptation to pull rank with my staff and pluck those prime assignments. From now on, I'll leave to other writers the task of untangling riddles of devilry and untimely demise.

Sorry. I've had my fill. At least for a while.

One last detail. As for that amethyst ear stud, Neil and I took Doug's advice and put it in a drawer. Specifically, we keep it in a little box, a jewel box we stow in a dresser in our bedroom—like hidden treasure. Neil has never, ever worn it again in public. But now and then, in the privacy of our bed, he wears it for me.

When he does, its purple fire never fails to work its magic.

Sparks always fly. ❑